"I th

me,"

"Sorry about that," Adam said. "I'm selfish sometimes, and all I think about is what I want or need."

She leaned back, surprised
After a minute, sh
of us."

"Yeah." A crooked s
mouth up. "But that
You're a good frienc
you down."

Friend. Why did that have a hollow sound to it? She set her computer on the side table and stood. "Is this another rescue for the underdog?"

When he looked sheepish, she turned away from the temptation to hug him. Imagine that big, hard-muscled body of Adam's, holding her, his smell and heat surrounding her. Her body trembled at the sudden, vivid image.

Dear Reader,

With every book I write I'm inevitably drawn to one character. I want to say it's Adam with this book, because in my mind he's not only the perfect hero, but I like him! If I met Adam in real life, I'd want to be his friend. But for all the heroic qualities he possesses, Sylvie is the character who fascinates me. As is often pointed out to her, unlike Adam, she has it all. How much harder it must be to admit failure when you appear successful to everyone around you.

I thought a lot about success while writing this book. More specifically, fear of success, which is one of Sylvie's challenges. It's not that Sylvie is afraid of succeeding; she's already a well-known artist. But the foundation or reason she pursues success is faulty, and eventually her world comes tumbling down. Luckily for her, Adam, and her family and friends, are there to help her rebuild her world.

I've always thought of success as a linear process. You set a goal, then work to achieve it. But human beings are rarely simple, and many of us set land mines along the way. Sylvie excels at sabotaging herself. In order for her to succeed, she must change not *what* she's doing, but *why* she's doing it.

Writing about Sylvie forced me to view my life from a different angle, and I wonder if when you read this book, you'll also look more closely at why you want to achieve something rather than concentrating on the end goal. The answers may surprise you!

I hope you enjoy reading Sylvie and Adam's story. I had a lovely time creating the village they live in and the characters who populate it. As always, I look forward to hearing from my readers. You can contact me at this address: kate@katekelly.ca or drop by my website for a visit : www.katekelly.ca.

Warm regards,

Kate Kelly

When Adam
Came to Town

—

Kate Kelly

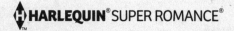
HARLEQUIN® SUPER ROMANCE®

Recycling programs
for this product may
not exist in your area.

ISBN-13: 978-0-373-71875-7

WHEN ADAM CAME TO TOWN

Printed in U.S.A.

ABOUT THE AUTHOR

Kate Kelly has had a love affair with books her entire life. Writing came in fits and starts, and she didn't take it seriously until her forties. Now she can't get along without it. She finaled in the RWA Golden Heart and won the RWA Daphne du Maurier contest. She has the good fortune to live on the east coast of Canada with her husband (the children have flown away). She writes, grows herbs and perennials, and sails when the wind blows her way.

Books by Kate Kelly

HARLEQUIN SUPERROMANCE

1751—A DELIBERATE FATHER

Other titles by this author available in ebook format.

To Teressa, Molly and Colleen.
The best sisters, one and all.
Thanks for always being there.

To Romeo
RIP

And as always, to my guys, Adrian, Reed and Rei

CHAPTER ONE

SYLVIE CARSON PUSHED the door to the family café open and made a beeline for the washrooms located at the front of the restaurant. She locked herself in a stall and thrust her head down between her knees. *Breathe*. She counted to seven before letting out her breath, blood rushing to her head.

Second breath. One, two, three, four, five, six, seven. And out. The door to the washroom burst open.

"They're taking bets out there on how many months along you are, and who the father is. Oliver's in the lead." Sylvie heard the scrape of a match as Teressa, head cook and childhood friend, lit a cigarette.

"No smoking in here," Sylvie croaked. She sat up and braced her hand against the side of the stall as she waited for her equilibrium to even out.

"Like you're going to fire me. You have a better chance of finding an available man who can support himself in this village than a professional cook. Unless you want to do my job. You'd have to learn how to boil water first, though." Teressa snickered.

Sylvie pushed the stall door open with her foot. "Very funny."

"For someone who has the perfect life, you're sure acting like you're at death's door a lot." Teressa frowned at her in the mirror. "Please tell me you're not pregnant. It would ruin my day. You're the golden girl, and golden girls do not mess up. Although having to marry the scrumptious Oliver…" Her friend looked away from her reflection in the mirror long enough to take another drag off her cigarette. "Hard to feel sorry for you, Syl."

Teressa had two small children to support, both from different fathers, which made her life a scheduling nightmare. So, yes, from Teressa's point of view, Sylvie's life probably looked pretty good. She was single, made enough money that she didn't have to worry about it and had even achieved a small amount of fame.

And it had all come to a crashing halt six months ago.

The curvy redhead took one last look at herself in the mirror and turned to face Sylvie. "No offense, but I don't get why you're still here. If I had your life, I'd be out of Collina like a shot. Your dad's getting stronger every day. He's out in the kitchen right now, trying to tell us all how to run a restaurant. You should stop torturing yourself and go back to Toronto and your cushy life."

Sylvie sighed. *Cushy life*. Why did people think being an artist was easy? "Wait 'til everyone finds out that I'm not pregnant…that I'm just…whatever."

Every day, that first step inside the café, the oh-my-God-what's-happened-to-my-life moment, stole the breath right out of her body. She'd tried blaming the whole fiasco on her father's heart attack and having to move home six months ago. Six months! Normal, well-adjusted people did not let their lives become gridlocked because their father got sick.

The first signs that her life had derailed came the day after her father's heart attack. She'd gone into her studio, picked up a brush and painted mud. Okay, not mud. She was a skilled craftswoman, after all. But the tingle of magic she'd always felt had been absent, and it showed.

She and Oliver, her agent boyfriend, had tried to keep

her problem under wraps, but rumors were starting to circulate about her inactivity. Oliver insisted she needed to return to Toronto, but Sylvie didn't know if she'd be able to paint, or—worse—if she even wanted to. Either way, she wasn't leaving until her father felt a hundred percent better. Then maybe they could discuss the real problem—the secrets her family had kept from her all these years.

Teressa stuck her cigarette under a stream of water, chucked it in the garbage and started washing her hands. "Well, boss, I came to tell you the customers are packing in for breakfast, and sweet little Tyler is hiding God knows where. I think he's been alley-catting all night again. If his mother wasn't the only decent hairdresser in town, I'd beg you to fire him. And, lentil soup, Sylvie? Again? Your father had the heart attack, *not* the entire village. We're going to have a revolution on our hands if you put too much healthy stuff on the menu." She stopped on her way to the door. "If I knew how to fix things for you, sweetie, you know I would, but I'm afraid you're on your own with this one. Oh, and there's a big bruiser of a guy waiting at the cash register. Haven't seen him around before. He'll start growing roots if he stands there much longer."

Sylvie rubbed her hands over her face and levered herself off the toilet. "I'm right behind you. I'm good now." But Teressa was already gone, the door swishing shut behind her.

Sylvie stood at the sink and scrubbed her hands. The panic attacks may have started after her father's heart attack, but having to move home for a while hadn't helped her being blocked and not able to paint. She knew her family and friends had her best interests at heart but she wished to God they'd stop asking if she had started painting again. Nothing like having your failure thrown in your face every day.

If she went back to Toronto—*when* she went back to Toronto... Her lungs seized up. Would it all come back to her? Her talent? Her bright, shining future? She'd lived and breathed painting for seventeen years and without it, she was lost.

Hell, at the moment she could hardly talk herself into leaving the washroom. Returning to Toronto seemed as inconceivable to her as swimming across the frigid Bay of Fundy that sat outside her door. No, for once in her life she had to make a decision completely on her own. She needed to stay home in Collina and figure out who she would have been if painting hadn't become the central focus of her life.

When she dragged herself back into the dining area, Tyler was leaning his forehead against the cool, stainless steel soda machine, ignoring the man waiting at the cash two feet behind him.

Sylvie hurried across the room. She felt sorry for Tyler, nineteen and nothing to look forward to but more of the same. It was enough to drive anyone to drink. But she couldn't afford to sympathize too much. Tyler had to pull his weight, or Pops would insist on spending even more time here. The heart specialist had been explicit last week, Pops was to work no more than two hours a day, and that was pushing it.

She was already desperate to find a second cook. But even though good help was slim pickings in the village, that didn't mean she could let Tyler get away with too much. And God forbid her family let *her* work in the kitchen or try her hand at bookkeeping—not the talented Sylvie Carson. They thought they were freeing her up to pursue her dreams, but every time they said *no,* she felt more and more limited as to what she could do. Instead she was expected to sit and stare at an empty canvas and pray for inspiration.

"Be with you in a second," she said to the man standing at the cash register. She huddled with Tyler in the corner. The tall, wiry teenager looked like he'd fall over if she breathed on him. "We're busy, Ty. I need your help."

He shot her a sheepish look. "My stomach's all jumped up this morning."

"Right." She sighed, checked out the guy at cash again. He looked like he was trying not to grin. Another tourist soaking up the local color. She lowered her voice. "Go tell Pops. He'll fix you up with his secret concoction. It'll probably burn your toenails off, but it'll settle your stomach."

Summoning a smile, she scooted over to the cash register. "Sorry to keep you waiting. What can I do for you?"

As she looked up at the man, his tawny gaze caught hers and pulled her in. He was tall and lean, his jean jacket outlining broad shoulders and a narrow waist. With an artist's eye, she automatically studied the way he held himself, as if taking care not to disturb the air around him. His nose had been broken at least once. She was guessing more than once. He didn't have the bright-eyed, ain't-life-grand look most visitors wore when they walked in the door. A stranger, but not a tourist.

"What's the fifty-fifty draw for?" The man's voice was soft and deep, and she caught herself wanting to lean closer to him.

"The what?"

He nodded at the glass gallon jar that sat beside the cash register. "The draw, what do you have to do to win?"

"Oh." Her cheeks heated up. "You have to guess what's been added to the mural." She waved a hand toward the back wall, where she'd painted a scene of the village. Folk art was not her usual style, and after years of treating art as a discipline, she'd felt like a kid with a new box of paints when she'd tackled the mural.

The fifty-fifty draw had started when she realized she'd forgotten to include the Hacheys' boat in the mural. Worried someone would interpret the omission as a sign of bad luck, she'd added the minor detail early one morning before the café opened. No one on earth was more superstitious than fishermen. Beanie, the local plumber, had noticed the change a few days later. It hadn't taken long for people to start placing bets on who could spot the newest addition. Not that she'd planned or wanted to keep adding to the mural, but it had been so good for business, she'd have been stupid not to run with the idea. Yet every time she looked at the damned thing now it was like a slap in the face. The mural was the last half-decent thing she'd painted. And it was folk art.

He squinted toward the back wall. "You'd have to spend a lot of time looking at it to see what had changed."

"Exactly."

He shot her an admiring look. "Who's the artist?"

"Me. So. Breakfast? Coffee? You can have it to go if you want. The coffee, that is." She tried holding his gaze, but felt herself being pulled in again and broke the connection. So he had pretty eyes—a solid band of black circled his gold-flecked, hazel irises. She already had an acceptable boyfriend. She may have only seen Oliver twice in the past half year, but they hadn't broken up…yet.

"Coffee to go would be great. Black, with a half teaspoon of sugar."

She spun around, slid a paper cup off the stack and grabbed the fresh carafe of coffee.

"I actually came in to ask for directions," the man said to her back.

A tourist after all.

"Two Briar Lane. Do you know where that is?"

Hot coffee spilled over her hand as surprise jolted through her.

"Hey, are you okay?"

"Yes." She thrust the coffeepot onto the hot plate and looked over her shoulder. "You wouldn't be the new owner, would you?"

He did the stillness thing again, like he was holding his breath. "That's right."

They'd often joked about who'd bought the old run-down house next to her family's house. One of the best things about returning home, other than watching her father grow stronger every day and the occasional romp with her brothers, was living on Briar Lane with no neighbors. Apparently life wasn't going to stand still for her, not even in Collina. What a pity.

Sylvie forced a smile as she turned back to the man and held out her good hand. "I'm Sylvie Carson. We're neighbors."

ADAM HUNTER FELT calluses on the woman's palm as they shook hands. Her hands belied her appearance. He'd never been good at describing things, but to him she looked like an angel. Almost. More like a tarnished angel, which was a helluva lot more appealing than a perfect one. It was her curly, white-gold hair that made him think of angels. And her sky-blue eyes. But that's where it stopped. Her mouth was too pouty, too full and ripe, and her body… Adam pulled his hand away from hers and doused the heat that flickered through him. Tarnished or not, she was somebody else's angel. He'd bet on it.

"Adam Hunter," he said. She probably hadn't lived beside his gram's house all those years ago. He'd have remembered, wouldn't he? Or maybe not. At eight years old, he'd been a lot more interested in snakes than girls.

"We've been wondering who bought the old Johnson place. Took you a while to get here." She slid his coffee across the counter.

He'd have arrived a day earlier if he'd had the sense to stop and ask for directions. Instead, he'd spent the night in Lancaster, the closest city. But she probably meant the nine months that had lapsed since he'd inherited his gram's summerhouse.

Adam's stomach knotted when she avoided looking him in the eye. He knew the place was run-down. He'd visited only a handful of times when he was a kid, and the house had been old then. If it was beyond repair, he didn't know what he would do. The promise of moving to the small fishing village, of restoring the old house and making a home, had kept his head above water for the past few months.

In a few minutes he'd see for himself what shape it was in, but it was just as important to get a feel for the village and the people living here. The café seemed like a good place to start. "Interesting place. Are you the owner?"

"My family owns it."

People were eating breakfast in the first half of the room. Past the crowded tables and chairs, several comfortable armchairs and a couch were loosely arranged around a woodstove with a glass door on the front. Everywhere he looked there were stacks of books; in columns leaning against a support beam, on several small tables positioned around the room. Two laptops stood open and ready for use on a long table in another corner. Available Wi-Fi. Great. It would probably take a while before he could get his systems up and running. In a little nook near the back was a kid's corner with a knee-high table holding paints and crayons and more books.

The morning sun spilled in through the large front windows that looked out on the street, and apart from the colorful mural, the walls had been painted a warm gold color. It was a room that tempted people to use it, and judging by its warm, lived-in look, people had accepted the invitation.

"How much for the coffee?" When his voice echoed through the suddenly hushed room, he kept his smile in place. He imagined small towns had their own set of rules, and one of those would be knowing your neighbor's business.

"First one's free." The angel smiled.

"Thanks, I appreciate it."

"You have a family?" she asked.

Not one he planned to tell anyone about. "Just me and my dog. So, Briar Lane?"

"Go back to the main street, turn right. Turn right again at Seaman Street. Briar Lane's at the end. We're the only two houses on it."

Adam felt a whoosh of air as the door opened behind him. "Hey, sis. I need a coffee to go." A man close to his age stepped up to the counter. He was an inch or two shorter than Adam and solid through the chest and upper arms. He had the same blond curls as his sister, but his eyes were a darker blue, edged with creases, like he spent a lot of time squinting into the sun. Adam thought he might remember the guy from the few times he'd visited his grandmother as a child.

The man turned to him. "That your dog in the half-ton?"

"Yeah."

"Beautiful animal. Oh, thanks, Syl." He grabbed a cup of coffee from his sister. "I never saw a shepherd with that much white in it. Is it a mix?"

"Haven't the faintest. I'm thinking part wolf."

"Must make a great attack dog."

"The only thing I've seen Romeo attack are bumble-bees."

"Romeo?" The guy laughed. "What kind of name is that for a dog?"

Adam cracked a grin. "He's a lover, not a fighter. He's got a deep bark, though." He turned to Sylvie. "I'll keep him in at night so he won't wake you up."

The brother's smile dried up as he looked from his sister to him. "What's going on?"

"Meet my nosy brother, Dusty Carson. This is the… guy who bought the old Johnson place. Adam Hunter."

Out of the corner of his eye he saw her smother a smile. Not only tarnished, but sassy, as well. Nice. He didn't like the way she'd hesitated, though, like there was a better way to describe him. Idiot? Rube? Take your pick. Adam stuck out his hand to shake Dusty's.

"Actually, I inherited the house from my grandmother."

After an eternity, the angel's brother shook his hand. "I think I remember you. You came once or twice when your grandmother was up from the States. You've got Ontario license plates."

"I'm from Toronto."

Dusty studied him over the rim of his coffee cup. "You plan on holding on to the house or selling it?"

"I'm hoping to fix it up so I can spend the winter. Install some windows, probably put on a new roof."

An older man barreled through the kitchen doors, wiping his hands on a towel. "Whose roof are we talking about?" He looked at Sylvie. "I thought you'd left already, Sylvie. Better get going. I don't like you driving back from Lancaster in the dark."

Sylvie's father or grandfather, if his looks were anything

to go by. He was as tall as Dusty but more solid, bulkier. Despite his age, he still had a full head of blond hair. He held himself with the casual authority of someone used to commanding respect.

"His roof." Dusty jerked his thumb in his direction. "Adam Hunter. Mrs. Johnson was his grandmother, and he inherited her house. This is our dad, Pops Carson."

Not big on authority figures, Adam tried not to flinch as he met the old man's stare straight on. "You've got a beautiful town here," he said to fill the heavy silence in the café.

Pops shook his hand. "Your grandmother was a lovely person. I was sorry to hear she died. You're from Toronto, aren't you?"

"That's where I grew up."

"Toronto's a long way from here."

"That it is. I'm looking forward to a bit of peace and quiet." He'd told himself that so many times, it had become a mantra. Peace and quiet. His salvation.

Pops switched his attention to the red patch on the back of Sylvie's hand. "What did you do to your hand?"

"It's nothing." She turned her hand so only the palm showed.

"That looks like a burn. It could blister and get infected if you don't take proper care of it. Let me see."

Sylvie rolled her eyes. "It's okay, Pops. My hand is not going to fall off because I spilled a bit of coffee on it." She put her hand up to stop her father's retort. "I'll go home before I head out for Lancaster and put some ointment on it. Okay? Your turn. Did you take your morning medication?"

A smile softened Pops's weather-lined face. "Just going to do that now, missy. You phone when you leave the city to come home so I'll know when to expect you."

"No, I won't," she responded over her shoulder as she sashayed toward the door. "You'll be too busy chasing all the women at the dance. Come on, Adam. I'll show you where your house is. I have to run back home now, anyway. See you later, all." She waved over her shoulder and led the way out of the café.

Adam bit back a smile, nodded to the two men and followed her. Sylvie's father and brother might like to think they held the upper hand, but he had a feeling the sassy little angel was used to getting her own way. Something to keep in mind.

He climbed into his truck and gave Romeo a hard scrub behind his ears. "This is it, Rom. What we've been waiting for." He started the motor, his leg jittering so much the truck almost stalled as he engaged the clutch. Cursing under his breath, he pulled out behind Sylvie's fire engine–red SUV.

He'd envisioned this moment a thousand times. In his mind, it had been him, alone, standing in front of the house and taking his time to soak in each and every detail before going inside to explore. He hadn't counted on having an audience. Still, he was grateful to Sylvie for rescuing him from her father's interrogation. He was so jacked up about seeing his house, he hadn't been paying as much attention as he should have to what he said. He wanted this to work. He needed it to.

He followed Sylvie's four-wheel drive down a short side street that was lined with wood frame houses, each one different from the other. The last one was a lumbering old beauty with a widow's walk on its roof and fanciful trim. Driving into the village, he'd noticed a couple of other houses with the same kind of intricate detail. Once he got to know some people, he'd ask what the story was behind the elaborate carpentry.

It had been over seventeen years since he'd been here, and the end of the street came up quicker than he remembered. A long stretch of beach and the wide gray ocean opened up in front of him. When Sylvie turned sharply to the right, he cranked his steering wheel and strained forward to catch his first glimpse of his gram's house. Sylvie drove past 2 Briar Lane and pulled into the gravel driveway of a cedar-shingled two-story. He pulled into the weedy, narrow driveway he barely remembered and turned his attention to the small box of a house that sat before him.

His gaze shot over to his neighbor's house, which had dormers and a huge veranda along the front, then back to his. His had cedar shingles, too, but they looked mottled, the white paint peeling from them, partially exposing the gray beneath. The windows and front door looked like they'd rattle in a light breeze, and the way the stunted spruce between the houses leaned drastically to one side suggested they got their share of gales here. A huge crescent beach crept up to meet the small patch of grass that formed his front yard.

"Hey." Sylvie rapped her knuckles against his fender.

He switched off the engine and climbed out of the truck. Romeo jumped out after him, his nose leading him straight to Sylvie.

"Gorgeous dog." She bent down to run her hand over Romeo's head.

"Thanks." He couldn't peel his eyes away from the house. *His house.*

Someone else might see crumbling and decay, but to him it was beautiful. Everything he'd hoped for.

Sylvie straightened up from patting Rom. "What do you think?"

He tore his gaze away from the house and looked at her. At her clear blue eyes and silken, blond curls. A woman like her, she'd have a husband or a boyfriend who kept her busy. He wasn't interested in distractions, and Sylvie, if she were free, which she probably wasn't, could become a major distraction if he let her. He was here to work on his house. Maybe make a couple of friends. That's all.

Her forehead furrowed. "It's pretty run-down. Probably too much work to fix up. Although my other brother, Cal, says the house has a solid foundation and framework."

She'd said that last bit almost grudgingly. "I think I remember Dusty, but not you or another brother. How many siblings do you have?"

"Just the two brothers."

"Do they live here with you?"

"Cal and Anita have a house on the hill, and Dusty bought his own house just a few weeks ago."

"So, it's you and your dad." As anxious as he was to go inside and explore, he wanted to know who lived beside him. Where he'd grown up, being aware of his neighbors had saved his hide several times.

"Just me at the moment." She folded her arms and tucked her chin into her chest, frown lines creasing her forehead.

Before he could wonder why that ticked her off, she gave him a sour smile. "I have to get going. Enjoy your... house."

A vague feeling of distress settled around him as he watched her scoot over to her house and slam the door shut. Why did he get the feeling she was slamming the door on him?

Hell, he'd only been in town half an hour and already there could be complications. Fitting in and being accepted was going to be more difficult than he'd imagined. Maybe he'd made a mistake; Collina was too small. People would want to know where he came from, who his folks were.

But he'd been running from the day he'd been born, and it was time to stop.

One thing he knew for certain. He'd keep his distance from Sylvie Carson. He hoped to ease his way into the community, get to know a few folk before the questions started in earnest. After watching Sylvie's dad fuss about the light burn on his daughter's hand and her driving home in the dark, he had no intention of riling up papa bear. Not that Sylvie seemed the least bit interested in him. The exact opposite, as a matter of fact. But still, he'd be smart to stay on his side of the fence.

He dragged his attention back to where it belonged—his new home. His future. His hand shaking, he stuck the key into the keyhole and turned the lock.

CHAPTER TWO

TWO DAYS LATER, Sylvie dropped the phone into its cradle and wandered over to the dormer window of the attic room Pops had made into a studio for her years ago.

She'd woken depressed and tried to convince herself the low pressure system moving in from the ocean was the reason for her foul mood. The clouds looked saturated with rain, but none had fallen yet. There wasn't a breath of wind outside. The ocean, for once, was a benign presence, still and crystalline. She should go for a brisk walk along the beach, get her heart pumping and clear her head of the debris left from her brief conversation with her now ex-boyfriend, Oliver, whom she'd left behind in Toronto.

Oliver was a sophisticated, cultured man, and everyone envied her relationship with him. Even her father and brothers, for Pete's sake. No matter how many times she explained to them that Oliver had a doctorate degree in museum studies, not medicine, they referred to him as Dr. Templeton. When he'd visited her two months ago, nothing had been too good for the doctor. Lobster, scallops, boat rides out to watch the whales. Her family had fallen in love with him. Which, now she thought about it, wasn't an unusual reaction to Oliver. *She* was the problem, not him. To make matters worse, he'd seemed genuinely interested in everything her father and brothers had talked about. But that was Oliver. He made everyone believe they were fascinating.

In fact, during the entire two years they'd been a couple, she had thought about breaking up with him on more than one occasion. But when she tried to talk about it with her girlfriends or her family, or even Oliver, they looked at her like she was crazy. Small wonder. Her sole reason was that her handsome, considerate boyfriend annoyed her to no end. She always felt she had to be on her best behavior around him. And if she ever did let her guard down, act snotty and throw a fit, he'd say it was her artistic temperament and would she like a back rub? She didn't want a back rub, and she didn't want him to be so damned nice. She wanted...well, that was the problem. She had no idea what it was she wanted, but it wasn't Oliver.

This morning she'd taken the coward's way out and ended the relationship over the phone. The gesture had been mostly a formality. She'd only seen him twice since she'd moved back home and had assumed he'd gotten on with his life.

To her surprise, he'd done his best to change her mind, just as he had every time she'd told him she needed a break from their relationship. Yet this time she'd sensed something different. He hadn't sounded upset as much as annoyed—probably because he was far too self-contained to blow up. Too bad. She'd have welcomed a shouting match. Something that she could rip into. Something...real. The only thing she felt was relief.

Their lives had dovetailed together perfectly in the beginning. He owned a respected art gallery, and took a chance on her as an unknown artist—a chance that had paid off for both of them. Her career had taken off under his guidance and had been capped off when a corporation commissioned her to paint six seascapes. She'd managed to paint four before she returned home to help take care of Pops.

How could she have guessed that here, at the edge of the ocean, her muse would desert her, and she wouldn't be able to complete the last two seascapes? This was where it had all begun. Where she'd won her first drawing contest. Where she'd spent endless hours learning and perfecting her craft.

And now Oliver was hinting that she'd run out of time. The buyers wanted their paintings, and if she couldn't come up with them, the damage to her reputation, not to mention *his* reputation, would be irreparable. Bottom line, either she pulled it together and started painting again, or she'd better start shopping around for another career. Which was a slight exaggeration, and beside the point, because if she couldn't paint, she couldn't paint. But damn, she wished she could get it all back. Well, not Oliver necessarily. But she truly loved painting.

A burning sensation shot through her chest, a sure sign of an oncoming panic attack. She plopped into the chair by her desk, stuck her head between her legs and started counting. Life was difficult enough with her father still not completely recovered and her being blocked, she didn't need this. The panic attacks had to stop. Maybe she should forget about her career for now. Forget about everything, except resolving her issues with her family.

Except she hadn't even told them what she'd remembered about the night her mother died. She was waiting for Pops to get stronger. And then she'd ask her questions, and maybe somehow magically, she'd get her life back. Problem was, the longer she stayed in limbo, the more she wondered if she wanted to go back to her old life.

When her equilibrium returned and she could breathe again, she grabbed her sketch pad from the desk where she'd flung it the day before and ripped out the first page without looking at it, tore it in half again and again. She tore out another useless sketch, scrunched it into a ball and jammed it into the wastepaper basket. Sentimental drivel. The lines in the drawings weren't bold enough, they left too much room for interpretation. She wanted to excite people, stir them up—not give them something to snivel over.

The miserable preliminary sketches she'd ripped to shreds were all she had to show for six months of anguish. She'd actually thought she was an artist...with a future. Hah! What she was—three more pages came loose in one pull—was a talentless nobody. A waitress in her family's café.

She tossed the pad on the desk and stared sightlessly out the window until a movement next door caught her eye. Adam Hunter strode into his backyard and started his tai chi routine. Yesterday, watching him go through his routine for the first time, she'd sat riveted for an entire half hour. She'd seen people do tai chi in the city parks, but the difference was like looking at a reproduction of a masterpiece and looking at the original. Adam was the real thing.

Her fingers itched for a pencil as he slowly glided through a complicated set of movements, his body moving with the sinuous elegance of a dancer. Romeo sat only three feet away from him, but didn't move. Interesting that a man, whose less-than-perfect nose suggested he'd been in a few fights, would choose to practice tai chi, not one of the more aggressive disciplines.

Not able to stop herself, she grabbed her book and started sketching. She'd thought she hadn't been able to stop thinking about him the past two days because of what she had remembered of her father's relationship with his grandmother, but maybe it was because she needed to draw him. Heaven knows he had an interesting face, but drawing his body in motion, the combination of the brute strength of his huge, well-muscled body tempered with grace...

She chucked the book on the table and paced the large, open room. She needed to sculpt him in clay, a medium she'd been playing with before *The Great Demise*. She'd make a small sculpture, no bigger than twelve inches— any larger, and it would be overwhelming. And it would be best if she could get him to pose in the nude. She stopped, laughed out loud. Like that would happen. Her father and brothers would probably take him for a long boat ride and not bring him back.

Still. She took another turn around the attic room. She'd start slow, ask him if he'd sit for her. Then maybe work her way up to no shirt, get him down to his boxers or whatever he wore for underwear. Her breath hitched in her throat. She felt almost giddy, ramped up like...

What was she doing? Sylvie looked at the sketch where it lay on the desk. Hideous. A three-year-old could do a better job. Adam didn't look graceful or sensual in the sketch. The proportions were all there, but the excitement he incited was missing. The magic. She'd lost her touch, and she didn't need Adonis next door reminding her of that fact.

Sylvie ripped the sketch out of the book and crammed it into the wastebasket. Disgusted with herself, she pulled the window shade down and stalked out of the room. It was time to admit her life had completely crapped out. Sooner or later, she would have to tell her family that she wasn't moving back to Toronto until...well, she didn't know. Until her father was better, and they could finally talk about her mother. Until whatever had blocked her was dislodged. Until Sylvie Carson finally knew who she wanted to be when she grew up.

ADAM STOOD LOOSE, but alert, as he transitioned from his meditative state back to the world around him. He'd grown addicted to seeing the world in bright detail while feeling a deep sense of peace inside. Never in a million years would he have imagined he'd end up getting into meditation and tai chi. As always, he gave thanks to Jake McCoy, the man who'd given him the tools to manage his anger. He took a final deep breath and turned to track Sylvie over the four-foot cedar-slab fence that separated their yards.

He knew she'd watched him the past two mornings, and he was curious to hear what she thought about his morning practice. He'd have done his exercises inside if there was room, but his little house was divided into three small rooms downstairs and three upstairs. None were big enough for him to perform his daily exercise routine.

Not that he was ashamed of practicing tai chi, but he suspected the male stereotype still reigned supreme in a village like Collina, where most of the men made a hard living at sea. He wanted to fit in, not alienate people.

Wearing clingy, black pants that came to just below her knees, and a formfitting, long-sleeved T-shirt the color of a plum, Sylvie sauntered into the back corner of her yard. When she crouched down and cooed, a white cat materialized out of the shrubs. Adam put his hand down by his side and rotated it, signing Romeo to his side. Sylvie alone was trouble, but put her together with a cat, and he and Rom could both be in trouble.

Against his better judgment, he drifted closer to the fence. He knew he should leave well enough alone. On the other hand, people would start asking questions if he holed up in his house and didn't talk to anyone.

He cleared his throat when she didn't look in his direction. "It feels like rain," he said. Brilliant, yet original. Hard to top that.

Sylvie obviously thought otherwise. He heard her sigh as she scooped the cat into her arms and turned to face him. The smile she offered looked like the leftovers that usually resided at the back of his refrigerator. Bland, wilted and dried up around the edges. Guess she wasn't thrilled about acquiring a new neighbor. Or maybe it was having *him* as a neighbor. He was aware he looked like he belonged in a dark alley on the wrong side of town rather than in a quaint coastal village.

She glanced at the sky as if just noticing the day. "Probably. This is Moonbeam." She held the cat up in front of her. The white puffball's eyes were as blue as her mistress's. "I kept her in yesterday so Romeo could get used to his surroundings, but she was getting twitchy, so I let her out earlier. She's used to coming and going as she pleases. Is he okay with cats?" She nodded at Romeo, who was straining to sniff the cat through the slats of the fence.

Adam leaned against the fence, catching a whiff of peaches. "I don't know. This is a first for us. What do you think, Rom? Are you going to be nice to Moonbeam?"

Romeo lay down on his belly, which, according to the books Adam had read, was a supplicant position. Yes, sir, that was his dog, ready to let a little kitty-cat walk all over him. The cat sprang out of Sylvie's arms and onto the top of the fence. With a graceful leap, she landed on the ground in front of Romeo and swiped at his nose. Having delivered her message, she sat back, looking pleased with herself as she started to lick her paw.

"Moonbeam!" Sylvie glared at her cat. "I had no idea she was going to attack him. Sorry, Romeo."

Romeo cringed away from them, whimpering, his nose buried under his paws. The old boy was going to have to toughen up if he was going to survive in this neighborhood. Adam patted the dog and stood. "I'm going to reinforce the fence so Rom can spend most of the day out here. I can't keep him inside with all the dust from the renos. They'll have to work things out for themselves, I guess."

Adam studied Sylvie's face as she stepped back from the fence. She had dark circles under her eyes and her beautiful mouth was turned down at the corners. When he'd first arrived she'd been so full of herself, she'd practically glowed. But this morning she looked preoccupied and kind of sad.

"For now, I'll try to keep Moonbeam inside during the day as much as I can and let her out at night to roam. Will that work?" she asked.

"Sure, but sooner or later they're going to have to make some kind of peace." He wanted to ask Sylvie what was wrong, but clamped his mouth shut. Neighborly was one thing, getting involved in a person's life, another. He didn't like that she was sad, though. He wished he could think of something to make her smile—she had a great smile.

"How's it going with the house?" She shifted from one foot to the other. Twitchy like her cat.

His house. He smiled. "I have a pretty clear idea of what I want to do. Matter of fact, I should get going. I have to drive to the city and buy some building materials today. Do you know anyone who would be interested in helping with the renos? I want to get started right away."

"I suppose I could ask Cal. He was supposed to go away, but I think his plans have changed. But if he's busy, he'll know if anyone else is available."

She made it sound like asking her brother was the last thing she wanted to do. Fine by him. He wasn't sure he wanted to work with Sylvie's brother, anyway. From the short exchange in the café, he could see her family watched out for her, and with him living right beside her, he didn't want anyone on his case or looking too closely at him.

Sooner or later, someone was going to get wise to the fact that he had a criminal record. He didn't want to make waves or draw attention to himself. He just wanted to fit in.

"Collina is small, in case you haven't noticed. Tell one person you're looking for a carpenter and everyone will know in the next half hour," she continued.

Which meant it would be damn near impossible to keep a secret in this village. He'd known going in it was going to be hard. He wasn't ready to give up on his dreams that easily.

He hesitated, wanting to say something to make them both feel better. "You...you look great."

Her head shot up. "Excuse me?"

Adam backed away, a flush scorching the back of his neck. "Just...you know. You look nice. I gotta go." He turned and sprinted inside his house. At the very least he'd given her something to laugh about. Mr. Smooth strikes again.

SEVEN HOURS LATER, Adam arrived home tired, but excited. He'd decided to put up with both his malfunctioning toilet and the rust-colored water, instead focusing his efforts on a new roof and windows before the cold weather arrived. Although it felt like it already had.

The hour drive from the city had taken twice as long thanks to the thick, syrupy fog that had rolled in after sunset. And yeah, he'd gotten lost again, but he'd realized pretty quickly and backtracked to the main road. Reducing his speed by half had made the long, twisty drive in the dark only marginally easier. No wonder Sylvie's father had wanted her home before dark the other night.

He was thinking of Sylvie again.

He climbed out of the truck, and Romeo bounded out after him, immediately starting his circuit of their yard to mark his territory. Even though his mind had been occupied today with learning how to navigate the city and tackling all the decisions he had to make, Sylvie still slipped into his thoughts way too often.

There was no doubt about it—the less contact he had with her, the better.

He had a ton of other things demanding his attention, anyway. Like replacing the lightbulb over his front door. Unlike the city, the darkness here was complete, penetrating every corner of the night. Only the main street in the village had lights, and they hadn't done much to dispel the fog on his way home.

There wasn't much more to the village other than that one street, and a few side streets, like his, which led to or away from the ocean. He imagined the local fishing wharf and the café were the hot spots for socializing. Not that he planned to become a party boy. He'd partied so enthusiastically in his youth that if he never had another beer, he wouldn't miss it. Okay, that was an exaggeration. He liked having a cold one once in a while, but he didn't plan his life around drinking binges. Not like some of his family.

He felt his way cautiously through the fog to his front door, wishing he was as adept as Romeo at finding his way through the dark. Behind him, the restless surf raked over the round stones that made up the beach, the ocean sounding much closer at night.

When he first learned he'd inherited Gram's summerhouse, he thought his mother was jerking his chain. Just a step from the beach in the picturesque fishing village, and filled with good memories of time spent with Gram, the house was exactly what he needed at this point in his life. Something he could put his heart and soul into. A place to call home.

It had taken him an entire day to summon the courage

to call the lawyer's number. If his mother was tripping on something and screwed up the message, he didn't think he could face the disappointment. Hope was a brittle concept to him. But finally, he phoned, and two weeks later, he was the proud owner of an ancient, decrepit house far away from everything he knew.

Moonbeam appeared out of the mist and twined herself around his ankles as he shoved the door open with his shoulder. "It's not all that nice out, so you can come in if you behave yourself. But give Rom a hard time, and you're on your own. Understand?" The cat followed him into the house and padded into the kitchen. Adam laughed. At least she knew what she wanted. He'd get her some milk in a minute.

Juggling an armload of groceries, he flicked on the light and grinned as he deposited the food on the kitchen counter. He didn't care if the rooms were so small you could barely sneeze in them, or that the whole house had to be gutted and just about everything replaced. It was all fixable. And it was all his.

A door slammed next door. When Moonbeam reappeared and stared at him, he ran his fingers along her spine before edging up to the window to look out. A man stood in Adam's front yard, staring at his house. Adam had expected a few curious souls to come around, but not on such a gloomy night. When he heard the man talking outside the door, he wondered if there was more than one person, then remembered Romeo was still outside and swung the door open.

"Hey." The man straightened up from petting the shepherd. "I'm Cal Carson. You met my brother and sister and dad the other day."

Cal's face was narrower than Sylvie's and Dusty's, and he had only a sprinkling of blond in his short, brown hair.

He looked intelligent around his eyes, which were as bright blue as the rest of his family's, but they held a hardness that hinted at disappointment.

"Adam Hunter. Come on in." Adam shook Cal's hand and stood back to let him through the door. Romeo brushed past him with hardly a wag, probably miffed to find Moonbeam hanging around.

"You babysitting Sylvie's cat?" Cal nodded at Moonbeam, who sat on the old trunk that he was using as a coffee table. The old, battered furniture that had come with the house was what you'd expect to find in a neglected summer home. He planned to replace it at some point, but it served its purpose for now.

"Nah. Rom and Moonbeam haven't worked things out between them yet. Sylvie keeps the cat in during the day so Romeo can stay outside, and she lets it out at night. It's lousy out tonight. So…" He ran his hand over Moonbeam again.

Cal smirked. "That bit of fluff can come and go as she pleases. She's got a cat door. She's just taking advantage of you. Give them enough rope, they all do."

Ouch. Sounded like the guy had been burned recently. "Want a beer?"

"Sure. Sylvie says you're looking for help to do some renovations." Cal followed him out to the kitchen, where Adam grabbed a couple of beers from the ancient green refrigerator.

He handed one to Cal. "That's right. I'm in a race against the weather at this time of year, but I'd like to get a new roof on, replace some windows before it gets too bad. Ideally I'd like to replace *all* the windows and doors."

Cal looked around the room while Adam took a saucer from the cupboard and poured some milk into it for the cat. He wouldn't blame Cal if he turned and walked out the door. Wood flooring showed through the worn linoleum in front of the green stove and rust-stained, white enamel sink. The cupboards were made of plywood, painted a non-intrusive beige. It was the largest room in the house, but unfortunately one third of the country kitchen had been walled off for a mudroom.

"What kind of roofing are you thinking about?"

"Metal. I checked out a couple places today, got some costs."

"I could probably get you a better price."

"You're free to do the renos?"

Cal's mouth tightened at the corners. "I am now." He drank deeply and set his bottle on the table with a thunk. "Let's take a closer look at the rest of the house. Tell me what you have in mind. One thing, though." He scowled at Adam. "I take the job, I'm the foreman. I don't mind if you want to help. Matter of fact, that would be good 'cause it's hard to scare up a crew at this time of year. Have you done much building?"

"Not much but I learn fast."

Cal narrowed his eyes as if trying to bring him into focus. "Most people wouldn't move to an isolated village like Collina and take on a project like this. Do you always jump in with both feet?"

Adam smiled as if Cal had made a joke. "Not always." Only when it felt as if his life depended on it.

"You win the lottery or something?"

He relaxed his tight grip on the beer bottle. At least he got to tell the truth with this one. "I inherited both of my grandmother's properties, but I'm not interested in living in the States, so I sold that house and decided to renovate this one."

He still hadn't forgiven himself that he'd been in jail and not free to attend her funeral last year. When he was a kid, he couldn't wait to leave Toronto in the summer to visit his gram. He'd always felt safe with her. Both his parents had such mercurial moods, but Gram was always the same. Kind and loving, and when he was with her, he felt good about himself. He'd often daydreamed about what life would be like if he lived with her, but then who would have taken care of his mother? Their visits had always been too brief, and once he hit his teenage years…she wouldn't have wanted him around, anyway. Thank God those years were behind him.

When he discovered she'd left both houses to him, he invested the money from the sale of her house in Maine before his mother could find a way to get her hands on the cash. She'd burn through it in a few months, which was probably why Gram had named him her heir. When, and if, his mom wanted to get clean, he'd made sure to put aside enough money to help her.

"You think I can take that wall out without the whole floor falling down on me?" he asked, shifting the conversation to safer ground. He outlined what he wanted to do with the kitchen, inquired how many walls he could knock out and what Cal's rate was.

He couldn't stop grinning when they'd gone over the entire house. His dream was coming together. It was finally happening. Cal was an okay guy, a bit grim, but Adam thought they'd work together just fine. He certainly sounded knowledgeable when it came to renovations.

"No reason not to start tomorrow," Cal said. "I'll order the steel for the roof. We can start stripping the old shingles off first thing in the morning. Shouldn't take too long, it's a small roof." His eyes roamed over the living room. "You'll never get back the amount of money you're planning to invest in this house. We're too far away from everything.

Not a lot of people are interested in moving here. Hell, most of the young people move away first chance they get."

Adam nodded. "It's not an investment thing for me." Not financially. "I appreciate you bringing it up, though. Thanks."

"One more thing." Cal pulled a piece of paper out of his jacket pocket. "You know anything about this?"

Adam took the wrinkled paper. Holy! It was a pencil sketch of him doing tai chi in his backyard. Pretty hard to pretend it was of anyone else. The artist had gotten his broken nose exactly right. A thrill shot through him before the horror set in. Had Sylvie done this? "Where did you find it?"

"You didn't know Sylvie was drawing you?"

"No." He passed the sketch back to Cal. "She's good enough to make a living from her drawings?" The drawing was good, not the best he'd ever seen, but what did he know about art? What he should be concentrating on was damage control. He didn't want Cal to think he'd been coming on to Sylvie. Hell, he didn't want him to think he'd even looked at his sister.

"She had quite the career going, but then Pops had his heart attack and things have been pretty rough for her the last few months. She stopped painting 'cause—I don't know why. I don't think she does, either. But this—" He fluttered the sketch in the air. "This is the only thing I've seen her draw in weeks." He studied Adam. "So, what's the deal?"

"Deal?" Adam choked out as he watched his plans sink out of sight. Finding a contractor with an open schedule at this time of year was a blessing. Finding one right in the village was a miracle. He knew Sylvie was trouble the minute he'd laid eyes on her.

The Carson men weren't going to be happy about a

stranger cozying up to their angel. Especially someone like him. He was the first to admit he'd done some stupid things in his life. He wasn't perfect; he had issues. But he had to believe if he kept working at it, someday he would become a good man. Right now his dreams were about to go down the toilet if he couldn't convince Cal he hadn't a clue about the sketch.

"Has she said anything to you?" Cal placed the sketch on the old trunk.

"Like what?"

"I don't know. She usually paints landscapes, and she hasn't done much except for that mural since she came home. Why you?"

"Haven't a clue." Adam tried to quell his desperation. "Don't you think you're overreacting? So, she drew a picture of me. Big deal."

Adam caught himself forming fists and forced his hands to relax and hang loosely at his side. He inhaled, held his breath and slowly released it. Only then did he allow himself to look Cal in the eye. Jake would be proud of him. "The only thing I'm interested in is fixing up my house."

After a minute, Cal smiled. "It wasn't a very good sketch, anyway. She used to be really good, but, like I said, she's messed up now. Can't paint. I was hoping that you inspired her or something. She'll be going back to Toronto soon, anyway. Oliver—that's her boyfriend, a doctor—is probably fed up with her staying away so long."

The last of Adam's tension slipped away. The only thing Cal had been concerned about was Sylvie's career. It probably hadn't even occurred to him that Sylvie would give someone like Adam a second look. Not with a doctor boyfriend. Which was good.

Adam forced his attention back to what Cal was saying about the renovations. His house was important; not

Sylvie nor her boyfriend. Or the fact that she was returning to Toronto soon. The only thing he cared about was making a new life for himself here.

CHAPTER THREE

THE AIR HAD a bite to it the next day when Sylvie finally ventured outside midmorning. Not cold, but not summer warm, either. She shivered as she walked along the beach. She'd always hated the change from summer to fall. It signified having to leave and go back to school. Although she'd completed her master's degree a couple of years ago, her family would still be expecting her to leave soon.

She was running out of reasons to stay. Since Pops had moved into a seniors apartment at the complex, he didn't need her as much. And all she did at the café was order supplies and fill in for Tyler.

Her family and friends believed all her problems would go away once she returned to her life in Toronto. But even before she'd come home it had become a daily struggle to go to her studio and produce something other people might be interested in. Not that she considered her audience when she was painting. Nothing killed an original idea or approach faster than letting public perception intrude.

Weeks before Pops's heart attack, the joy she'd once felt from creating had shriveled into a hard knot of anxiety. Her therapist hadn't helped. Dr. Carmichael had managed to get her to admit she hated living in Toronto, and that Oliver was as much a prop in her life as her studio and her Yorkville apartment. Who wouldn't be depressed by an admission like that?

She stopped walking and watched as the sun dappled

gold on the ocean surface. Losing your mother was a turning point in anyone's life. But to discover her father and brothers had lied about her mom's death—or at the very least, not told the entire truth—was devastating. Sylvie couldn't even decide what they'd done or not done, but she knew they would have made any decision with her best interests at heart—which was wonderful when you were nine years old. But at twenty-six years of age she needed the whole truth if she had a hope of dealing with this new view of their not-so-idyllic family life. They'd had more than a few years to come clean, and yet they hadn't.

As recently as last week, she'd stopped by Dusty's with a six-pack of beer, hoping to loosen his tongue. She'd wasted her money because he'd been on to her scheme before he'd finished one beer and made up a fantastic story about Pops joining a cult of mermaids. She laughed out loud. Maybe she hadn't wasted her money after all. They'd had a great time, just the two of them, kicking back and trying to best the other with how silly they could be.

But to have Adam Hunter move in right next door… If her memories that had surfaced from the shock of almost losing her father were true, then his grandmother was responsible for wrecking her parents' marriage, and thereby indirectly responsible for her mother's death. That long-ago night, she'd overheard her parents fighting about Adam's grandmother, and soon afterward her mother had stormed out of the house and died in a head-on collision with a truck not even two miles out of Collina. Sylvie shivered. Had it really been an accident or had her mother killed herself?

She wished Adam would go back to where he came from instead of hanging around her backyard.

Maybe she wasn't being fair, but she hated the constant reminder of how things weren't right with her family.

She turned when she heard a sound behind her and plowed into her father. "Pops!"

"There now." He engulfed her in a hug, surrounding her with all things safe, the smell of Old Spice and the feel of rough wool against her cheek. "You were off in a world all your own." He patted her affectionately on the back and released her. "How's my little Em this morning?"

Sylvie forced a smile. Her father had given her the nickname when the critics noted her work was reminiscent of Emily Carr's art. "What are you doing here, Pops?"

"I need to get in my two kilometers a day, so I thought I'd join you for your walk on the beach." He slipped his arm through hers, and they started down the beach. "I wanted to check out the new neighbor, as well. Cal likes him." Pops smiled. "That's high praise coming from your brother."

They strolled amicably along the beach for a few minutes before Pops tugged her closer to his side. "There's something I need to talk to you about, honey. You see, I'm thinking of putting the café up for sale. I thought I should tell you first, even though you'll be heading back to Toronto soon, anyway."

"What?" She stumbled and almost fell. Not only was he expecting her to return to Toronto any day now, but he also wanted to sell the café.

"It doesn't make sense to keep the old place. You're living in Toronto, the boys are both settled in their careers, and I'm tired, hon. I don't want the responsibility of taking care of the café. I never did, really. When Mrs. Marley ran it, I didn't have to do much, but since she's retired, it's like I've got a whole new job. Plus, the money from the sale will make my life a lot easier."

Tears rushed her. She'd never seen her father look embarrassed before.

"The last few months I've been dipping into the profit

margin from the café because my pension doesn't cover all my medical expenses. That works in the summer when we're doing a good trade, but now the season's over, I've got to find money somewhere. The boys think it's a good idea."

"But, Pops—"

"Now, honey, don't cry. I know we've owned the old joint forever, but it's either that or sell the house. I can't hang on to both."

Sylvie gulped for air. The café was called Plain Jane's, named after her mother, the Jane part, anyway. Twenty years younger than Pops, her mother had been a stunning beauty. Sylvie sometimes wondered why her mother, so young and beautiful, had married such a gruff old fisherman. Pops had a heart of gold. But still.

The café was the last link she had to her mom, and in her mind, Plain Jane's had always been her backup if life tipped out of control. Just as the house was her refuge. Between the two, she'd believed she had a safety net. If Pops sold the café that would mean...she supposed it would mean she'd have to finally grow up. No more *I can always go home.*

"I'm not going back to Toronto." The words spilled out before she could censor herself. She'd rehearsed this conversation over and over and had been waiting for the perfect time to talk to her father about what was troubling her. Guess the perfect time had arrived.

"What?"

"I hate living there. It's not working for me. I want to move home full-time."

"Don't be silly. You're...you're famous. You can't walk away from everything you've worked so hard for."

"I'm not famous, Pops." But she loved him for believing she was.

"Well, you can't move back here."

"Why not? It's my home."

Pops ran a hand over his chest. "Of course it's your home. But there's nothing here, except your family. What would you do?"

"I'll run the café." She'd been playing with the idea off and on for the last few weeks, but it didn't feel like play now. The idea fit. It felt inspired.

"You're an artist, Sylvie. You don't know the first thing about running a business."

"Then teach me." Her voice rose as the words tumbled out. "I'm no longer an artist. You know I'm stuck—I can't paint anymore.… I'm twenty-six years old, and I've got nothing except my family, and even you don't want me."

"That's not true. Of course I—" Pops's face contorted with pain. "I don't feel so good. Maybe we should head back to the house."

"God, I'm sorry. I shouldn't have shouted at you. Are you okay, Pops? We could sit down for a minute, or I can run home and get my car. I'm so sorry." Sylvie beat back the burning sensation in her chest. No time for a panic attack now. If anything happened to Pops…

Pops smiled gently at her. "You're going to give yourself a heart attack if you don't slow down. I'm fine. I get a little winded sometimes. The doc says I push too hard."

"You always have." Sylvie slipped her arm through his and guided them slowly toward the house. She hated seeing her father vulnerable and weak; his fragility was the first hint that things couldn't continue as they were. But that didn't mean he had to sell the café. If they'd only give her a chance, she knew she could make the business even more successful.

"I have some money saved," she said after a few minutes of silence.

Pops patted her hand. "It's not only the money but also the responsibility of running a business. It weighs on me."

"I've been giving it some thought. It would be good for me to try something other than painting for a change. I could run the café business. I know I could. I've got lots of ideas."

Pops laughed. "Of course you do. You're our genius."

"I'm not a genius, Pops. I'm just an ordinary person with a gift."

He wasn't listening. No one listened to her. The familiar pang of disappointment tightened inside as she followed her father's gaze out to where a fishing boat was taking its time winding through the marked channel. By the bright blue hull, she could tell it was Ron Hachey's boat. Lobster season was just around the corner, and the fishermen were anxious to get their traps in the water. Yesterday in the café, she'd heard Ron say he planned to try out his new motor today.

Pops turned his attention back to her. "There's not an ordinary bone in your body, honey. That's why you can't stay. Collina is too small for you. I know you get homesick from time to time, and that you love us. But to live here full-time? I honestly can't see you being happy."

Hard to argue against such certainty. Maybe Pops was right, maybe living in Collina would drive her nuts. But she'd been here six months already, and despite the frustration of people thinking they knew what was best for her, she hadn't been bored. Much. The fact was Toronto didn't feel right to her anymore; the city didn't fit. She was better off here for the time being.

As they approached the house, she noted her father's normally robust complexion had turned gray, and his breathing was coming in short, harsh gasps. She'd phone the doctor later and ask if Pops's fatigue was to be expected at this point of his recovery. Maybe they'd missed something in the last checkup. It didn't feel right to her that he still struggled to do normal, everyday things. And she likely wasn't helping his recovery; it must have weighed on his mind, knowing he had to tell her about putting the business up for sale.

He was right about one thing. Other than her family, there wasn't much holding her here. If the café didn't prove challenging enough, she'd have to leave and find something else to do.

An insidious pounding stabbed her left temple. It felt as if her skin had shrunk two sizes too small for her head. God. She squinted, trying to ease the pain. No wonder she had panic attacks. Twenty-six years old, and she didn't have a clue what to do next. But she was getting ahead of herself. If the café was her sole responsibility, that would be enough to keep her busy, right?

And she wouldn't stay just for the sake of staying—not after Pops was completely recovered, and they'd had their father-daughter talk and straightened things out between them. But that was one conversation that would have to wait. She'd upset him enough today.

She kissed his cheek. "Why don't you come inside for a cup of tea, and I'll drive you back to the apartment after?" She still couldn't bring herself to call the seniors apartments his home.

"I'm going to see what the boys got done this morning on Adam's house. Cal'll drive me back." He hugged her.

"Would you consider not putting the café up for sale right away? I'd like to stay a few more weeks, and…it would just be nice to hold on to it for a bit longer."

He narrowed his eyes, reminding her of Cal when he was trying to suss out the truth. Her older brother had ridden herd on her and Dusty in their teen years when Pops was busy fishing. They never could get anything past him because Cal had learned from the master—Pops.

"I guess I could hold off for a bit. It's not the best time of year to sell, anyway. But I'd like to get it on the market soon. Give folks some time to think about buying."

"Thanks, Pops. I just need to get used to the idea." And time to prove to her family she could run the business successfully. "Are you sure you don't want me to drive you home?"

He waved her off. "I want to ask Adam a couple of questions. Cal will drive me."

Adam again. Surely Pops wasn't going to ask Adam if he wanted to buy the café. Unless he was fabulously wealthy, and by the look of his older truck and the way he dressed, she didn't think he was, Adam would probably have to look for work eventually. The lack of job opportunities in town was laughable. But wouldn't that be rotten luck? Her father decides to sell the café, and Adam turns up on their doorstep with enough cash in hand to buy it.

She hurried to keep up to her father. If Pops started talking about selling the café, she'd steer the conversation in another direction. "I've got a few minutes before I have to go to work. I'll come with you."

Other than raising his eyebrows, Pops didn't say anything. She never could get much past the old man. She loved her brothers and father, but her eyes often glazed over two minutes into one of their conversations about… whatever. Building, fishing, fixing engines. But this was one conversation she planned on paying attention to.

When they walked around the corner of Adam's house, Romeo bounded over to greet them. Sylvie bent down to scratch behind his ears and Rom leaned against her leg like he'd been waiting all day just for her. What a beautiful dog. She looked around the yard. Moonbeam hadn't been around this morning. Actually, since Adam had moved in, the shameless hussy had barely been home at all.

An armload of old roofing shingles slid off the roof and landed in a pile of debris ten feet in front of them. "Have you seen Moonbeam?" she shouted up at Adam and Cal.

They both stopped ripping at the shingles. "What do you want, Sylvie?" Cal looked impatient. "Oh, hey, Pops. What's up?"

Nice. She got a snarl, while Pops rated a hello. She bit her tongue to hold back a snappy retort.

"It's almost lunchtime. I thought you could drive me home, Cal."

Cal shot a look in her direction.

"I offered," she said, defending herself. She hated that she still craved her older brother's approval.

Pops sat on a paint-stained wooden workhorse while he waited for the men to climb down. "What's the use of living in the same village if I can't spend any time with you? You work too hard," he said to his son as Cal climbed down, followed by Adam.

"Have you seen Moonbeam?" When Sylvie turned to Adam, she faltered back a step. She'd been so focused on Cal, she hadn't really looked at her neighbor.

He wore a sleeveless gray sweatshirt and his faded jeans, weighed down by his tool belt, hung low on his hips. When he raised his hand to wipe a trickle of sweat from his forehead, his biceps bunched into a solid mass of muscle.

Sylvie swallowed and tried to look away from the tuft of underarm hair that peeked out of his sweatshirt and the startling white skin on the underside of his arm. The stark contrast of masculinity and vulnerability, hard muscle covered with velvet skin, thrilled her. She wanted to trace her hand down the underside of his arm and follow the prominent blue vein down to his wrist. She wanted, *no,* she needed, to get it all down on paper. Everything about this man… The sweat-streaked dirt on his face, his muscles. God, his neck. He had a beautiful neck. Even the shape of his—

"Sylvie, child, are you in there?" Pops shook her shoulder and smiled quizzically into her face.

She blinked and tore her gaze away from Adam's armpit. Oh, help. She was mesmerized by a man's armpit. Maybe Pops was right. Maybe she was going stir-crazy and didn't even know it.

"Sorry. I was just thinking…" She glanced at Adam and hoped like hell she wasn't blushing.

Pops put his arm around her shoulders and gave her a hug. "She does that sometimes, goes off into a cloud. Back to earth now, honey?"

She made herself smile. "I'm back."

"Moonbeam's inside," Adam said.

He'd stepped back a pace, as if he knew exactly where she'd drifted off to and didn't want to go there with her. "She kept hanging around, and I was afraid one of the shingles would hit her, so I put her in my house. I should have told you. Sorry."

In case some of her rapture of studying his armpit still lingered, she kept her gaze trained over his right shoulder. Pathetic. If she was going to stay in Collina, she'd have to get a social life and start dating because lusting after Adam Hunter didn't work for her. She needed someone else to drool over. "Thanks for looking out for her."

"That cat spends more time over here than she does at home." Cal grabbed an old towel draped over the workhorse and brushed the dirt off his arms as he squinted up at the roof. "We're almost done this side. We should get a good start on the other side today."

"Then you can spare a few minutes for your old man," Pops said before turning to Adam. "I was thinking of your grandmother this morning."

Sylvie stiffened and watched Adam from the corner of her eye as he hesitated before hanging his tool belt over the workhorse. Did Adam know anything about his grandmother and Pops's friendship? Probably not. How could he? She hadn't known and she'd lived right here at the time.

It wasn't his fault what had happened, but still, the situation was uncomfortable. Except as far as she could tell, she was the only one who had a problem with it. She sighed. She was acting like a bitch, taking her resentment out on Adam. She could at least act neighborly toward him. Maybe even offer the use of her kitchen and bathroom while he was working on his house.

And maybe when she got everything straightened out, she could paint his portrait. It would be a sin not to try to capture something of Adam's… What?

Well, body for one thing. But the appeal was more than that. He was a delicious mixture of contrasts that intrigued her. He was, in a word, a challenge. Maybe that was what her problem was. She'd been stuck doing seascapes for so long, she needed new, fertile ground to mine.

When she heard a note of longing in Pops's voice, she forced herself to concentrate on what he was saying about Adam's grandmother. Not exactly the confirmation she sought, but something had definitely happened between them.

"She was always excited when you came to visit. You were her only grandchild, weren't you?" Pops said.

Adam smiled. "Yeah. I loved spending time with Gram."

Pops stretched his legs out in front of him as he leaned

back against the workhorse. "Your parents still live in Toronto?"

"My mom's in Vancouver." Adam shoved some of the discarded shingles to one side with his foot. "My dad's dead."

"Sorry to hear that, son. No doubt he'd be proud of you, coming here and making a home."

Adam shot him a look from under his brow. "Maybe."

Sylvie could see he didn't like talking about his family from the way his shoulders had drawn together, and how his hands made a couple of spastic fists before he relaxed them.

"What kind of work was your dad in?" A question Pops had asked every one of their friends at some point.

But Adam had gone somewhere deep inside himself. He did his stillness thing, as though if he didn't breathe or take up space, they wouldn't notice him. Silly to feel that she should protect him. And from what? Her father?

"He was in security," Adam said.

"Ah." Pops smiled. "You mean like a security cop?"

"Something like that."

Pops nodded, looked at the roof. "You boys are making good progress. I won't hold you up. Ready to go, Cal?"

Cal slung his tool belt beside Adam's. "I'll be back in a bit. We'll start on the other side after you eat."

"Great." Adam scratched his arm as both he and Sylvie watched Cal back his truck out of the driveway.

"I'll get Moonbeam if you want." Adam didn't look at her as he brushed dirt off his jeans.

"If she's happy where she is, leave her. I've got to go to work, anyway. I was just worried she'd get hit by a shingle. I see Romeo's smart enough to stay out of the way. Just so you know, you don't have to feed Moonbeam. She has lots of food at home." *Shut up*. She had the urge to babble about anything but…armpits.

She looked at the debris on the ground, at the roof and finally at Adam. Why did the workingman thing look so fantastic on some men? Oliver would just look dirty. Adam looked manly. Scrumptious, if she was being honest.

Sylvie tore her gaze away. Oh, God, she wasn't getting a *thing* for him, was she? Of course not. He was a healthy, vibrant male in his prime, and she…

She was an artist and couldn't help noticing details about people. Like how Adam withdrew at times or how he did that thing with his hands. She had no intention of adding to her messy life by becoming attracted to another man. Going out on a few dates with a guy was fine. But an intense attraction? No way.

"Are you all right?" Adam frowned at her.

"Me?" Her smile faltered. "Of course. I was thinking… well, I haven't actually thought it out, but if the inside of your house is going to look like this." She pointed at the exposed roof. "You're welcome to use my kitchen and bathroom for cooking and stuff. If you want." That hadn't been so hard. She could act neighborly.

Adam folded his arms. "I don't know. It's nice of you to offer, but um…your family. They might not think it's such a great idea."

She laughed. "I haven't had to ask their permission to do anything for a long time. I don't need their stamp of approval."

"Thanks." He nodded. "I'll, ah…think about it. Appreciate the offer."

"Right." Was that a yes or a no? "I've gotta go." She dipped her head toward the village and the café. "Have a good day."

She sprinted over to her car and climbed in. *Have a*

good day? How lame could she get? He probably thought she was a spastic dweeb. And if he didn't yet, her brothers would make sure he did by the end of the week. Knowing them, they probably already had plans to introduce him to the available women in town.

Which was a good thing, because Collina needed more people living here. And she needed Collina. That was where she wanted to direct her time and energy, making a place for herself here. She already had several ideas of how to increase business at the café at this time of the year. If she could stage one successful event, maybe Pops and her brothers would take her more seriously and agree she was capable of running the café.

Feeling more optimistic than she had in months, she whistled on her way to work.

THE SUN PEEKED over the horizon as Adam knocked softly on Sylvie's door, then slipped inside and deposited his two bags of food on the counter. Cal had told him no one locked their doors here. Details like that—unlocked doors, wide-open, deserted beaches, and people stopping on the street to talk to each other—reinforced his decision that this was where he wanted to live.

According to Cal, Sylvie wasn't an early riser. He liked that Sylvie had suggested he use her home for cooking and washing up, but hadn't seriously considered the offer until he mentioned the idea to Cal, who agreed, albeit a tad reluctantly.

Adam's water was a rusty brown. He could buy water to drink and cook with, but he hadn't figured out what he was going to do about having a shower. Collina was too small to have any public facilities like a community center with showers or a Y. Plus, this way he didn't have to waste time putting stuff away every day before they continued ripping his house apart.

After giving it some thought, he'd realized that using the kitchen and bathroom next door sounded like the perfect solution. But now that he was in Sylvie's kitchen, he realized he should have given the idea *more* thought.

With her working nights at the café, he figured he should be able to avoid her most of the time. But it felt weird tiptoeing around her kitchen while she was still in bed. Sylvie and bed—intriguing, but not an image he wanted stuck in his head.

He pulled out the coffee beans he'd thought to grind before leaving his house. He'd make enough coffee for both him and Sylvie. Same with the blueberry pancakes he had planned. If she didn't want them, he'd leave a note for her to put the batter in the fridge, and he'd use it for tomorrow's breakfast.

After whipping up the batter and covering it, he crept into the hallway to find the bathroom. He stopped, listened for sounds of Sylvie moving around upstairs and continued on to the bathroom when all remained silent.

Moonbeam sat square in the middle of the hallway when he came out of the bathroom after the fastest shower he'd ever taken. The shower shelves had been full of Sylvie's stuff, and the room had smelled like peaches. He swore the girly smell still clung to him.

The cat's tiny pink tongue slipped out once as she practiced her cat stare on him. "You've got my number, don't you?" He scooped her up and laid her across his shoulder as he shoved the kitchen door open.

"Oh. Hey." He halted in the doorway.

Sylvie leaned a hip against the counter, sipping coffee. She wore those tight black pants she seemed to favor and a faded, blue-and-white flannel shirt that had probably belonged to one of her brothers or her father.

The curious expression on her face closed down. "I thought you were Pops."

"Sorry." He stopped, tried to form his thoughts into a cohesive sentence.

She looked warm and sleep-tousled, and he was back to thinking about how great she'd look in bed. Not a direction he wanted his thoughts to go. What the hell had he been thinking—that he could ignore a woman like Sylvie?

He slipped Moonbeam off his shoulder and edged toward the coffee, planning to grab a cup and run. With his back safely to her, he continued, "It didn't occur to me to tell you I decided to take you up on your offer to use the house until I walked in this morning. Sorry."

"Make yourself at home."

He stiffened. Was she being sarcastic? Had he crossed some invisible boundary? People questioning his integrity was a by-product of the life he'd lived, but somehow he'd gotten it into his head that life would be different here. *He* would be different. Resigned to the inevitable, he put a half teaspoon of sugar in his coffee and turned to face her.

"I'll get out of your way. Sorry to wake you."

"No, I'm sorry. That sounded rude. I didn't mean to imply you weren't welcome. I'm not my best in the morning." She smiled. "Where's Romeo?"

"Outside." He allowed himself to relax against the counter as he suppressed a laugh. Wow. It suddenly dawned on him that he was playing in a whole new ball game now. One where people didn't automatically assume the worst of each other. That someone would apologize to him for *indicating,* not assuming, but only *hinting* he may be out of line, brought home how much he wanted to live here. "We went for a five-K run already, so he's pretty pooped. That's such a great beach. It's amazing not many people use it."

"One of the perks of living in a sparsely populated area, I guess. Romeo's a great dog. Did you train him?"

"No. I got him from the animal shelter when I knew I was moving to the country. The previous owners loved shepherds, but having a large dog in the city is difficult for even the biggest dog lover." He sipped his coffee. "Cal says you live in Toronto."

"Yeah." She let out a weary sigh.

He watched as she slipped into a chair at the table and leaned her head on her hand. Either she hadn't completely woken up yet or living in T.O. wasn't doing it for her.

"What part?"

"Yorkville."

He raised his eyebrows. "That's a classy part of town."

"It's okay." She stared into her coffee.

He moved to the stove and turned the heat on under the frying pan. He might as well cook the pancakes he'd started. Sylvie didn't seem to mind him being there, and he could use a big breakfast to start his day. He poured a scoop of batter into the pan and watched it sizzle along the edges. "Any idea when you're moving back?" *None of his business.*

"Haven't a clue." When she continued to stare into her coffee, he felt a wrench in his gut. The same feeling he'd had a couple of days ago in the backyard when she'd looked sad. He flipped the pancake over. She had a family to support her—hell, she probably had the whole village at her beck and call. It wasn't his responsibility to cheer her up.

He slipped the pancake on a plate and placed it in front of her, then poured more batter into the pan. "You don't want to move back to Toronto?"

Her head jerked up. "I didn't say that."

No, she didn't, and if he were smart he'd stop talking right now. What Sylvie felt or didn't feel was none of his business. "You don't sound very enthusiastic at the prospect."

"There's nothing to go back to."

"Cal said you have a boyfriend. A doctor?"

"You and Cal had quite the conversation."

He turned his attention back to the stove. "Cal—" did *not* find a halfhearted sketch of him doing tai chi "—just mentioned you were a really good artist and lived in Toronto."

She lathered butter and maple syrup on her pancake. "That's all in the past. I'm going to have to figure out something else to do now. Mmm," she said around a mouthful of pancake. "These are fantastic. I don't suppose you want to work at the café? We're desperate to hire a second cook."

"Sorry. I'm too busy right now." But once his house was finished, he'd consider it. The café was probably the hub of the village, and that was the kind of thing he'd like to get involved with.

He put another pancake on her plate, poured more batter into the pan and expertly cooked up a stack of pancakes as Sylvie ate hers. When he had what he hoped would be enough, he sat at the table, slipped a couple more to her and added syrup to his.

"Thanks."

Adam forked up a mouthful and sat back to watch her eat. He was a good cook and he liked feeding people. He might not be able to help Sylvie with her problem, but at least he'd made sure she started the day with a good breakfast.

When she finished eating, Sylvie shoved her plate to one side and leaned toward him. "Would you teach me how to cook?"

Feeling as if he'd been dropped into the middle of a minefield, Adam placed his forkful of pancake back on his plate. "You don't know how?"

"No, and I want to learn."

"Um…" He looked everywhere but at the hint of sadness in her eyes. "Teressa. Ask her. She's a cook."

"Teressa hates me. She won't teach me."

"I met her yesterday. She seemed like a nice person. I doubt she hates you." When Sylvie skewered him with a snarky look, Adam smothered a smile. He liked her sass.

"Okay, she doesn't hate me. She thinks I've got it made, and her life stinks. She loves her kids, but having two different fathers for them is hard. Nothing's ever come easy for her."

"And it has for you?"

"No. I've worked my butt off. But no one sees that, or at least wants to see it. I'm the one who left and made it in that big, cold world out there." The corners of her mouth crimped tight. "Sorry. I don't usually indulge in self-pity."

He had to admit that he didn't understand what her problem was—she was young, beautiful and apparently successful. What he did know was he needed to come up with a reason why he couldn't teach her how to cook.

No way could he spend time around this woman and not have rampant fantasies about her. She was just too damned hot. It wouldn't take long for him to want to act on those fantasies, and then he'd be back to the Carson men wanting to know exactly who he was and where he'd come from. Assuming, of course, Sylvie was interested in him. "Your father and brothers don't know how to cook?"

"They do, and they won't teach me, either. Everyone either thinks I should be painting all the time, or they're afraid I'm going to slice a finger or hurt myself if I work in the kitchen. But they don't get it. I need to know I can do something other than paint." As Sylvie paused, the pleading in her eyes damn near broke his heart. "We don't have to tell anyone. It would be our little secret."

No. He tore his gaze away from her angel-blue eyes and said the word inside his head again to make sure he got it right. *No.*

"Sylvie, I—"

"Please don't say no." She reached across the table and grabbed his hand. "I'll get up early, and I'll clean up whatever mess we make. And I promise I'll be really, really careful so I don't hurt myself."

Because if she did, the Carson men would fry him alive. "You don't know how to cook anything?"

"I can make coffee. And scramble eggs. Sandwiches, of course." She shot him a crooked smile. "And I excel at ordering takeout."

Her smile hooked into him and his resolve softened. "You'd think your family would want you to know how to take care of yourself."

"I was always good at drawing." She dipped her finger into the pool of syrup on her plate. "I won an art contest when I was nine. That's the year my mom died, and somehow my family saw that contest as my consolation prize for losing Mom. Or so my therapist tells me. After that, Pops and Dusty and Cal couldn't do enough to…I don't know, nurture my talent, I guess. I was the baby of the family and the only girl, so… They were all hurting, and maybe it was easier to concentrate on me rather than deal with their own pain."

She stared at the pattern she'd drawn in the syrup. "It eased their grief every time I drew a picture, so I kept drawing and drawing and drawing. I thought—I don't know—that if I kept it up everything would be okay, and we'd be happy again. I drew my way into a scholarship when I was sixteen, and I've been living away from home ever since."

He'd left home at fifteen for entirely different reasons, and he was sure he'd been a lot tougher than her. Even with his false bravado, it had been a rough go sometimes. Sixteen was a tender age. Too young to leave home.

His unexpected anger at her family caught him by surprise, and he stood and picked up the plates to dispel the feeling. The world was full of nasty, dangerous people. What had her family been thinking to let Sylvie leave at such a tender age?

He let the dishes clatter into the sink and turned on the water as he did his deep breathing exercise. *Okay.* None of this was his business. Keep things on track and get out.

"They never had a chance to teach you how to cook," he said as he started washing the dishes. "Doesn't mean they won't now. You should ask them."

"I have."

Adam closed his eyes and prayed he hadn't heard her voice tremble. He grabbed the frying pan, scrubbed it with more gusto than necessary. "I gotta go. Cal's going to be here soon." He drained the sink and bolted for the door, keeping his back to the table where Sylvie sat.

Not sat, *huddled.*

Man, why did he look at her? He'd almost made it out the door. What was it about this woman that unhinged him? He liked women well enough, had even fallen victim to a few and had a couple of semiserious relationships. But he'd always felt a measure of reserve with them, because truthfully, he didn't quite get women, and that usually resulted in him saying as little as possible. So far, that didn't seem to be happening with Sylvie. If anything he had to work at keeping his mouth shut.

He walked back to the table. "I'm not saying I'll be

available every morning, but okay, maybe tomorrow. I'll show you how to make an omelet. You'll have to get up early, though."

Her eyes twinkled as she beamed up at him. He sighed in resignation and tore his gaze away from the stunning picture she made, with the morning sun kissing her face. "And you'll have to clear it with your father first," he added.

Her twinkle dimmed at the same time the delicate line of her jaw hardened. "I'm twenty-six years old. I do not need my father's permission."

But *he* did. If he pissed off her family, he could lose Cal's help, and work on his house would grind to a halt. Things were getting off track, and he'd just started working on his house. "We'll try one morning, then."

"And go from there."

Adam backed up fast when Sylvie jumped up from her chair, looking grateful enough to give him a hug. *Not going to happen.*

"I'm not making any promises. Just so you know." He rushed the door and escaped outside.

Teach her how to cook. He shook his head and headed toward his house. Most people when they met him kept their distance because of his size and because he looked like a scrapper. But for some reason Sylvie seemed to have locked right into the fact that he was a pushover. He didn't want people to be afraid of him, but neither did he want it getting around that he was an easy mark. Saying no to anyone had never been his strong suit—another reason to stay away from Sylvie. Half an hour, and she'd convinced him to teach her how to cook. What next?

CHAPTER FOUR

THE LIGHT WAS fading from the sky when Adam made his way over to Sylvie's house later that day. In many ways, it had been a good day. The sun had shone all day, and he and Cal had ripped the last of the shingles off the roof. Tomorrow they'd prep for putting the steel on.

Cal was a man of few words, but despite his reticence, Adam liked him. He was smart, and he had a confidence that came from knowing who he was and where he belonged. Adam had never possessed that quality. Because though he knew where he came from, he was doing everything in his power to leave that past behind. He'd always dreamed of belonging, and Collina was as good a place as any. Maybe better. Wouldn't it be something if someday the folks of Collina accepted him as one of their own.

He knocked, waited a beat in case Sylvie was home, then shouldered his way through the unlocked door, his arms full of groceries.

He paused to listen to the quiet house. Sylvie was still working, he supposed. Hopefully he could shower, cook supper and leave before she returned home. Not that he didn't like seeing her, but she was an unnecessary complication. Life would be a lot easier if Cal or Dusty lived next door, not their sister.

As for teaching her how to cook? Man, he still didn't know how she'd roped him into that one. He planned on keeping his word, but he wasn't going to go out of his way to do so. No sense looking for trouble.

It wasn't hard to see how protective her brothers and father felt toward her, and he didn't want them getting crazy ideas about him and Sylvie. He came with a lot of baggage, and once people realized who they were dealing with, his dream of fitting in and being a regular joe could be lost forever.

He'd done time for assault, and if his record ever surfaced, he'd hope to have the opportunity to explain how and why the fight had happened. But he'd never confess that his immediate and brutal reaction to his mother's abusive boyfriend had confirmed what he'd always feared—he harbored the potential for violence.

His dad, Paulie Hunter, had been an enforcer for the dreaded biker gang Sons of Lethe. For the first ten years of Adam's life, brutality, in one form or another, toward him, toward other people, toward the damned pet rabbit he'd tried to hide from his father, had been a daily occurrence.

As a child, he'd been dragged from his bed several times each year to flee with his mother and father, leaving everything he owned behind. He'd grown up looking over his shoulder, and it wasn't always for the cops. The Raiders, the sworn enemy of the Sons of Lethe, had a price on Paulie's head for years. They figured if they could get to his father through him, all the better.

What they hadn't understood was Paulie wouldn't have cared. He'd told his son straight-out if he was stupid enough to get caught by the Raiders, or any of his father's other enemies, not to count on his old man for help. Paulie Hunter damned well wouldn't have sacrificed his life for his son.

It had taken longer than it should have for Adam to admit his dad was a killer, probably a psychopath. Or sociopath. It didn't matter what you called him, he'd been one sick dude who relished violence. Adam had not only feared his father, he'd also been ashamed of him. Still was, when you got right down to it. And yet, what secretly shamed him was that, in a weird way, he loved his dad. Which caused him to wonder what that made him? How was it possible to love a monster? And Adam had been running away from the thought that he could be like this monster, his father, until the day he'd almost killed a man.

A few months ago, before coming to Collina to see his newly inherited house, he'd made the mistake of visiting his mother. He'd had the crazy notion that with the money he'd made from the sale of his grandmother's house in the States he could get his mom help to kick her drug habit. Never mind that she'd switched to using prescription drugs—a junkie was a junkie.

Instead of helping his mother he'd ended up almost killing her current boyfriend. Bruised almost beyond recognition, his mother couldn't even pull herself out of her drug haze long enough to report her condition to the police, but then again most of his family would die before asking the cops for help.

Horrified at the violence he'd unleashed on her boyfriend, Adam had turned himself in to the police and found the help he sought in the form of Jake McCoy, an ex-con who ran a center against violence.

The cops got a kick out of Adam turning himself in for a crime that hadn't been reported, but he'd needed help, and he didn't know where else to go. It had worked out okay in the end. His mother's boyfriend wound up doing time for assaulting Adam's mother. Adam had served a few months for assault, and then spent the last few months of his sentence doing community service, working with juvenile boys who came from similar backgrounds as him. He met Jake at the drop-in center for street kids, and that was when he began to see his way out of the shit pile of his life.

Adam dumped his groceries on the kitchen table and continued on to the bathroom. Now here he was, months later, ready to get on with his life. And he'd do damned near anything to fit into Collina.

Like Cal said, he'd never get back the money he was investing in the house. Which meant if things didn't work out in Collina, he wouldn't have the money to start over somewhere else. Sure, he could get a job and a mortgage in another town, but his heart had already picked this spot to make his home, probably because he associated it with his gram. He doubted he had the courage to start again somewhere else if things didn't work out.

He shouldn't have caved this morning and promised Sylvie he'd teach her how to cook. But it had struck him, despite all the talk about her talent and success, that her family hadn't taken into account Sylvie or what she wanted. Maybe she'd change her mind and go back to Toronto like Cal said she would. If she did, it sounded like it would be better for all of them—except, maybe, Sylvie. The thought made him feel lousy, but then he'd always been a sucker for the underdog.

He grabbed a quick shower and returned to the kitchen. Over the past year, cooking had become his secret passion. Lots of men cooked these days, but every time he indulged, he heard his father sneering over his shoulder. Old Paulie would not have approved of his son cooking anything more than a hamburger on a grill.

He laid out three chicken breasts, sprinkled olive oil and rosemary over them and slid them in the oven along with a scrubbed potato. Halfway through mixing the greens for a salad, Dusty burst through the door. He grabbed a chair, turned it backward and straddled it.

The Carson boys might be interested in becoming friends with Adam, but apparently they also planned to keep close watch on him. He didn't know if they were just curious or watching over their little sister.

"Smells good. Got any extra? I haven't eaten yet."

"There're more potatoes in that paper bag." Adam nodded at the counter. "Scrub one and toss it in the oven."

"So, you cook, huh?" Dusty washed two potatoes and rolled them into the oven.

"Yeah. You?"

"Some."

Adam slid the salad into the refrigerator and leaned against the counter. "Hey, I don't know if you can help me out with this, but I've got a bike in the back of my truck. I need a place to park it, a shed or old barn, doesn't matter, just somewhere to get it out of the weather. You know of anyone who's not using their garage or shed?" He hated asking for help, but he didn't have a choice.

"I've got a shed at my hunting camp where I keep my four-wheeler when I'm hunting. It's not far from here. Fifteen minutes." Dusty pulled himself out of his slouch. "What kind of bike have you got?"

"Harley." He pushed the word out. He didn't want to tell anyone about his dad's bike, but he needed to find a place to stash it. He should have asked Cal, not Dusty. Cal might have kept it to himself.

"Cool."

"I'd like to unload it somewhere so I can use my truck to pick up building supplies. Do you think we could shoot up there now?" Best to do it with as few people around as possible. He didn't welcome questions about the bike.

"What about supper?"

"No problem. I'll put the oven timer on, and the food will be ready when we get back."

"That thing has a timer?"

Adam laughed. "Yeah, they're great. I'll show you how it works." He explained how to set the oven to turn off in thirty minutes and followed Dusty out the door.

When they crossed the yard to Adam's truck, the sky was clear, lit up by a gazillion stars. Adam looked longingly at the beach. He'd love to drag out an old blanket, lie down and soak it all up—the stars, the restless sound of the waves, the smell of salt in the air. Not tonight, though. But the good news was the beach wasn't going anywhere and neither was he. He grinned at the thought. Life was good and getting better.

Dusty's hunting camp wasn't much more than a plywood shack set deep in the forest. By the number of beer cases that lined one wall of the shed, it was evident a lot more drinking than hunting went on there.

"You ever gone deer hunting?" Dusty asked as they moved the empties out of the shed to make room for the bike.

"Nah." He hated guns.

"The season starts in a few weeks. You wanna give it a try, we can go together."

"Hunting's not my thing, but thanks."

"I like it 'cause Pops taught me, and the three of us—Cal, me and Pops—go every year. You know, do the guy thing." He laughed. "But it's not for everyone."

When Adam was eight, his dad had started taking him to the dump to shoot rats. He'd taught him how to use a knife as well, but it had been about survival, not sport. As Paulie Hunter's son, his dad had been giving him a running start against his enemies, that's all. He supposed it was his dad's idea of fatherly love.

Adam rested a two-by-eight board against the lowered tailgate of his truck and hopped up under the truck cap.

To avoid questions, he'd have preferred to stash the bike out of sight by himself, but it was too heavy and awkward to move without help. "Can you climb up in here? She's heavy. I'll wheel her out if you hang onto the rear so it doesn't get away on me."

Dusty whistled when he saw the bike in the yard light. "Sweet wheels. Is it custom built?"

"Yeah."

"You ride often?"

"Not much." He grabbed the handlebars and pushed the bike into the shed. Romeo gave a soft woof from inside the truck. He didn't know how the dog would react to the wilderness, so he'd left him in the cab.

Dusty followed him. "It's a lot of bike for an occasional ride."

"It was my dad's." He should have sold it before leaving Toronto. But it was the only thing he had of his father's, and he wasn't ready to let it go. Ironic that it was that same kind of sentimentality that used to drive old Paulie crazy.

"You decide to take it for a ride, let me know. I'm not crazy about riding shotgun, but it would be worth it with that machine. Your dad, he's not alive anymore?"

"No." Adam closed the shed door, relieved to have the bike out of sight. It stirred up too many unresolved feelings. Maybe Paulie'd been right—being sentimental would sink you every time.

"I can't imagine my old man not being around," Dusty said as they backed out of the driveway a few minutes later. "We used to whine about him being too strict when we were kids, but he's always been there for us, you know? When I was six, these two kids started tormenting me. I guess you'd call it bullying now. When Pops found out…" He whistled through his teeth. "I don't know what he said to their parents, but those kids never picked on me again."

Dusty scooted sideways in his seat and peered through the dark cab at Adam. "How about your dad? Was he a weekend warrior?"

Adam choked. "Excuse me?"

"You never heard that expression? All those old farts riding bikes they can barely hold up. Weekend warriors. No disrespect to your dad, of course."

Adam wanted to laugh. What would Dusty say if he told him that his father could have killed someone for calling him that? He slowed the truck as he crept through a deep pothole that had eaten a good part out of the road. Hopefully, the hole would discourage people from driving down this route.

"Is there much crime around here?" he asked as he picked up speed.

"Crime? Like what?"

Dusty had said that like he'd never heard the word before. Adam grinned. Would it always feel like he'd fallen down a rabbit hole and ended up on the other side of the rainbow?

"Like breaking into your camp or stealing my bike. It's pretty isolated out here."

"Just about everyone's been out to my camp, and they know there's nothing there to steal. Too far to go for too little. We won't tell anyone your bike's there."

"Sounds good to me."

"You never answered about your dad."

And therein lay the danger of getting too comfortable around anyone. He'd thought Dusty was talking for the sake of talking, but this time Adam caught the curiosity in his voice.

"My parents divorced when I was ten, and my mom and I moved out West a couple of years after that. My dad wasn't around much." Thank God. Handling his mother's addictions had been tough enough.

"That's too bad. Nice that he left you his bike, though."

Old Paulie didn't do nice. If Paulie could have taken it to the great beyond, he would have. Adam ended up with it by default.

Dusty chatted on the way back to the house, leaving Adam free to chase images of his father from his mind. When his mother had left his father he'd dreamed of life getting better without Paulie around. He'd imagined he and his mom buying a house, having a real home—one they wouldn't have to desert in the dead of the night. But his mother was a junkie, and it didn't take long for Adam to realize that without his father's questionable but lavish income, they were in trouble.

And trouble led to more trouble. At twelve, Adam joined a gang so he could make money to feed his mother and himself. By the time he turned fifteen he'd graduated to stealing cars. Everything—the lifestyle, the brotherhood— had felt right. Familiar. Until a street gunfight broke out between his gang and another. His best friend had died in his arms. The cops picked him up, more for his own safety than anything, and he'd served six months in a juvie hall. By the time he'd gotten out, his mother had a new douche-bag boyfriend, and he realized it was time for him to move on. He'd been on his own since.

With heavy memories weighing down his footsteps, Adam followed Dusty into the house and silently served up supper. As Dusty chatted about the upcoming fishing season, his last hunting trip and this winter's local hockey team, Adam only half listened.

Was Adam crazy to think he could settle here and live a normal life? Every time someone asked him about his family, he felt as though they were shining a spotlight on his past. He had too much baggage, and it was too damned hard to leave it all behind.

They had just sat down to eat when Sylvie waltzed in. She had a lot of color in her cheeks and her eyes made him think of how the blue ocean looked with sunlight on it. Geez, he was turning into a regular poet. He dug into his potato, hoping to distract himself from the plunging neckline of her pink T-shirt.

"What smells so good?" She pulled up a chair beside her brother and filched a piece of chicken from his plate. "Yum. Is this your own recipe?" She directed her question to Adam.

"Yeah."

"He even made his own salad dressing," Dusty said around a full mouth of potato.

She picked a tiny tomato out of his salad and popped it into her mouth.

Dusty jerked his plate out of Sylvie's reach. "Get your own."

Adam grinned as he got up from the table, grabbed a plate out of the cupboard and put it in front of Sylvie. Sylvie and Dusty had no idea how lucky they were to have each other. "There's another potato in the oven and lots of salad. You can have the last piece of chicken, too."

"Are you sure? We shouldn't be eating your supper." Despite her polite inquiry, she slipped the chicken on her plate as she spoke and started cutting it into small pieces. She closed her eyes as she savored the first bite. "Superb."

Then opened her eyes and skewered him with a look. "I'd love to know how to cook this."

Heat crept up his neck. He couldn't teach her if she wasn't around when he was cooking, now could he? He stabbed a piece of lettuce. "It's real simple. I'll write it down for you."

Dusty looked from Adam to Sylvie. "Why?"

"Very funny, bro. Did it ever occur to you I'd like to know how to cook a meal for myself?"

"Why bother when you can afford to pay people to do that stuff. You should concentrate on what you're good at and get back to painting."

"Why exactly are you here, Dusty?" Sylvie asked without missing a beat.

Adam slid his chair back a few inches from the table. Sylvie may look sweet, but she sounded like she knew how to hold her own against her brothers. Why did he find that reassuring?

Dusty choked on his food. He made a big deal of clearing his throat and taking several gulps of water. "I stopped by to see Adam," he said after the obvious stall. "He was cooking supper, and I begged him to feed me." He grinned at Adam. "Good stuff, man. Lobster season doesn't start for a few more weeks, but I've got scallops back at my place. You want some?"

"That'd be great. Thanks."

"I'll bring you some tomorrow night."

"Tomorrow night?" Sylvie sounded annoyed.

Dusty got up and took his empty plate to the sink. "Or the next night. Whatever."

"Call before you drop by the next time." Sylvie continued eating.

"Yeah, right." Dusty laughed, then frowned at her. "Are you serious?"

Sylvie put her fork down and sighed. Adam watched affection deepen the blue of her eyes as she looked at her brother. "Not really. It's just…I'm not used to coming home from work and tripping over you. Every night. If you want to hang out with Adam, you can invite him to go for a beer. Or, here's an idea. Hang out at *your* house. Sometimes I like to come home and soak in the tub with a glass of wine and a good book. Alone."

With candlelight. Adam rubbed his forehead to banish the image from his mind. Think of something else. Think… Romeo barked from his yard, and Adam clambered to his feet.

"Fair enough." Dusty headed for the door.

"But I still want those scallops," Sylvie responded to her brother's back.

"Only if you promise to let Adam cook them, not you." Dusty turned to Adam. "I'll check on Romeo for you. Relax. You worked hard today. See ya, man."

Adam had planned to eat and leave, but now he felt awkward, as if he were a dinner guest. "I'll wash the dishes before I go." He scooped up the dishes from the table, pleased he'd thought of an exit line. Better to not examine why he felt ill at ease left alone with Sylvie. All he wanted to do was clean up his mess and leave.

Sylvie jumped to her feet and grabbed a dish towel. "You wash. I'll dry. Or, I'll wash and dry, and you write that recipe down for me."

He glanced sideways at her, then looked away.

"What? Do I have gunk on my face from the café?" She watched Adam scrub the plate harder than necessary.

"You look great. Was the café busy tonight?"

"Why? Did my father talk to you?"

Adam stopped scrubbing. She took the plate from him, a tingle shooting up her arm as their fingers met. She almost dropped the plate.

"He did, but you were there, too, sort of, yesterday afternoon."

She snapped her teeth together to keep the snark inside.

It was exactly the kind of gibe her brothers would make. "I meant today."

"Haven't seen him today." He grabbed a dish towel and dried his hands. "I don't think this is such a great arrangement, Sylvie. It's gotta be a drag for you to come home and find a stranger in your house. I can do all this stuff at my place."

He didn't feel like a stranger to her. He felt like...like someone she wanted to lean against. Right now. Standing side by side at the sink, she wanted to just lean against him. Maybe he'd put his arm around her and kiss the top of her head, and they'd make a silly joke about—

"Here's the recipe. Told you it was simple." Adam handed her a piece of paper he'd ripped from the notepad by the telephone. He pulled on his jean jacket. "Sorry you weren't here when I made supper. Maybe another time." He backed toward the door.

The one person in the village who was willing to help her was about to escape out the door. Couldn't she have one person on her team? Did everyone have to work against her?

Sylvie blinked back tears of frustration. Tears would have him out the door quicker than a house fire. "I liked coming home and finding you here. Really." In truth, she'd had to concentrate on not thinking about him all day. "The house smells so nice and the lights were on and..." She looked around the kitchen, trying to think of more positive stuff to say.

"And I need to talk to someone." She smiled, hoping he'd be pleased. But his face darkened as he narrowed his gaze. He stayed close to the door.

"About what?"

Geez, could he sound any more suspicious? What did he think? That she needed help planning a murder?

"Well…" She went back to the sink and pulled the plug. "I'm going to plan a cycling event for the café, and I need to bounce some ideas around." She sprayed water around the sink and turned to face him. Still with the suspicion.

She didn't consider herself vain, but she knew she was a reasonably attractive woman, and when she smiled at a man, the response was usually somewhat warmer than what she was getting from Adam right now. She was tempted to remind him she'd missed out on cooking lessons tonight, through no fault of his, but still, surely he could stay and talk for a few minutes. Not that he owed her anything.

"It'd be better to talk to someone who knows more about the village or café than I do."

"No, you're exactly who I need." She blushed and turned away. Grabbed the notepad and pencil and sat at the table. She didn't *need* to smell his scent of ocean and sunlight. Just as she didn't *need* to feel his arms around her, as much as the idea intrigued her. "People get stuck in ruts. They see things the same old way. But you're new, and that makes you the perfect person to help me."

And he was. What did Adam care if she stayed in Collina or left? He was impartial to her just as she was impartial to him.

She wrote CYCLING EVENT in block, capital letters across the top of the sheet and checked to make sure she had his attention. Adam still stood close to the door, but looked resigned to the inevitable. She beamed up at him. "Want a coffee or a beer?"

She thought she heard him sigh as he moved to the counter. "I'll make the coffee. But I have to grind the beans. Hope you don't mind the noise."

Sylvie watched as he moved gracefully around the kitchen. He was such a big man, and with his broken nose and that stealthy thing he had going on, he looked like he was a trained killer or something. Sylvie shivered. What did she really know about him? One thing was for sure, he shouldn't have looked so at home in a kitchen. But he did.

She picked up the pencil and started sketching him, trying to catch whatever it was that made her feel as if she could sit all day and watch him work. When Adam placed two full mugs of coffee on the table, she ripped the drawing from the notepad and scrunched it into a ball. She should know by now to leave well enough alone.

"My idea is to have an all-day event for cyclers. Is that what you call them? Cyclers? Bicyclists? I should look that up." She scribbled a note to herself.

"Cycling would probably do it." He pushed a mug in front of her. "Cream? Sugar?"

"Just cream, thanks. Okay, so what things can we do to keep them here? See, that's the point. Or one of them. First, they need to have a good time. Second, they have to stay around long enough to want to eat. The café will be the headquarters for all the events, so everyone will gravitate to it. What do you think?"

Adam sat and stirred sugar into his coffee. "Sounds good so far. What kind of events do you have planned?"

"I don't. Not yet." The interest in his eyes dimmed, and she scrambled to come up with an idea. "Okay, how about we map out different routes for different levels of biking? Like, beginners, intermediate and senior level." She scribbled the words on the notepad.

"Beginners would bike through the village, go to the wharf and the swimming hole. Maybe across the covered bridge, then back to the café," he added.

"Perfect." She grinned across the table at him. Not only because of his suggestion for a beginner's run, but he also hadn't once said a cycling event was a stupid idea or that no one would come. How great was that?

"You'll have to do something about traffic," Adam added.

"I'll talk to Tommy at the highway depot. And we'll need to come up with at least two more routes. Do you have a bike?"

His interest faded into sudden detachment. She pushed on, hoping to keep him engaged. "Dusty has an old bike kicking around, I think. I'll ask if he'll lend it to you." She made another note. "We should fix up the bikes and try out some of the routes ourselves. And…" She bounced in her seat as another idea hit her. "We could have some bikes here. Not just for this event, but all the time for people to rent. No, to loan out to customers. This is great. People are going to love this."

As she laughed across the table at him, their gazes connected, and she felt a solid thunk inside her chest. She hadn't realized they'd been avoiding looking into each other's eyes, and no wonder. A glimmer of affection and admiration shone in his. Her own gaze faltered, and she felt her smile dim.

A dozen different ideas crowded in as she looked away. Adam Hunter was a really special man, but he didn't let people see that part of him. Or at least he didn't let *her* see it. He was the perfect antidote to everyone's set expectations of who she was and what she could do because he didn't know her.

Could he be her muse? She'd heard of that happening to other artists. Why not with her? And why not Adam?

She stood, circled the kitchen, her fingers itching to draw him. But no, she'd tried only minutes earlier and it hadn't worked. For once in her life she had no choice but to *wait* for inspiration to come to her.

"Are you okay? You look like dinner didn't agree with you."

She stood beside the table, drawing circles on the notepad. Circles that were really question marks. Why Adam? And why now after all these months?

"I'm fine. Let's get back to the cycling event."

A corner of his mouth hitched up. "I thought that's what we were talking about."

She shoved everything else out of her head and smiled back. "Of course we were."

"Good to know we're thinking about the same thing." A wicked gleam sparked in his eyes momentarily, then disappeared.

Her heart did a funny little leap, as if jumping for joy. *Were* they thinking the same thing?

"I was wondering," Adam continued, "what do they win?"

"You think we need a prize?"

He wrapped his large hands around the empty coffee mug. A scab covered a nick on his knuckles. His mouth curved upward as he looked at her lips. "I can think of one or two things I wouldn't mind winning."

Heat washed over her. She tore her gaze away from his and cleared her throat. "How about a…a free lobster dinner at the café? Ties right in with promoting the café."

"How about an original poster of the event."

She grew still. "A poster?"

"You're going to make posters to advertise, right?"

"I guess. I hadn't thought of it." She crossed her arms, feeling suddenly exposed.

"I'd think that a poster by Sylvie Carson would bring a lot of people to the village. But it wouldn't be like a painting," he added. "You could paint it on…whatever you use for posters. Something simple. You could do that, right?"

She stared at her folded hands, trying to ignore the fist in her stomach. She should tell him it was a stupid idea—except it was brilliant. Lots of people recognized her name, yet until now, the village hadn't capitalized on her fame much.

But what if she couldn't draw a simple poster?

"I'll have to think about it." She went to the sink, poured a glass of water and drank deeply.

"It was just a suggestion, Sylvie. You don't have to do it."

Her muscles locked into place when she heard pity in his voice. How embarrassing. He felt sorry for her. That's how everyone would look at her if she failed to produce an acceptable poster, as if she were a pitiful failure. If they didn't already.

Adam wasn't her muse. He wasn't even her friend. He was a neighbor and a stranger, and damn, she hated feeling like a loser. Especially around him.

She plastered a polite smile on her face and turned to face him. "I think I just hit a wall. I'm bushed. But that was a good start. Thanks."

Adam stood but didn't move away from the table. "When were you thinking of having the cycling weekend?"

"I don't know." She massaged the small of her back with her thumbs. "It's just in the planning stages."

"It's a good idea, Sylvie. I think it'll work."

"You think so?"

"Yeah, I do." He headed for the door. "Let me know when you find Dusty's bike, and we'll try out a couple of routes."

"Okay. I'll do that. And thanks, Adam. I appreciate your help. We're still on for a cooking lesson tomorrow morning, right?" At least she'd be a loser who knew how to cook.

Geez, did he have to look so grim? Maybe she should let him off the hook about the lessons. But then she wouldn't learn how to cook.

"I suppose. We both have to eat." He nodded and left. Sylvie smiled as she picked up their mugs and put them in the sink. Adam may not be her muse but he was interesting to work with. Maybe between the two of them they could actually pull off the cycling event. And an omelet. She certainly couldn't do all that by herself, and so far, no one else had volunteered. Adam hadn't, either, but he was too polite to say no to her. For a second she considered feeling guilty about taking advantage of his good nature but ended up laughing at herself. Yeah, Adam Hunter looked like a pushover. Not.

CHAPTER FIVE

ADAM SLOWED HIS PACE as he approached Sylvie's back door. When he stopped by the step, Romeo woofed once as if asking *what about him?* Adam squatted down to give the dog an affectionate rubdown. They'd had a rip-roaring run on the beach and watched the sun come up. What a way to start the day.

With one last pat, Adam straightened up and eyed the house. He had to go inside and teach Sylvie how to cook an omelet. For the hundredth time since he'd made the promise, he wondered what had possessed him to agree. Not only to the cooking lessons, but last night he'd also promised to help with the cycling event. He wanted to become involved with the village, but…but what? Not with Sylvie?

Fair enough. Neighbors were one thing. A wave over the fence, a nod as they passed each other in their vehicles. But Sylvie seemed determined to involve him in her life. Dear God, she wasn't attracted to him, was she? He already struggled to keep a lid on his attraction for her. If she came on to him… He swallowed. Yeah, not going there.

Either way, he'd made promises he planned to keep. But he'd watch her for clues on how she felt about him. If he saw any indication she was interested in being more than neighbors, he'd have to let her know he wasn't looking for that kind of involvement. Not yet, anyway. And by the time he was settled enough to have a relationship, she'd be gone back to Toronto. Adam grabbed his bag of clean clothes and wash-up gear he'd left on her porch before going for his run, rapped once and opened the door, on full alert.

And felt like he'd been sucker punched the second he entered the kitchen. Sylvie was curled up in the old armchair in the corner with Moonbeam on her lap, both of them sound asleep. She looked young and unguarded—the sight of her took his breath away. Her long, golden eyelashes fanned out over her skin and the curve of her cheek struck an ache deep inside him.

He shook his head. Good thing he was on guard against her advances. If she so much as opened her eyes, and oh, say, smiled at him, he'd be on his knees.

Moonbeam opened one eye and twitched her nose. Damned if it didn't look like she winked at him as he tiptoed past. The damned cat was as sassy as her owner.

He ran his shower hot, then cold at the end because he needed to clear his head and start thinking straight. Sylvie was an attractive woman, and he was a normal guy. Of course he'd noticed how beautiful she was. But it didn't have to go any further than noticing. He still had the upper hand.

When he entered the kitchen, Sylvie was awake. And stretching her arms above her head. Her blue sweater, made out of some kind of soft-looking stuff, skimmed over her generous curves and started another, more familiar ache. An I-want-but-can't-have ache.

"Morning," he barked. "Sorry if I woke you." He grabbed the coffee mill and tossed in some beans.

"I got up aeons ago so I wouldn't miss you. I must have fallen asleep again. How many of those did you put in?" She crossed the room to where he stood at the counter, bringing with her the smell of peaches.

"How many what?" he asked, tearing his gaze away

from how her clingy pants hugged her behind. Why couldn't she wear jeans like everyone else?

She smiled. Brilliantly. He pressed the button, drowning out all chance of conversation. Seemingly undeterred, she pulled herself up onto the countertop and sat, swinging her legs. When he turned off the grinder, she continued as if he hadn't interrupted.

"Beans. I was going to make coffee, but you make the best coffee I've ever tasted. So I decided to wait. What kind of beans do you use and how many?"

"Doesn't matter how many." Though you couldn't tell by the way he stared at the beans in the jar he'd left on the counter, as if he were counting each one. "The kind of beans do. I use fair trade. Costa Rica. Whatever I grind now but don't use, I save for later."

"And how much do you put in the coffee machine?"

Adam glanced over at her. She was taking notes. He relaxed and rubbed a hand over his mouth to hide his smile. "A tablespoon for each cup."

She looked up from her notes. "Are you laughing at me?"

"Who? Me? Nah."

"You are, too. I'm serious about learning how to cook."

"Yeah, I got that. But taking notes on how to make coffee? You've gotta know how. Everyone does."

Sylvie let out a huff of air. "Of course I do. But I want to get this right."

"You're a perfectionist."

"Sometimes."

He rolled his eyes and started pulling ingredients from the refrigerator. Perfectionists didn't take a day off. "That's what makes you a good artist."

"I'm not an artist. Not anymore." She slid a sly smile

in his direction. "But I could learn to be a good cook with a little direction."

He turned his chuckle into a cough. He had to toughen up. Let her know he had limits on what he'd help her with. "You could try out a few recipes on your own, you know. That's what recipe books are for."

"I'm a visual person, and I learn much quicker when someone shows me how to do something."

God, she was quick. Hard to get anything past her. "What kind of omelet do you want to cook?" On the counter he lined up an onion, a green pepper and a brown bag of mushrooms. Good thing he'd stocked up on fresh veggies the other day.

"The kind that oozes out yummy ingredients." She smacked her lips.

He laughed. "I'm not sure about the ooze part, that'd be lots of cheese, I guess. You can start chopping those." He nodded at the veggies on the counter, and moved out of her way when she hopped down. "Small pieces. And take your time, so you don't cut yourself."

"Aye, aye, captain. What are you going to do?"

"Drink a coffee." He grabbed a mug from the cupboard, poured his first cup of the day and sauntered over to the window. Romeo was lying on the ground outside the door. Moonbeam sat a foot away from his, swishing her full tail as she studied him. Adam grinned. Looked like Romeo had met his nemesis.

"You're not going to help?"

He continued looking out at the bright morning. A fog bank was building a mile or two out to sea. No sense torturing himself by standing close to Sylvie if he didn't have to. "Only if you need me to. What do the fishermen do when it's foggy out?"

"Use their radar and their chart plotters and GPSs.

There's not much guess work with navigation these days. Are these onions the right size?"

He glanced over his shoulder. "Perfect. They don't all have to be the exact same size."

"Right." She pushed the chopped onions into a neat pile on one corner of the chopping board.

Adam sighed. Breakfast would take hours if he didn't help. Which he'd been trying to avoid. After the rush he'd gotten this morning when he first walked into Sylvie's house, there was no doubt it would be easier all around if he kept his distance.

"I'll chop. You get the eggs, the milk and a bowl." He put his coffee down and washed his hands.

Sylvie stood by his side. "Didn't I chop the onions okay?"

"Yeah, but I don't have much time. Sorry." He started chopping the pepper.

"Holy mackerel. I didn't know I was supposed to go that fast." She reached for the knife.

He held it out of her reach. "No way. I've had tons of practice. You'd slice a finger, and then your father would have to kill me. You can beat the eggs."

"How many?"

"Two." He made the mistake of looking at her as she bent over to rummage in the refrigerator. He suppressed a groan. This cooking lesson had been a really, really bad idea.

"So what happens if their navigation equipment fails? That could happen, couldn't it? If they lost battery power or had an engine failure?" he asked, more to distract himself than from any real worry. The local fishermen had been working at their trade forever. They could probably find their way home blindfolded.

"Then they get lost at sea and all of us go out to look for them and start praying."

He kicked himself mentally when he heard the stress in her voice. "Sorry. Stupid question."

He bit back a curse when he felt a stab of pain. Great. He'd cut himself.

Sylvie set the carton of eggs on the counter as he grabbed a paper towel and wrapped it around his middle finger. "Are you okay?"

"Yup. Just need a bandage."

"I'll get you one. Shouldn't you run cold water over the cut or something?"

"Sure."

As Sylvie left the room, anger exploded inside him. He didn't know why he was mad— Well, he did, but he didn't know what to do about it.

He must have been a lunatic to think he could pull off this lifestyle. A sweet woman like Sylvie asked for his help with something as simple as cooking a damned omelet, and suddenly it felt like he was walking on eggs. *Don't think this. Don't say that.* Only an hour into his day, and already he was exhausted. He should have bought a cabin in the wilderness, away from civilized people. He didn't know the first thing about acting like a normal, decent person.

He sank onto a chair and rested his arm on the table, his finger throbbing. Or maybe he should have stayed in Toronto, where people didn't care who he was or what his father had done for a living.

"I brought different-size bandages and the peroxide." She smiled sweetly. "It doesn't sting as much as iodine. You didn't run water over the cut yet?"

He stood, grabbed the bandages from her and went over to the sink. "I'll take care of it."

"Are you mad?" Sylvie asked in a subdued voice.

"No." Yes, but it had nothing to do with Sylvie. Or not much.

"You are. I can hear it in your voice."

"Why don't we just drop the subject?" He turned on the tap and watched the water wash the blood away. The cut was deeper than he'd thought, but it didn't need stitches.

"You're mad at me because I asked for your help." She slid up beside him at the sink.

"I'm just not in a good mood."

"Because of the cooking thing."

He remained silent as he grabbed a handful of paper towels and dried his hand. The bandage proved tricky to get on with one hand.

"It's always better to discuss things when you're mad. My brothers yell at me all the time."

He wished she'd back up a foot or two. He could feel the heat from her body, and he didn't want to be aware of her in that way. "I'm not your brother."

A nervous laugh escaped her. "No kidding. But it's still better to talk about things than keep them bottled up inside."

"For God's sake, Sylvie. Will you let it go?" Horrified, he watched her stumble backward, her face white and pinched with surprise. What the hell was wrong with him?

"I'm sorry. I'm an idiot." It took all of his self-control to keep from pulling her into his arms to comfort her.

"No, it's okay. Sometimes I don't know when to back off." Color seeped back into her face. "This is good. I mean, we can't be friends if we're not honest with each other."

The rotten feeling in his gut intensified. Then they'd never be friends because he couldn't envision ever telling her the truth about who he was.

"I can't believe I snapped at you. I'm sorry." What was

it about her that got under his skin? He worked hard at managing his anger, and it was unforgivable that it had gotten away from him.

"It's done. Over. Let's get back to cooking breakfast." She tried on a smile. "I'm looking forward to cracking a few eggs. Any tips?"

Really? That was it? Adam paused. True, he didn't feel as agitated anymore. But what about Sylvie? Embarrassed that he'd snapped at her, but relieved to move on, he tried to make up for his gaffe by showing her how to crack eggs using one hand.

A dozen eggs and a partially burnt omelet later, Sylvie looked pleased with herself as she insisted on cleaning up the mess she'd made. Adam checked the clock on the wall. Cal would be arriving soon, and Adam had planned to get a few things done before he showed up.

He poured another cup of coffee and leaned against the door, watching a smile play over Sylvie's lips. She was humming an unrecognizable tune under her breath, and the oversize brick-red apron she'd put on halfway through cooking breakfast was smeared with food. He smiled as he sipped his coffee. She was a sloppy, but happy, cook. After he'd put his doubts behind him, he'd laughed more this morning than he had in a long time.

"Did you talk to Dusty about his bicycle?" Adam marveled at his inability to keep his mouth shut around her. He was usually pretty good at letting sleeping dogs lie. But not today. Not with Sylvie.

"I did. He's going to bring it over in a day or two. Along with some scallops." She sent him a worried look. "He probably expects you to cook supper for him again. You should say no if you don't want to."

"I don't mind, especially if I'm cooking, anyway. Did you tell him about the cycling event?"

She went back to scrubbing the stove top clean of onion bits and eggs. "No."

She wasn't afraid of her family, was she? He hadn't been able to stop thinking about her last night after he'd left. It didn't make sense that someone with a successful career as an artist would spend so much time planning an event for the café. It seemed like such small potatoes in comparison. Unless she really was in trouble with her art.

Cal and Dusty had been very vocal on how she just needed to snap out of whatever snit she was in, but he had to wonder. He couldn't imagine being given a special talent, only to have it taken away. Sylvie had done nothing else all her life. If she really had lost her talent she must be afraid.

"This cycling event. It's important to you." He told himself he was asking because he wanted to know exactly what he was getting into. But part of him needed to know if she was hurting and how much.

She stopped scrubbing, pushed a curl behind her ear. "Yes."

"Because?"

"Because no one thinks I can do it, and I need to prove to myself that I can." Bleakness dimmed the sparkle in her eyes. "I don't want to go back to Toronto, so I need to find a reason to stay here."

"But Collina's your home. What other reason do you need?"

SYLVIE COCKED HER head and studied Adam. Funny how she barely noticed his rough edges anymore. His broken nose looked…not sexy, exactly. But it suited him. She loved his eyes. Except for right now as he peered at her as if looking into her soul. She realized with a start that she liked him. Not just the physical thing—that, too—but he was sort of fun to hang out with, and she could tell he was kind. She enjoyed spending time with him.

"Tell that to my family. Every time I mention moving home for good, you'd think I said the ocean had dried up. The tide goes in and out twice a day, lobster season starts late in the fall, and I go back to Toronto when summer ends. Heaven forbid anything should change."

Adam drank the last of his coffee and rinsed his cup. "Maybe they're afraid."

"Of what?"

"I don't know. Have you asked them?"

"Of course I have. You ask some really dumb questions sometimes." She slapped her hand over her mouth. "I can't believe I just said that."

The corner of his mouth quirked upward. "Guess we're even now."

"Yeah," she said with satisfaction. "You're the perfect antidote for being with my boyfriend Oliver. He was so perfect, and you—" She started giggling. "I'm doing it again."

"Yeah. I got it the first time." This time he didn't look amused, and she grabbed his arm to stop him from leaving before she could explain. They both stilled, stunned by the current that arced between them. Sylvie snatched her hand away at the same time Adam took a step back.

"It was always so stressful being with Oliver," she babbled on. "Because he was perfect, and trust me, I'm not."

He grunted a noncommittal sound.

She laughed. It felt great not having to mince her words. "He's gorgeous and so successful, but it took me a while to realize how wound up I was whenever we were together. I think I'm allergic to him." Why was she making Oliver sound spectacular? Granted, he was great, but he had his faults.

"Allergic to a guy because he's too good to be true? That's a new one." Despite his skepticism, she could see he was intrigued.

"It's true. See here?" She showed him the white patch on her left arm. "After three months of dating him, I started scratching my arm. It wasn't even itchy, but I couldn't stop."

"I don't think it's possible to be allergic to someone, Sylvie."

"The doctor said it was stress. I was always trying to keep up to Oliver's standards. I think Oliver was as relieved as I when I told him last week I wasn't returning to Toronto. Of course, he's perfect so he didn't say so. But I could hear the relief in his voice."

"What if you're wrong? What if he's in love with you, but being the nice guy he is, he said what he thought you wanted to hear?"

"Maybe you don't know what you're talking about." She felt a frisson of discomfort when she realized she was talking to Adam the same way she spoke to Dusty and Cal. What was that about? She didn't bother apologizing, and he didn't look the least bit surprised or insulted.

They both turned as the outside door opened. "You ready to work?" Cal asked from the doorway.

"Absolutely. Gorgeous day, isn't it?" Adam nodded to Sylvie and followed Cal out the door.

"Cal." Sylvie followed the men outside. Adam was right. With no breeze and the sun climbing the cloudless sky, the day looked like a picture from a calendar. Maybe she'd go for a hike later. No, a bike ride. Perfect.

"What's up?" Cal smiled, his sunglasses reflecting her image back to her.

"I'm planning a cycling event to bring more customers

to the café, and we're having a meeting about it Wednesday night at the café. Eight o'clock. Can you be there?"

Cal's smile disappeared. "Not this again." He took off his sunglasses and squinted at her. "Didn't Pops tell you about selling the business?"

Adam shifted his weight from one foot to the other. "Sounds like family business. I'll go get a start on the roof."

"It's okay." Sylvie put out her hand as if to grab him, but stopped herself. "You said you'd help, Adam, so you have to be at the meeting, too."

Cal shot him a pitying look and shook his head.

"Pops said he'd hold off on the sale for a bit," she informed her brother. "What can it possibly hurt to bring in more business at this time of year?" She hated that she was coming close to pleading with Cal, but his opinion meant a lot to her.

"It's you I'm worried about. And Pops. Not the café," Cal murmured.

Sylvie smiled. "Stop being such a worrywart. I'm fine. I'm better than fine. And Pops is getting stronger every day. What's the worst that could happen? That the café might look even better on the books?"

Cal's mouth tightened. "Or you put all your energy into something that doesn't matter while your career goes down the toilet. How about that for a worst-case scenario?"

She kept her smile plastered to her face. "I'm one step ahead of you, bro. My career is already down the toilet."

"Come on, Syl. It is not. All that time and energy and talent, it doesn't disappear. You're just…I don't know, off track or something. It'll all come back. And it seems to me it'll come back sooner if you concentrate on painting, and not all this other stuff."

Sylvie blinked back tears. He had such faith in her.

What would happen if she failed him and never painted again? Failed all of them?

But what would happen if her talent kick-started again? Would she be happy? The thought leapt out of a dark, hidden corner. What a ridiculous idea. She'd be ecstatic if she could paint again.

"I'm going to start painting." She strove to keep the wobble out of her voice. "Adam suggested I paint a poster to advertise the cycling event. Some lucky cyclist is going to win an original Sylvie Carson."

Cal studied her face. "Not a bad idea. Okay. I'll see you Wednesday. But don't expect much help from me. I'm busy."

As he and Adam walked away, he said something that made Adam laugh. How like Cal to trivialize any idea she came up with. But she'd learned how to create a buzz from watching Oliver put shows on at his gallery. She knew she could plan this event and make it a success. All she needed was a little cooperation.

She strode purposefully inside the house and made a list of names before she picked up the phone and started calling.

As EIGHT O'CLOCK and the meeting drew closer on Wednesday night, Sylvie's mood deteriorated. She'd been excited all day. Pops and Dusty had promised to show up tonight, and even Teressa agreed the cycling event was a good idea, as long as Sylvie found another cook to help. It turned out Mrs. Marley, anxious to earn some extra money to go on a cruise with her sister, was happy to help out anytime between now and December.

But best of all, Sylvie had outdone herself designing a poster for the event. Deciding to appeal to family values, she'd painted a poster mimicking Norman Rockwell's style. Admittedly, it wasn't a true Sylvie Carson, but she was pleased with the result.

Sylvie wandered through the almost-empty café and frowned at the mural. It was past time for her to put something new into the village scene. She grinned, suddenly knowing what she wanted to add. Maybe later, after the meeting. Right now she had to check that the coffee and pie were ready in the kitchen. It never hurt to sweeten everyone's mood.

"Do you know the last time I was free to go out without children?" Teressa said as if they'd been talking all along when Sylvie entered the kitchen. "April. It's September now, in case you haven't noticed." Teressa stabbed the air with her knife to emphasis her point. "Almost five months. I need you to go with me to the bonfire, Sylvie. Do not screw this up for me, or I'll never forgive you."

"I'm not talking to you until you put that knife down." Teressa wouldn't hurt a fly—okay, she would if it were buzzing around her kitchen—but Sylvie wasn't taking any chances. She hung close to the door that opened onto the dining area.

Sylvie had always missed the annual bonfire, but doubted it was worth getting steamed up about. Every summer the locals stacked driftwood that they found along the beach on an ever-growing pile and then put a match to it, marking the end of tourist season and the return to normal village life. Many of the townspeople were too busy during the summer months to visit each other, and they looked forward to the bonfire as a time to catch up on everyone's news and enjoy a laugh and a beer with their neighbors. Always having to return to school, Sylvie hadn't attended a bonfire since she was sixteen. Teressa would laugh at her if she told her that she felt shy about going. People still treated her like she was from *away*.

"Is it happening close to the cycling event?"

"You and your *event*." Teressa squiggled her fingers in the air as if making quotation marks around the word. "No, it's a few weeks later."

"Just this once, it wouldn't hurt to be positive. I'm trying to make a life for myself, and I could use a little support."

Teressa hung her head. "I'm sorry. At least you're trying to do stuff. Which is something for this village. I just don't get what was so bad about your life in T.O. You had it all."

"With the emphasis on *had*."

"I dunno. The poster looks great to me. I don't see what your problem is." She nodded toward the poster sitting upright on the desk they used to order supplies and write out the daily menu.

"Doesn't count. I'm copying someone else's style." Sylvie plopped down in front of the poster. "The mural doesn't, either. No one takes folk art seriously."

"Unless you're Maud Lewis."

"Not even. That can only happen once."

"The hell with all of them. Come with me to the bonfire, and we'll get roaring drunk and make fun of everyone like we used to in the good old days."

The good old days. She didn't bother pointing out she hadn't been part of the good old days. She'd been too busy honing her craft.

"I don't know." Sylvie stood and sidled closer to the door. Looking at Teressa's long reddish-gold hair, now held back in a hairnet, and her chocolate-brown eyes, a person would never suspect how fearsome she could get when riled up. "There must be someone else who'll go with you. You know everyone there, anyway. Why do you need me?"

Teressa drew out another knife, a bigger one, yanked the side of ribs in front of her and swung the knife down, cleaving off several ribs. "Because they're all couples."

Whack. "If I have to feel like a loser, I want company."
Several more whacks, and a row of neatly chopped ribs
sat on the cutting board.

This town. Sylvie felt a pang of solicitude for Teressa.
The chances of her being able to move somewhere else
with both fathers' blessing was pretty much nonexistent.
Teressa was stuck here until Sarah and Brendan turned
eighteen. They'd celebrated Brendan's second birthday
last month.

Teressa was a lonely woman who made the best of her
situation. The problem was there weren't many available
men, and the ones who were free were that way for a reason. Dusty, for instance, was emotionally stuck in teenage
mode. But at least he wasn't married, and he made a good
living as a fisherman. "Ask Dusty. He's free, and he'll be
going, anyway."

"Dusty?" Teressa spat the name out. "Puh-lease. I might
as well take my kids if I go with him. It's either you or
Adam. Which is it going to be?"

Sylvie tried to control her burst of annoyance. Not that
it made any sense, but to her Adam seemed…off-limits.
"Fine. Ask Adam. Excuse me, I have tables to wait on."

"When's the best time to catch him?" Teressa called
after her.

Halfway through the doorway, Sylvie shrugged a shoulder. "I have no idea. I haven't seen him around lately."

She swung out of the kitchen and ignored the table of
four who had just sat down. Tyler was AWOL again. She
was going to have to fire him, which meant having to hire
someone new and then train them. Even if she wanted to
paint, she wouldn't be able to find the time.

She picked up a cloth and swiped the counter in front
of her. She'd been looking forward to Adam teaching her
how to cook more dishes while they discussed the cycling

event, but he'd been avoiding her the past three days. Not that she was counting.

Reluctantly, she grabbed an armload of menus and made her way over to the customers. She'd gone over the conversation she and Adam had had the last morning she'd seen him. True, they'd spoken sharply to each other, but she thought it was refreshing to be able to say what was on her mind, and she assumed Adam had, as well. Obviously, she was wrong. No matter how early she'd gotten up in the morning, he hadn't shown. That was what she got for speaking her mind. At least she knew where she stood with him—nowhere.

He was doing her a favor, really. Adam was a nice guy, but come on, she wasn't interested in getting involved with another man. Her life was a mess. She had so many things to sort out, why would she even consider adding another problem to her list? Not that there was even a remote chance of anything developing between them other than a neighborly friendship. The words tasted like sawdust in her mouth.

She didn't bother smiling at the two windswept couples as she slapped the menus on the table. "What'll it be, folks?"

"We haven't looked at the menus yet. What's the special?" Doughboy, with a thick Bostonian accent.

"The special." She frowned. "It's ah…on the board." Where she'd written it a few hours earlier. Bad enough her career had bombed. Now she was taking the café down with her.

"Sorry." She plastered a smile on her face. "The special is a bowl of chili with corn bread. Dessert and coffee included. Dessert is blueberry buckle."

"Blueberry buckle." Doughboy's wife smacked her lips. "Sounds delicious. What is it?"

Fattening. Sylvie caught the word before it escaped. She explained blueberry buckle, took their drinks order and escaped behind the counter. Teressa hissed at her through a crack of the kitchen door.

"Quit pissing off the customers. Tyler's around here somewhere. He'll take the table."

She wouldn't fire Tyler, at least not today, because the kid was much better at his job than she was—when he showed up. She prepared a tray of water, coffee and beer and was about to deliver the drinks when Dusty walked in, followed by Adam.

"Hey, sis. What's Teressa got cooking?" He swung his leg over the stool at the counter and sat. Adam sat beside him, nodded at Sylvie, then spun his stool around so he could look at the room. Apparently, she didn't even rate a hello.

"Ask her yourself." She picked up the heavy tray and pushed the kitchen door open with her hip. "Teressa. Someone here to see you."

She made her way over to the Boston folks and delivered their drinks, making sure to keep her back to the counter. If Teressa wanted to ask Adam out, it wasn't any of her business. She took longer than needed to write down the food orders and listened to the tourists gush about Collina. In another month, when the biting north wind left no doubt that summer was officially over, they'd be singing another tune. But most of the tourists would be gone by then, and the village would settle in for a long winter's nap.

She loved the idea of long, lazy winter days, curled up in a chair by the window and reading a book, a cup of tea by her elbow, the sun glinting on the water.... One of the women at the table cleared her throat, and Sylvie's daydream evaporated. All four were looking at her as if expecting her to say something.

"Food will be ready in a jiffy."

When she returned with the order, she was surprised to see Teressa still at the counter, watching the two men dig in to her chili. A food snob, Teressa believed cooking for people in Collina a waste of her talent. She rarely came out of the kitchen and absolutely refused to wait on customers. Guess she'd been serious about getting a date to the bonfire.

"This is delicious, Teressa," Dusty said, his mouth full of chili. "If you didn't have kids, I'd ask you to marry me."

Teressa snorted, somehow managing to hold on to her cool Julianne Moore look. "Just what I need. Another kid to take care of."

Dusty placed his hand over his heart. "My feelings are hurt. You know, you're getting ornerier by the day. It wouldn't hurt you to be nicer to people."

"Ornerier?" Teressa's freckles looked like they were going to pop off her face as she dragged Sylvie into the mix. "Is that even a word?"

"Unfortunately. Could you two keep your voices down or take it outside?"

"Cinnamon," Adam said as he looked up from his bowl.

A smile softened Teressa's face. "Bingo."

Adam smiled back at her. "I'll have to remember to use it next time I make chili."

"Don't bother. I make a batch every couple of weeks. Just come on over to the café for a bowl."

Sylvie shoved the menus under the counter, ripped the order off her book and handed it to Teressa. "Tyler's on his way?"

"Yes, ma'am."

"All right. I've got stuff to organize then." She pulled the navy-and-gold-striped apron she'd thought was so cute a lifetime ago over her head and chucked it in the laundry bin behind the counter.

"Hang on." Teressa caught her arm. "We were just talking about the bonfire."

"Nothing to talk about. I'm not going." God, she was pouting. She hated pouting.

"You promised."

Sylvie pulled her arm away. "I did not. I said to ask Dusty. Or Adam." Making sure she kept her back to him so she didn't have to make eye contact, she waved her hand in Adam's general direction.

"Geez, Syl. She hasn't been out in forever. Give her a break. Go with her," Dusty said.

Sylvie whirled on her brother. "You go with her." She didn't even know what she was mad about, just that she was.

"Okay." Dusty wiped his mouth on a napkin. "We'll double-date. I was going to drag Adam to the bonfire, anyway. No reason we can't all go together."

"You're not serious," Sylvie protested. "You—" Hate Teressa. Didn't he? Every time they were in the same room, they started sniping at each other. She looked from Teressa to Dusty. They were both staring at her like she had antennae growing out of her head.

"Okay. But it's not a date," she added for Adam's benefit. She didn't want him getting any ideas. As if that were likely.

"Tyler." She sighed with relief when the teenager slinked through the door. "So glad you could come."

She tossed him a clean apron and headed for the kitchen, without once looking in Adam's direction. She stacked coffee mugs, plates and cutlery on a tray. She wanted everyone to be paying attention to what she had to say, not wandering around the café looking for a fork or a napkin.

She grabbed a handful of napkins and placed them on top of the dessert plates.

Teressa's laugh, coming from the front room, drilled into her nerves. Why wasn't she in here, dishing up the chili so they could get the Boston customers fed and on their way?

Sylvie eyed the pot of chili on the stove. She'd be happy to get the order ready, but Teressa was a tyrant in the kitchen. Sylvie hadn't even been allowed in the room until she'd sworn on her mother's grave she'd never, ever touch any of the food. Maybe it was time to revisit that promise.

Teressa swung through the kitchen door, beaming and looking beautiful even with the hairnet. "Don't even think about it." She bumped Sylvie away from the chili pot with her hip.

"I want to renegotiate our deal."

"Talk to your father." She hit the bell sitting on the shelf above the stove to summon Tyler.

"Are you all hoping I'll get so bored that I'll finally leave?"

"Yeah, that's it." Teressa placed four bowls of chili and chunks of corn bread on a tray. "Table five, kid," she said to Tyler as he slouched into the room. "And move them along. Sylvie's got her precious meeting in a few minutes."

"Can I come to the meeting, Syl? I've never been to one," Tyler said.

"It's just a boring meeting." She should have had the meeting at home. That way if her family laughed at her idea, the entire village wouldn't know. But she'd wanted everyone to look at the event not as her family and friends, but as people who could benefit from the idea.

"If Beanie's going, I don't see why I can't," Tyler whined.

"Beanie's not invited to the meeting."

"He's out there, sitting with Pops, and you know he's not going to leave until he's heard everything that's been said."

Sylvie closed her eyes in frustration. A person couldn't fart in this village without everyone knowing they'd eaten beans for lunch. "Okay." She waved her hand at the door. "Try to get rid of the Boston crowd first, please."

Teressa patted her on the shoulder, which was her idea of support, and wandered back out to the café. The murmur of voices sounded much louder than the handful of people she'd invited. Did no one in this village have a life? She slid the pie back into the refrigerator. There wouldn't be enough to go around if there were as many people out there as she thought. If this had been Saturday night, and the hockey game was on, she wouldn't have this problem.

At the moment she didn't know which she preferred— low attendance due to disinterest or the whole village showing up to satisfy their curiosity. She stood in front of the poster and tried to view it with fresh eyes. Why had she thought that storm cloud would add drama to the picture? The picture looked ominous, not the fun-filled family-day theme she'd been trying for. She should trash it. People were going to laugh at her.

She turned as the door swished open behind her. Tyler, looking almost skeletal in his teenage lankiness, beamed at her from the door. "It's showtime."

CHAPTER SIX

ADAM HAD WANTED to sit at a table farther back in the room, but the Carson men dragged him along in their wake to the front table. Sylvie kept her back to them as she arranged charts. He hoped the promised poster was included in her pile of presentation materials. He craned his neck, anxious to see how she'd made out.

Even from behind Sylvie looked great. She wore a knee-length skirt that made him think of a field of wildflowers and a sleeveless, silky top the same delicate pink as the inside of a seashell. Her sandals—he swallowed and looked away—had three-inch heels and were sparkly. A remnant from a more glamorous life, he imagined. They conjured up X-rated images of slow dancing in candlelight, just the two of them. Not the kind of picture he needed stuck in his head, sitting beside her father.

But the shoes were also a good reminder why he'd kept his distance the past few days. Yeah, he was busy with his house. But if he'd wanted to, he could have made time for breakfast or dinner. Instead, he'd stocked up on granola and fruit, and in the evenings, went for long drives, looking for restaurants that weren't there. He hadn't appreciated how isolated Collina was before now.

He couldn't imagine Sylvie being content to live here for any length of time. Her family was right, she was a tourist in her own town. As soon as she recovered from whatever bump in the road she'd run into and started painting again, she'd be on her way.

While he knew in his gut he'd found his home.

When Sylvie turned and smiled tentatively at everyone, Adam picked up on her nervousness and started fidgeting. The cycling event was a good idea. No reason the community wouldn't get behind her. Just because he'd taken a step back didn't mean he didn't like the idea. And he planned to help. But it had to be more than just him and Sylvie, because... He kneaded his knuckles. Because it had to be. That was all.

"Let's jump right in, shall we?" Sylvie tried to smile, but it didn't stick. Adam's stomach started aching.

"First, thanks to everyone for showing up. Second, I've been working on an idea to bring tourists to the village now that summer's over. More and more people have been visiting in the fall the past few years, so I thought we'd give them a focus." Her gaze lit on Adam's and skittered away. She compressed her lips.

"Added value," someone piped up from the back. Adam looked around with everyone else. He'd seen the white-haired, slightly overweight guy washing windows on one of the grand old houses used as a B and B on Main Street.

Sylvie's face lit up. "Exactly, Thornton. I thought we could issue an invitation to bikers to participate in Collina's First Great Annual Cycling Event. I don't have the name down just yet. So, if anyone can come up with a better one, I'm open to suggestions."

"Bikers." Dusty stirred beside him. "I like that. Lots of bikers are looking for day trips." He leaned toward Adam. "You could take your baby for a spin."

No. He couldn't. Riding his dad's Harley around a group of enthusiasts would be like waving a flag. Hard-core biker over here! Someone in the crowd would start asking questions.

Sylvie frowned. "I meant cyclists. Bikers is a good idea, too," she said to Dusty. "But I like the idea of cyclists. The café could even have a few spare bikes around to borrow. Not just for the event, but always. So could some of the other businesses. Okay, moving along. I've mapped out three different routes."

She moved and a collective gasp rippled through the room. Her poster. It was beautiful. Eye-catching. The picture evoked all kinds of emotions, telling a story about kids biking to their favorite swimming hole on a hot summer day. It made him long to be young again, although he'd never known innocence like the kids in the poster. A pang of regret pinched tight inside for all he'd missed during his childhood.

Someone in the back started clapping. Everyone joined in. He clapped as well, but his hands didn't seem to fit together.

"I gotta get me a bike. What do I gotta do to win that picture?" The man the locals called Beanie shouted.

Sylvie laughed and blushed a pretty shade of pink. "It's a poster, not a picture. And I don't know. I'm open to suggestions on how someone can win the original. Like I said," she went on as everyone started talking to their neighbor, "I have three routes mapped out. One for beginners and children. An intermediate one." She pointed to a second map. "And an extreme route. This one will take you to the lighthouse." She smiled. "And I'm thinking we'll need a couple of volunteers with trucks or SUVs to bring some of those bikers back."

"You have a plan how to set this event up, honey?" Pops asked over the murmuring crowd.

She beamed at her father and explained how the café

would be the headquarters for the day. People had to come here to sign up. She suggested setting up a small, historic walk around town for those who didn't bike and trimming the café's menu to showcase the best and easiest recipes. Teressa's chili topped the list.

Sylvie listed in detail all the things she'd thought of. Adam glanced around the room at the interested faces. She was thorough and had everyone's undivided attention. So why did he feel like he was waiting for the other shoe to drop?

"Everyone should write down their suggestions for the event and I, with a few of my helpers, will go through them. I think it's best if we keep the emphasis on biking, so please keep that in mind while you're jotting down your ideas." She grinned. "Next time, who knows, maybe a treasure hunt."

People chatted with each other as they stood. Adam could tell most of them were excited about the possibilities for the day.

"This is a volunteer list," Sylvie said over the babble of voices. "I'm putting it on the bulletin board. To make this a successful day, we're going to need help with lots of different things. Please make sure you sign up for something."

"Have you set a date?" Still sitting, Pops's deep voice carried over the room.

"The last weekend of September."

Her father nodded and looked down at his hands, frowning. The enthusiasm didn't carry over to the Carson men. Pops looked worried. Cal, grim. Dusty had a puzzled expression on his face, but it vanished when Teressa walked by, stopping long enough to nudge his foot.

Adam eased to the edge of the crowd, not sure what was up as Cal and Pops talked quietly. He had the irrational impulse to stand between Sylvie and her father and brother.

Protect her from whatever was coming. Because something was coming. Something not good. Hopefully they'd wait until the crowd thinned before speaking their mind.

Adam wandered over to get a coffee and leaned against the wall. If he were smart he'd go home now. He'd had a hard day and needed sleep. Plus he had no business getting involved with the Carson family problems. *No business,* he repeated to himself. But the message didn't reach his feet, and he remained glued to the wall. He could no sooner leave Sylvie to face her family on her own as he could walk away from the life he'd begun to make for himself here.

Beanie, a tall man and so thin his bones rattled, shuffled over to introduce himself, reminding Adam he was a plumber, and if, or when, he needed work done, he was the man to call. Adam politely answered Beanie's questions about where he was from and how long he was staying, but when the conversation turned more personal—where his family was from, where they were now—Adam decided it was time to mingle. If he kept moving, no one could pin him down with specific questions. Someday his past would have to come out, but not tonight.

The room cleared more quickly than he expected. Ten minutes later, he was left alone in the restaurant with the Carsons. Sylvie flitted around, collecting her maps and lists, stacking up dirty coffee cups and casting surreptitious glances over her shoulder at her father.

Pops got to his feet and went over to her. He looked tired, the skin on his face sagging into pouches. "Honey." He put his hand on her arm to make her stand still. She hugged her maps to her chest and looked up at him. Adam didn't know what to do. She looked so damned brave, it hurt to watch her.

"I'm proud of you, Sylvie. The cycling event is a brilliant idea."

Adam watched her shoulders slump as her tension leaked away. "Thanks, Pops. I wasn't sure… If you'd think…" A nervous giggle escaped her. "I'm glad you like the idea. I'm going to need your help to pull it off."

"Look at that." He moved in front of the poster. All of them turned to stare at the painting. "Your inspiration's starting to come back, isn't it?"

Adam tensed as she bit her lower lip and frowned at the poster. "Not really. I imitated Rockwell's style. You can't really consider this an original."

Pops took her elbow. "Look at it, Sylvie. Everyone in this room felt something when they saw it. Nostalgia for their childhood. Regret of never having one." Adam looked away. "They felt something. That's art, honey.

"Now…" He turned her away from the painting to face him. "Cal and I were talking. You know his Anita hasn't had enough to keep her busy lately, and she studied PR. She'd be the perfect person to take over organizing your little event."

Sylvie turned red. "But—"

"This has gone on long enough, Sylvie. The only thing you've lost is your will to paint. You're as talented as you've always been."

Adam stepped toward Sylvie, but Cal's flinty glare cut into him. Adam flexed his hands. Damn it. Couldn't they see what they were doing to her? Her beautiful glow had turned waxen.

"I don't mind if Anita helps. That would be great. But this is my idea, and I'm going through with it."

"Give it up, Syl." For once, Dusty sounded concerned for his sister. "It's just a stupid fund-raising event."

She whirled on him. "You didn't even listen. I'm making money for the café. For Pops."

Dusty raised both hands, palms facing up. "Let him sell the café, and he'll have all the money he needs."

"But Sylvie won't have what she needs." Was he stupid? Adam couldn't believe he'd interrupted the family dispute. But Sylvie's family had pissed him off. Once again, no one was talking about what Sylvie needed. Someone needed to stand up for her.

Pops emitted a weary sigh and shot Adam an irritated look. "We appreciate you helping Sylvie develop her idea, but with all due respect, you have no idea what you're talking about."

Oh, and they did. "I know that this cycling day is important to her. And that she needs to know she can do something besides paint. And that no one seems to be listening to her."

Pops looked at Cal. Cal shook his head as if to say *I told you so.* "You're a good man, Adam, but this is one time you need to step down, son."

And let them walk all over Sylvie? If she wanted her damned day in the sun, then she should have it. What the hell was the problem? He pushed back his building anger. He was not going to lose it over something as stupid as a cycling event. He dragged in a deep breath and reached for reason.

"Look, I'll admit that I sometimes go overboard championing the underdog, but in this case—"

"Underdog?" Sylvie grabbed his arm to pull him away from her father and face her. "Is that what you think of me?"

God help him. Heat stung the back of his neck. "No, of course not. But you have to admit they're ganging up on you."

"Phfft." She flung his arm away from her with a look of disgust. "I can hold my own with my family. What did you think? That I was a helpless female pining away for some big strong guy to come along and rescue me?" She punched him in the shoulder as even Cal started laughing. "I am not an underdog, you sap."

He felt his blush spread up to the roots of his hair. Man, he had to learn to keep his mouth shut around this woman. "I apologize," he said, stiffly. "I won't make the same mistake again."

"That's enough for tonight." Pops pulled on his jacket as he made his way to the door. "Go home, everyone. Tomorrow's another day. Coming, boys?" He didn't look back as Cal and Dusty followed their father out the door.

Sylvie snatched up the poster and marched out after them, leaving Adam alone in the café. Burning with embarrassment, he waited for someone to realize they hadn't locked up, but no one came back. Guess it was up to him to close up shop.

The Carsons must think him an idiot, running off at the mouth like that when he obviously didn't have a clue what he was talking about. To make things worse, Pops had been so damned nice, telling him he was a good man. What he really was was an idiot, and he planned to stay the hell away from Sylvie from now on. Just as he'd figured the first time he met her, she was nothing but trouble.

He wandered over to the mural and studied the huge painting. Now that he knew a few more people in the village, he appreciated Sylvie's sense of humor. A figure who could be no one but Pops looked a little like Popeye. One person he assumed was Tyler was drawn as a stick figure. Adam's house was there, but leaned to one side and looked old and derelict. It still looked that way, but they'd finished the roof today and would be installing two new doors and a few windows tomorrow. He should go home and get some sleep. Except he knew that would be near impossible—he felt restless and on edge.

He whirled around when he heard a noise from the kitchen. There had to be a second door into the place for fire regulations. Had someone sneaked into the kitchen through the back door?

A second later, Teressa swung out of the kitchen and stumbled to a sudden stop when she saw Adam.

"Lord, you scared me." She put her hand on her chest. "I thought everyone had left."

"So did I. Now I understand why everyone walked out without locking up. I was just wondering how to go about locking the doors."

Teressa came to stand beside him and looked at the mural. "She's something else, our Sylvie. If I had a tenth of her talent…" She sighed.

Adam turned back to the mural. It was a fun painting, but he couldn't imagine anyone cutting down the wall to ship it to an art gallery or museum.

Teressa elbowed him. "I heard you stand up for Sylvie. That was nice of you. Misguided, but nice." She went over to the cooler behind the cash, grabbed two beers and twisted the tops off.

He accepted a beer and turned the bottle around in his hands. "I don't understand. It's obvious her family loves her, but they're determined that she leave. What's wrong with Sylvie living here and running the café if she wants?"

Teressa took a drink. "You've been in their house, right?"

"Some of it. The kitchen and the bathroom."

"Ah." Her puzzled expression cleared up. "That explains a lot."

It did? She watched him expectedly, as if waiting for

him to ask her something, but Adam hadn't a clue as to what that was. "Sylvie said you have two kids?"

She half smiled. "That's right. Sarah's five, and Brendan just turned two."

"Must be tough at times." He couldn't imagine having kids, let alone being a single parent.

"A lot of people in this village have helped me. And the Carsons pay me really well. Probably more than I'm worth, but they know my situation. Pops is going to sell the café. Did you know that?"

"Someone mentioned it. Cal or Dusty."

She took another drink and looked at him. "Dusty says you're a good cook. Have you cooked commercially?"

"Not really." Unless you counted institutional cooking. He'd been on kitchen detail when he served time in juvie hall.

"So, buying a café, is that something you'd be interested in doing?"

Adam choked on his mouthful of beer. "Do you mean this café?"

"Duh. Where else? You're young. Even if you're rich as Hades and don't have to work another day in your life, you don't strike me as the kind of guy who would be happy doing nothing."

"For the record, I'm not rich. I'll definitely have to look for work at some point. But the café?" He looked around the room, a spark of excitement igniting inside. It would be a pretty cool place to work. *Own. Man.* Would that even be possible?

"If I could get a mortgage on this place I could come up with half the payment. I need a partner, though. So I thought…" She gulped a mouthful of beer. "Doesn't hurt to put a bug in your ear. Pops hasn't listed it yet, and he won't until Sylvie sorts herself out. You've got time to chew on the idea."

Adam's excitement shriveled. Sylvie. How quickly they all forgot. "I'd never buy this place as long as Sylvie wanted it. I wouldn't do that to her."

"Of course you wouldn't. You're one of the good guys." She patted his arm. "Drink up and come with me. I've got something to show you."

He hung back when she scooted to the door and held it open. He liked Teressa, but he wasn't attracted to her. Not in that way. And he didn't like how she'd dismissed Sylvie so easily. "Is this going to take long? I've got a big day tomorrow."

"Relax, big guy. I want you to walk me home. I live just up the block." She slid him a sideways glance when he moved past her out the door. "I'm not going to jump your bones. Not tonight, anyway."

Adam laughed as he waited for her to lock the door. He liked Teressa's spunk, and he hoped they could be friends. In his midteens, he'd had a female friend. Not a girlfriend, though he'd had plenty of those, too, but Sherry had been a friend-friend. Sometimes he missed her company.

Teressa slipped her arm through his and turned them both to the right. The street was empty and silent and most of the houses dark, although in a few you could see the blue flicker of TV screens through the window. He couldn't see any stars. If it rained tomorrow would that interfere with installing the new doors in his house?

"I live there." She pointed up the street to one of the old monster homes. He'd noticed it the first day he'd driven through the village because it was painted a burnt orange.

"That's a remarkable house."

Teressa groaned. "It's a beast and costs the earth to heat. Every five years or so, my mom wants to burn it down.

Last year she painted it the color of a pumpkin. I guess she thought it might turn into a magic carriage one day, Cinderella style. She inherited it from her parents."

Adam laughed. "Someday all this will be yours?"

"God, I hope not. I rent the carriage house behind Mom and Dad's. Come on." She slipped her hand into his and tugged him up the driveway. "You need to see this."

Not knowing how to say no without offending her, he followed her past the pumpkin house that looked like something out of *The Munsters* and spotted a friendly light twinkle through the trees. Adam peered at the small carriage house. He'd have to come back during the day to check out the detailed trim that hung from the eaves.

"You should call this the gingerbread house," he said in a hushed voice.

"That's a good one." Teressa unlocked the door and stepped inside. "Hey, Eliza. How did it go tonight?"

A teenage girl with long brown hair, wearing tight clothes that drew attention to her round belly, eyed him from the doorway to the living room. "S'okay. Brendan was a little cranky, and I had to read him *The Tale of Custard the Dragon* two times before he fell asleep. Other than that everything was quiet."

"Eliza, this is Adam. He owns the house beside the Carsons. Adam, Eliza Newton. She's my primo babysitter. The kids love her."

"Hello, Eliza." Adam nodded from the door. If the village grapevine worked nearly as well as he suspected, he and Teressa would be rumored to be having a torrid affair by tomorrow morning. He flashed on Sylvie, but pushed the image away. What difference did it make what she thought?

"Did you find someone to go to the bonfire with you?"

When Eliza moved toward the door, Adam eased out of her way.

"Sure did." She grinned at Adam. Yeah, he was going with her, but so were Dusty and Sylvie. Was she trying to start rumors about them?

Money changed hands between Teressa and Eliza while Adam looked around the kitchen. Red-and-white-checked curtains and a red tablecloth draped over the table gave the room a warm, homey feel. There was a rocking chair in one corner and a stack of kids' books on the floor between the rocking chair and a soft cushion that looked big enough for a small child to curl up on. If he'd thought about it at all, he'd have imagined Teressa to be less cluttered. More streamlined. He wasn't sure what he was doing at her place and wanted to leave, but didn't want to hurt Teressa's feelings.

"I have to peek in on the kids. Come on." Before he could reply, she tiptoed down the hallway, and he was forced to follow.

He glanced over her shoulder as she looked into the bedroom. A night-light gave off barely enough light for him to see a tiny, sleep-tousled boy in one bed, his blankets kicked off, and a beautiful redheaded girl curled up on her side in a bed that had a lot of pink. Pink pillows and blankets. Even the bed frame was painted pink.

Kids. Wow. His admiration for Teressa rose. "They're beautiful," he said when she closed the door. And so was she. She glowed with pride.

"Thanks. I know I complain a lot but I'm crazy about them. Come on." She stopped by the next door in the hallway. "You want another beer?"

"Nah. I'm good. Thanks."

"Of course you are." She sent him a sardonic look. "I

want to show you something, but it's in my bedroom. Give me a sec to clean up."

As Adam waited in the hallway, he tried to remember why she'd thought he should come to her house. It had something to do with Sylvie, didn't it? Teressa seemed to be pretty down-to-earth. Surely, she didn't think—

He breathed a sigh of relief when she opened the bedroom door, still fully clothed. "Prepare to meet the real Sylvie." She ushered him into the room.

At first he was so nervous his eyes couldn't settle on anything but her bed. Finally he was drawn to the huge painting on the end wall above the headboard. *Holy mother of God*. Without realizing it, he sank down onto the bed.

"It's amazing, isn't it?"

The painting was four feet by six feet. It was all the colors of the ocean, and he leaned toward it as if there were an undercurrent, and he was being pulled in. Energy rolled out at him in waves. He thought he could hear the ocean.

It wasn't exactly an abstract. He could see…something…in the depths of the waves, but couldn't quite identify what it was. He was looking at an original Sylvie Carson seascape.

"Wow." He tried to swallow but his throat hurt.

"It's incredible, isn't it? All that energy. I don't know how she does it."

"Sylvie painted this." He stated the obvious.

"She gave it to me, if you can believe that. She said it's my insurance. If things ever got bad, I should sell the painting. As if."

Adam couldn't stop looking at the turbulent masterpiece in front of him. "How much is it worth?"

"Around twenty grand. If she really can't paint anymore, who knows?"

"If you ever need to sell, I'll buy it."

"That's good to know, I guess, but I'm not planning on selling. Maybe now you can understand why we discourage her from wasting time running a little nothing of a café in the middle of nowhere. Talent like this shouldn't be wasted."

"Right." He took one last look and tore his gaze away as he stood up. He felt as if he'd looked into a part of Sylvie so deeply personal, he had no business knowing about it.

They walked silently out to the kitchen. He stopped by the door. "Thanks for showing me the painting. It explains a lot."

Teressa leaned against the counter and drew her sweater tight around her. "I thought it might. They have one hanging in the living room at their house, and maybe another upstairs. Cal has one, too, at his place."

"But not Dusty?"

She smiled. "Not yet, but he just bought his house. If he ever fixes it up, which is unlikely, maybe she'll gift him one, as well."

He rubbed the back of his neck. "I can see what all the fuss is about now. Just because she's blocked, doesn't mean she won't paint again. But you know, I also understand why she…" What was he talking about? He didn't understand a damned thing. Yet he'd wanted to say maybe Sylvie needed a balance in her life. How did someone survive, creating a hurricane of colors and emotions like the one in Teressa's painting? It was amazing her talent hadn't totally consumed her. Of course she needed to step out of all that swirling color and energy to take a break. His blood had pounded just looking at the painting. Imagine what it took to create the masterpiece.

"What?" Teressa prompted him.

"Nothing. I obviously haven't a clue about Sylvie. Thanks again. See you."

He slipped out the door before she could say anything else. The weight of Sylvie's talent bore down on him as he walked the silent streets home. He felt the vastness of the sky above him, and the turbulence of the fathomless ocean when he arrived at his house. He'd never felt so alone in his life.

CHAPTER SEVEN

THE NEXT MORNING Sylvie looked up from her laptop at the sound of a knock on the door. She ran a hand through her hair and adjusted the old flannel shirt she liked to sleep in just as the door opened. She hadn't expected Adam. "Hey."

"Good morning. Ready for a lesson on making pancakes?" He put the frying pan he'd brought with him on the stove. "Mind if I have a cup of coffee?"

"It's your coffee. Go ahead."

She closed her laptop and waited while he added sugar to his cup. She'd thought her family had scared him off—especially after the meeting last night. She was still smarting from the underdog comment, but if he taught her how to cook, she might consider forgiving him.

"Good coffee." He toasted her with his mug.

"Why are you here?"

"You don't want another cooking lesson?"

She shifted in the old armchair. "I thought you'd given up on me."

"Sorry about that. I'm selfish sometimes, and all I think about is what *I* want or need."

She leaned back, surprised by his honesty. After a minute she laughed. "You and the rest of us."

"Yeah." A crooked smile hooked onto the corner of his mouth. "But that doesn't excuse my behavior. You're a good friend, and I shouldn't have let you down."

Friend. Why did that have a hollow sound to it? She set

her computer on the side table and stood. "Is this another rescue for the underdog?"

When he looked sheepish, she turned away from the temptation to hug him. Imagine that big, hard-muscled body holding her, his smell and heat surrounding her. Her body trembled at the sudden, vivid image.

Yes, that was what she needed, to have a torrid affair with the man next door. Her family would probably crucify Adam, if only because she'd found another reason to stay in Collina. And really, did she need another complication? Until she sorted out her own life, she couldn't afford to become involved with anyone. Going out on a casual date here and there, sure, but there was nothing casual about her feelings for Adam.

And there was still that bit about his grandmother and her father. If what she believed was true, she'd feel as if she were betraying her own mother. Which was totally illogical, since Adam had been just a kid then and hardly ever around. Still, warranted or not, she harbored a nugget of resentment about the whole thing.

"I should get dressed if we're going to cook," she said in a too-high voice.

"You look good to me."

"Yeah, old flannel shirts are really hot this year. I won't be long." She sprinted up the stairs.

She twirled around her bedroom and laughed. Adam hadn't given up on her. He was going to teach her how to cook and maybe she could even convince him to help more with the cycling competition–event. Whatever. Her reaction was over-the-top for a silly cooking lesson, but she didn't care. And she wasn't excited because it was Adam, she assured herself.

Finally, *someone* understood that she needed help to climb out of the rut she'd sunk into. She hated that she couldn't rescue herself, but she'd been trying for months and nothing had budged. Maybe Adam's small act of kindness was the push she needed. Life would be simpler if someone else other than Adam had held out a helping hand, but with summer behind her and her family gearing up to convince her it was time to leave, she couldn't afford to be choosy. She needed all the help she could get.

She dug in her dresser for a clean T-shirt and pulled out a Toronto Symphony shirt, black with glittery silver lettering. Oliver had bought it for her at a fund-raiser they'd attended. She put the shirt on and checked her reflection in the mirror. It had been months since she'd gotten all glammed up and went out. She didn't miss attending functions or dinners, except for the dressing-up part— she wouldn't mind doing that for the fun of it every now and then.

"I need to find a name for the biking event," she said as she walked into the kitchen. The empty kitchen. Maybe he was in the bathroom or he'd forgotten something and had gone back to his house.

A noise from the living room pulled her in that direction. Adam was standing in the middle of the room, looking at the painting she'd given to her father on his sixtieth birthday.

Adam glanced over his shoulder. "I hope you don't mind. Teressa told me I'd find one of your paintings here."

She perched on the arm of the old corduroy couch and slipped her hands under her legs. Adam wasn't a world-renowned critic. No need for her to feel so nervous.

"Is this the first one of my paintings you've seen?" Sometimes she forgot he'd just moved here.

He turned back to the painting. "Teressa showed me the one in her house last night."

Sylvie's stomach clenched. What had he been doing in

Teressa's bedroom at that time of night? Unless it had been earlier. It could have been earlier.

"Did you meet her kids?"

"They were asleep. Cute kids, though."

So, after the meeting then. Well, good for Teressa. She deserved to be happy. It wasn't like she'd hoped to become involved with Adam. She'd already decided she needed to keep her distance. So why did she feel a weight settle in the pit of her stomach, as if she'd swallowed a ball of iron?

"Sylvie?" She jumped when Adam touched her shoulder.

He pulled his hand away. "I was talking to you, but you didn't hear me."

"Sorry. You said…?"

"This is of a seashell." He gestured toward the painting on the wall.

"Basically. There's a wash over the painting." She stood and went over to the stand in front of it. "It's sundrenched." She swept her hand downward as if she were washing the painting. "Sea-drenched. The shell is separate from its environment in that you can distinguish it, while at the same time remaining a part of its surroundings.

"I was walking on the beach one day, and it struck me how remarkable—miraculous, really—a small seashell, absolutely perfect in design, was lying there, cast aside. I'd love to be able to do that just once, you know? Create something as perfect and beautiful as a waterfall or a seashell."

She stuck her hands in her back pockets. She never explained her paintings. Never. Because the words she used to explain didn't compare to what she was feeling inside while she was painting. "I probably sound crazy to you."

"You sound like a visionary." His eyes lit up with admiration. "Like an artist. I kind of understand what you mean, though. Me, I can see the beauty, but that's all. I don't think beyond that." He looked at the painting again, then turned to the kitchen. "I'd love to talk more about this, but I have to go to work in a bit, so if we're going to cook those pancakes…" He nodded toward the kitchen.

"Geez. I hope I didn't blow my lesson. When's Cal coming?" She followed him into the kitchen, embarrassed by her outburst of the painting.

"Half an hour or so. We've got enough time." He found a mixing bowl in the bottom cupboard and opened his recipe book to an earmarked page. "You're doing all the work this morning. I'm only here as a consultant."

"Gotcha." She gave him the thumbs-up sign before washing her hands. Honestly, what was with her today? First the discourse on her work, now she sounded like a cowgirl at a roundup. She felt all bubbly inside, like a teenager crushing on a guy.

His soft, deep voice drifted over her as he explained how to mix the liquids together in one bowl and the floury stuff in the other, then grabbed a second coffee and wandered over to the window. She glanced in his direction. Between the gray sky and the gray sea, fog scuttled over the surface of the water—it was a dismal day.

"Everyone seemed excited about your idea," Adam said without looking around.

She measured the buttermilk and poured it into the glass bowl. "Except Pops and Cal."

He turned around. "Why wasn't Anita at the meeting? I don't think I've met her yet."

She weighed an egg in her hand. "You'd remember if you had. She's gorgeous. Looks like a model. She's not interested in mingling with us common folk."

Adam laughed and came over to watch her mix the egg in the milk. "Nothing common about you, Peaches.

If you want to have super fluffy pancakes, you separate the whites from the yolk and whip up the whites and fold them in last."

"Right." She hadn't a clue what he was talking about except the bit about her not being common and that for some reason, he'd called her Peaches. Did that mean he thought she was special? Not *special*, special. But unique.

"This is the difficult part." He put down his coffee, moved up close behind her and reached around, encircling her. She gripped the spoon hard to resist running her hand up and down his sinewy arms. Gosh, he smelled good.

"Make a hole in the center of the flour." His deep voice vibrated through her. "Pour in the milk."

A nervous giggle escaped when she dumped the milk in too quickly, drops splattering the counter and the front of her T-shirt.

"Here's the secret to making good pancakes." He put his hands over hers and folded the ingredients together. "You mix the batter gently only until everything is dampened. Don't beat it."

"Right." Was that breathless voice hers? If she leaned back a mere inch, their bodies would be touching. The heat from his body would mingle with hers, and she could see for herself what all that hard muscle felt like and if his heart was pounding as hard as hers. She stiffened when she felt a movement above her head.

"Are you smelling my hair?"

Adam was quiet for a minute, then nuzzled her hair just above her ear. "You always smell delicious. Like peaches."

"My shampoo," she croaked. His breath warmed her ear as he buried his face in her hair.

"Thought so." He sounded distracted. Lost.

"What were you doing at Teressa's last night?"

Adam jerked away from her as if she'd thrown ice water at him.

"Sorry," he said. "I didn't mean to…"

She smiled to herself as she watched his face turn red. He didn't mean to what? Smell her hair. A giggle escaped her, and she glanced at him.

A grin spread over his face. "I didn't mean to upset you. You smell really good, Peaches. I could get addicted to that smell." He reached out, twisted one of her curls around his finger, his gaze resting on her lips. "I love peaches, especially ripe, juicy ones."

Heat flared inside her. If she didn't stop looking at him, she was going to do something really stupid. Like jump into his arms. Her glow dimmed. She wouldn't do that. Couldn't, really. He had his own agenda, and she had hers. If she hoped to get back to painting, she couldn't afford to let her energy disperse in too many other directions. "We better cook these pancakes or you won't have time to eat before Cal shows up."

He nodded, the twinkle in his gorgeous eyes becoming muted. He switched on a burner and poured a drop of oil into his frying pan. "I use a medium heat to start. If it gets too hot as you go along, turn it down. Do you have a soup ladle? I find that works best for pouring the batter into the pan."

He stepped way back when she approached the stove with the bowl of batter and ladle. Okay, he'd obviously picked up on the fact that she wanted to jump him. No surprise he'd want to keep his distance, and that was what she wanted, anyway. So, it was all good. Right?

"Like this?" She poured the batter. "So what changed your mind about teaching me how to cook?" She watched the edges of the pancake sizzle. "I thought after last night…" She peeked at him. He was frowning at the pancake. "I'm sorry I blew up at you over the underdog comment. I know it looked like my family was ganging up on me, but I can handle them. I'm not completely pathetic."

"You're the exact opposite of pathetic, Sylvie." He drained the dregs of his coffee and put the mug in the sink. "I decided I'd give you some cooking lessons because you painted those beautiful paintings. I don't completely understand them. Not yet. But I can see how much of yourself you invest in them." He looked away from her. "I guess this is my way of saying thank you. Thank you for sharing that huge talent you have."

Tears stung her eyes, and she blinked to chase them away. Wow, and wow. "No one's ever said that to me before. That's...that's beautiful."

He rolled back on his heels. "Um...the pancake's burning." He nodded toward the stove behind her.

She whirled around and pulled the pan off of the stove. "I need a flipper thingy."

"Spatula. Here." He handed her the utensil. "Cal just pulled up. I've gotta go."

"But you haven't eaten. It'll just take a minute to cook a couple of pancakes. Cal knows what he's doing."

"Actually he doesn't. I changed my mind about a couple of things, so I really do have to go."

"Okay, here." She thrust a banana at him. "I need to bounce a few more ideas off of you later about the cycling day. And—" She snapped her mouth shut. She didn't want him to leave. Not good news.

"Go." She tried to ignore his puzzled expression as she flapped her hand at the door. "I'll see you around."

"Yeah, see ya," he said as he turned to leave

"And thanks, Adam," she called after him. "I'll return your frying pan and recipe later."

Shut up. Let the poor man leave.

He hesitated at the door. "I walked her home. Teressa. She thought I needed to see one of your paintings. She was right. What is it in the painting that I almost see but can't?"

A warm glow unfurled inside her. "A mermaid. Do you know that poem by T. S. Eliot where he says that he heard the mermaids singing to each other but he didn't think they would sing to him? I'm paraphrasing but that's the gist of it. I've always been afraid they'll stop singing to me, and now they have." The weight of her failure to paint the past few months settled on her shoulders.

"Go." She waved her hand in the direction of his house.

Sylvie watched through the glass in the door as he strode across the yard to his house. When Romeo met him halfway, he stopped to pet him. Out of nowhere, Moonbeam appeared and twined herself around Adam's ankles, then walked under Romeo's belly, rubbing her tail against him. What a hussy. Looked like Moonbeam and Romeo had become best friends.

She started humming as she turned back to the stove and lifted the burnt pancake out of the frying pan. Interesting way to start a day. Imagine. Someone wanting to thank her for painting. People had been happy to buy her paintings. And a chosen few grateful to receive one as a gift. But to want to thank her? Could you get any more considerate? Not to mention he liked how she smelled.

Like a song winding down midnote, her pleasant buzz dimmed. Except she hadn't painted anything worth looking at for over six months. And what did it matter that Adam liked how she smelled? The scent came out of a bottle. It didn't mean a thing.

She wasn't here to fall in love, or whatever this was. She needed to straighten out the business with her family about how they'd betrayed her by not telling her the truth about her mother's death. It was all mixed up in her head—being blocked artistically, her father's heart attack and the jarring revelation about her mother's death. If she wanted to get her life back on track or even start a new chapter, she had to keep her focus.

Still. Her smile flickered on again. She now possessed the secret of how to make fluffy pancakes. One step in front of the other just may get her to where she wanted to go.

SYLVIE SWORE SHE'D scrubbed that café table clean fifteen minutes ago. Just as she'd used a hand brush to get rid of the paint under her fingernails. The immaculate Anita, tall and so slender to be delicate, with honey-brown hair and doelike eyes, always made her feel like a kid who'd been playing out in the hot sun too long. Sylvie had yet to discover what the quiet, refined woman had in common with Cal.

Sylvie rubbed her hands down the side of her jeans. "Anita. Thanks for coming." Not that she wanted or needed her here, but Pops and Cal had pushed until she'd agreed to let Anita help with the cycling event. Sylvie had been geared up to dig her heels in about being in charge until it struck her that maybe this wasn't about her at all. Imagine that.

Cal and Anita's marriage was in trouble. They were scheduled to go on a European tour for the month of October, but that seemed up in the air now. A few weeks ago Cal had gotten so grim, Sylvie thought he'd snap in two, and Anita had disappeared. Not run away, but disappeared into the showpiece of a house that Cal had built for her and she'd designed. Sylvie had never really connected with her sister-in-law, but she could see Cal was hurting big-time, and he wouldn't let anyone get close enough to help him. So if letting Anita help plan the cycling event somehow eased Cal's hurt, then it was the least she could do. She'd do anything for her brother—except return to Toronto.

"Nice jacket." Cashmere. Beige. Tailored. Sylvie studied the brittle woman. The jacket was more suited to an afternoon of shopping in the city than a meeting in an end-of-the-road café. Why did she always feel the need to prop up Anita's confidence when the woman was so well turned out and a hundred times better-looking than anyone Sylvie knew?

Anita gave her a tight smile. "Thanks. Were you adding something to the mural?"

For anyone else in the village, news that she'd painted on the mural would be a major scoop. Anita was mildly curious.

"Caught me. I always have to wait until everyone's gone home for the day. Want a beer?"

"No, thank you."

Sylvie stuck her head in the cooler behind the cash. "There's a bottle of white wine open. It's from Chile, I think."

Anita hesitated. "Sure. Why not?"

Sylvie grabbed two wineglasses and the bottle and set them on the table. "Are you hungry?"

"I'm fine. Thank you." She sat upright, her ankles crossed, princess-style, her hands neatly folded in her lap.

It must be a laugh a minute when Cal went home at the end of the day, dog-tired and filthy. Was he even allowed in the house before showering? She poured a healthy amount of wine into each glass.

"Cheers." She gulped a mouthful. "Haven't seen you for a while."

"No." Anita sipped her wine.

"Cal and Adam are moving forward fast on Adam's house. Have you seen it?"

Anita shifted in her chair. "No."

She was the only one in the village who hadn't. "Met Adam yet?"

"Yes. He was up to the house one evening. He's... unusual."

Sylvie bristled. "He's a nice guy."

"I'm sure he is. He just doesn't seem like the kind of man who would settle in Collina, that's all."

Sylvie swigged more wine. "He inherited his grand-mother's place."

"Yes, Cal told me."

"You think it's weird he moved here?" Now that she was thinking about it, it did seem kind of strange. Adam was probably in his early thirties. Way too young to be content walking beaches for the rest of his life, and he didn't have family here like the rest of them.

"I only met him briefly when he came to talk to Cal. I don't know him." Anita pushed her wineglass away. "What's this about a cycling event you have planned?"

"What did Cal tell you about it?" That had come out louder than she intended.

Anita raised her eyebrows. "That you would appreci-ate some help?"

"Oh." Relieved, Sylvie sipped more wine before she pulled out her notes.

"This is what I have planned so far." She handed Anita the list of events. "We've got a lot of volunteers already, but I guess I could use help coordinating the whole thing. There're a lot of details to follow up on."

The wine was making her stupid. Anita had probably guessed she was just making stuff up about needing help, and it hadn't been her intention to make her sister-in-law feel bad.

"These all look like great ideas." Anita handed the sheets back to her.

"Thanks." That was the first positive thing she'd heard Anita say in the two years she'd been married to Cal.

"What do you want me to do?"

"Uh…" Sylvie put down her wineglass, which she'd been about to drain. "What are you good at?"

"Nothing."

Slack-jawed, Sylvie stared at her perfect sister-in-law. Then she laughed and got up to retrieve the bottle of wine. "Yeah, right."

"I'm serious, Sylvie. I'm not brilliant like you. I can't seem to get anything right."

"Except design a house that's exceptional and look drop-dead gorgeous every day of your life. Cal says you're a fantastic cook, too." He'd said no such thing, but knowing the little she did of Anita, she was probably a gourmet cook.

"Adam's teaching me how to cook," Sylvie confided. "But it's a secret." She poured more wine into her glass.

"That's nice of him."

Sylvie leaned toward Anita. "I may have taken advantage of his good nature. He's a teddy bear but he wants people to think he's a grizzly."

"Are you certain of that?"

Anita's question sobered her up. No, she wasn't. She actually knew very little about Adam. So why did she feel as if she'd known him for years? The thought disturbed her. Later she'd think about all that—maybe. She had lots of other things to occupy her attention, thank goodness. "About the cycling event. I'm sure I can find some things for you to do if you really want to help."

Anita's mouth twisted, as if she'd swallowed a mouthful of broken glass. Oh, yikes. Something was terribly wrong. Anita looked brittle, as if she might fracture into pieces right in front of her.

"You probably know Cal and I are going through a rough time," Anita whispered, staring at her wineglass. "I won't burden you with the details. But when Cal mentioned this cycling event, I thought—" She spread her hands out in front of her. "I have to do something or I'll go crazy."

Anita pulled her hanky out of her purse and dabbed at her eyes. Even with the little Sylvie knew of her sister-in-law, she realized that for Anita this gesture was the equivalent of another person breaking down and sobbing. "I thought if I tried to get involved with the community more it would make Cal happy. And maybe me, too." Anita made a very un-Anita-like gulp, as if she were drowning.

Aw, hell. Why couldn't Anita and Cal sit down and thrash out their problems? Why did they have to hitch a ride on the back of her grand scheme? She'd never prove to her family, and herself, she could do anything other than paint if she passed most of the work over to Anita.

Sylvie caught the dim ray of hope in Anita's face and immediately felt ashamed. Of course she'd make room for her sister-in-law. She knew what it was like to be treated like an outsider, and while she didn't understand what Anita and Cal's problems were, people here for the most part were kindhearted, and maybe both Anita and Cal needed to let some of those kind souls into their life. What better way than to help out with Collina's First Great Annual Cycling Event.

And, hey, so what if she didn't get full credit for pulling off the event? At least she knew how to make fluffy pancakes. That ought to come in handy someday.

"If you think you're up to it, you could handle the PR for the event for starters. I'm terrible with reporters. I'm always blurting out things I don't mean. Plus, if I try to do the PR, they're going to want to ask questions about my painting, and we all know that's a dead end. I want this to be about the café and the village, not me. I'd really appreciate it if you'd take over that end of things."

She hadn't thought about that angle before, but it was the truth. When reporters realized who she was there was a chance they'd be more interested in why she wasn't painting than what was happening in the village.

Anita reached across the table and patted Sylvie's hand. "I haven't had the opportunity to tell you how sorry I am you're having trouble. It must be very difficult for you not to be able to paint."

Sylvie blinked back the sudden rush of tears. Damn wine made her weepy. "Thanks, Anita."

She patted her hand again. "And you really need me to do the PR?"

"Absolutely."

"Okay, I'll give it a try." She scooped up Sylvie's lists. "If you don't mind, I'd like to read over what you have planned so far. Do you have copies of these?"

"Not yet."

Anita shuffled the papers into a neat pile. "Okay if I take them home and look them over? I'll photocopy them and get them back to you in a day or so."

"Sure." Sylvie hesitated as she watched Anita slip the notes into her shoulder bag. She had most of the information in her head, so it didn't really matter. But it felt as if she'd just handed over more than a couple of pages of notes. If it made Anita and Cal happy, she guessed she could make one small sacrifice. Except it wasn't small. Planning this event was supposed to carry her into her new future.

Anita smiled. "Don't worry. I'm not trying to take over, Sylvie. I understand you need to do this, too. And…I know you're close to Cal, but I'd appreciate it if you didn't mention to him that I said we're having trouble." Her face tightened. "He thinks if we just ignore our problems, they'll go away."

Wine sloshed in Sylvie's stomach as she watched her sister-in-law stride out of the café. What kind of relationship could you have if you didn't talk to each other? She couldn't imagine what Anita's life must be like. She was stuck in her castle on the hill, waiting every day for her Prince Charming to come home. Cal was a nice guy, and he loved Anita, but he was no Prince Charming.

How far would they let things go before both of them admitted they were in trouble? Why didn't people tell the truth about what was bothering them?

She got up and slapped off the café lights. Okay, so she hadn't confronted her family about the discrepancy between what she'd remembered of the night her mother died and what they'd told her. But she planned to—soon. The same with Adam. The next time she saw him, she'd tell him about his grandmother and her father. No more evading the truth.

CHAPTER EIGHT

ADAM CURSED UNDER his breath when he saw the small feminine figure stride toward him. Sylvie, of course. He'd hiked a mile down the beach before he'd found the perfect spot for a bonfire—far enough away that hopefully no one would notice him, yet close enough that he could find his way home in the dark. He'd been living in Collina for nine days already, and it had been an incredible nine days. Time to celebrate.

The number of stars overhead dazzled him. He didn't need company tonight—and he definitely didn't need Sylvie's company. He wanted to be grateful for all the good fortune that had come his way. But Sylvie stirred him up, made him wish for more and it was hard to feel grateful when all the good things you had didn't feel like enough.

He pushed Moonbeam off his lap and poked at the fire as he watched her march toward him. Aw, hell. She looked like a woman with a mission, and he was in deep enough already. He didn't want to get involved with any more of her projects, but he'd yet to discover how to say no to her.

He'd known before he'd put his arms around her this morning that it was a mistake. Hadn't stopped him, though. *No sirree*, he cuddled right up to her and sniffed her hair like some kind of pervert. She was probably ready to kick his ass now. Wouldn't stop him from doing it again, though. He figured he'd been doing pretty good keeping his hands off her so far.

But tonight? Out here, under the stars with the ocean at his feet? Maybe she'd pick up on his mood, not come too close.

She marched right up to him and plunked down on his blanket, her thighs brushing against his jean-clad legs. He suppressed a groan and scooted over a foot onto the damp sand when she wiggled her behind like a little hen roosting for the night.

"Nice night." She pulled her legs up to her chest and hugged them. "You're a ways down the beach."

"I wanted to see the stars."

"It's best when there's no moon like tonight. Hey, Rom." She ran her hand down over the dog's shoulders when he nuzzled her side.

Damn fickle dog. Wasn't he supposed to be tuned in to his master's needs? Romeo was snuggling up to Sylvie like he couldn't stand to be alone with Adam. He wiped a hand over his face. Crap. He was jealous of a dog. Adam looked away, tried concentrating on the stars instead of how it would feel to have Sylvie run her hands over him. "Ever done a painting of the stars?"

"Van Gogh beat me to it."

"I'm sure your painting would be beautiful, too."

"I didn't come here to talk about painting, Adam."

No, he supposed not. By the pained look on her face, Sylvie had something definite on her mind. He admired her determination, but that didn't stop him from not wanting to be dragged into another one of her schemes.

As much as he hated to admit the truth, because it complicated his life, he realized he was falling for her. Not head over heels falling, but enough of a tumble that he needed to pull back. He'd drive himself crazy if he started thinking about how incredible life could be with Sylvie at his side. Because a life with Sylvie wasn't going to happen. Not in this lifetime.

"I'd offer you a drink, but all I have is water."

She rested her cheek on her knee and peered at him. "S'okay. I had some wine earlier."

She continued to look at him as if… He didn't have a clue. But from the frown on her face he didn't get the impression she liked what she saw. "Something wrong?" he finally ventured.

"This is nice. The fire and the beach." She straightened her back and waved her hand in front of her. "The stars."

"Yeah." Adam relaxed. Maybe he'd read her wrong. Maybe she just wanted to look at the stars, too.

"Your grandmother was having an affair with my father."

"Excuse me?"

"You heard me."

He clenched his hands into fists. What the hell was she talking about? "Are you high or something?"

As she studied her bare toes, he realized she must have kicked off her shoes partway here. She'd painted her toenails siren-red. They looked delicious.

"I wish. I don't mean I wish I was high. I wish it was that easy to dismiss."

He rolled to his knees and knelt in front of her. "My grandmother did not have an affair with your father, and you're crazy if you think she did. Gram was the sweetest, most honorable woman I've ever known."

Gram had been the only bit of goodness in his whole miserable life. "She'd never do anything to purposely hurt another person. I don't know where you got that crazy-ass idea but you can drop it right now. Why are you telling me this, anyway?"

"Because of a conversation I had tonight with someone

else. It made me realize it's not good to keep things to yourself. Pops and Dusty and Cal lied to me about my mother's death for years. I buried the memory, and it wasn't until Pops had his heart attack that I remembered the night my mom died, I overheard my parents fight about your grandmother. My mother stormed out in the middle of the fight. She died in a car accident a couple hours later.

"I'm sorry, Adam. I know you loved your grandmother and I don't mean to tarnish her memory. But I spent years trying to be who my family wanted me to be because I thought that made them happy or compensated for Mom's death or something, and the entire time they'd lied to me. Betrayed me. And now here you are, and we're getting to be friends, and I'm having a hard time because I like you. I mean really like you, but I don't want to. And it's not just me. You spend your days with Cal, and Pops likes you, too. So does Dusty. It's almost as if you're part of the family."

She put her hand on his arm. "I am sorry to hurt you, but how would you feel if you found out years from now that we all knew and didn't tell you?"

Adam shook off her hand and jumped to his feet. The air had grown too dense to breathe. "I gotta go." He grabbed his knapsack and stuffed his water bottle in it. Sylvie could keep the blanket she was sitting on.

Sylvie stood. "I've upset you. I'm sorry."

"Upset me?" He clenched his teeth to keep from yelling at her. "You didn't upset me because I know you're wrong. Gram didn't have an affair with your father. Anyway, shouldn't you be talking to your family about your stupid theory, not me?"

Sylvie raised her hand to her face as if he'd hit her. Damn it. He hadn't meant to hurt her. Or maybe he did. Maybe he wanted to push her away. He needed to get away and think. Not about his gram. He knew that delusion wasn't true. But he had so many damned secrets, he could hardly keep them straight.

Sylvie wanted full disclosure? She wanted to be his friend? He bit back a bitter laugh. If he told her the truth about who he was, what he'd done, she'd be appalled. Now there's an image he should keep in his head to cure himself from getting crazy ideas about fitting in—the look of horror on her face when she found out who her neighbor really was.

"See you." He turned and jogged down the beach.

Sylvie was struggling to come to terms with her own messed-up life, and what did he do? Tell her to get lost. He was an idiot and a coward and he didn't deserve her as a friend. He didn't deserve anything this town had to offer, and he never would, because he was Paulie Hunter's son. Worse, he was Adam Hunter—gang member, car thief, almost-murderer.

He'd thought he'd made progress in his life. But out here, under the vastness of the stars, it was hard to avoid the truth. It was also hard to ignore the reason why he was so upset. He slowed to a walk and used his wrist to wipe the sweat off his forehead. Despite all his resolutions, Sylvie's life and his had become far too entwined. He liked her. More than liked her, but he could never be the man she needed. He could only be himself, and that was never going to be good enough.

A HALF HOUR later, Sylvie trudged up to the door of her father's apartment and knocked. A month ago Pops had moved from home, where she'd been taking care of him, and she could count on one hand the number of times she'd stopped by to visit him in his new apartment. She understood he felt safer having a nurse living on the premises, but she also suspected he'd moved to prove she was free to return to Toronto. For that reason alone, she hated his apartment.

She turned the doorknob and, finding it unlocked, opened the door wide enough to stick her head in. Pops was sitting in his favorite recliner, sleeping. She peeked at her watch. Only eight o'clock. Had he been falling asleep this early since moving here? Was that normal or was it something she should worry about?

She needed to talk to her father. Adam's certainty about his grandmother's innocence made her question what she remembered. She'd be up all night thinking about it if she didn't find out the truth, but she hated to wake Pops. She started to close the door but heard his old recliner creak as he shifted in his chair and snapped on a light.

"Who's there?" His voice wobbled. Sylvie bit her lip. Her father had always sounded so strong and certain before his heart attack.

"It's me." She pushed the door all the way open and strode inside. Oh, God. Her heart sank as she studied her father. His features looked vague and out of focus, as if part of him was missing.

"Sylvie. I was just thinking of you." He smiled as he sat forward and held out one hand to her. "What brings you here?"

Sylvie grabbed her father's hand and held on tight. "Do I need a reason to visit you?"

"Of course you don't. Pull up a chair. Would you like something to drink? They frown on me having beer, but I think there's some juice in the fridge."

"I'm good." She sat on the sage-green love seat she'd insisted on buying for him. She'd wanted to buy a new recliner as well, but he insisted on keeping his ten-year-old one, since he'd only just broken it in.

"Is it nice out tonight?"

"Nice enough. I walked up from the house." She'd come straight from the beach and Adam, but no need to mention that. Apparently she was in a confrontational mood tonight. First Adam, now Pops. This evening may not be the best time to ask about her mother's death, but if not now, when?

"I was talking to Adam tonight about his grandmother," she began.

"Mirabelle."

"Excuse me?"

"That was her name, Mirabelle Johnson. Nice woman. Adam must miss her."

Sylvie scuffed the toe of her sneaker against the tile floor. "Were you good friends with her?"

Pops gazed off into the distance. "I suppose I was. Way back when, she used to stay for a full month, then she cut back to a couple weeks, then one." He smiled at her. "When I see all the summer visitors, I always think how lucky I am to live exactly where I want to be. I don't have to go anywhere else to be happy."

"Have you been happy with your life?"

"What kind of question is that? What's wrong, Sylvie?"

Her stomach twisted into a knot. "I've been thinking about when mom died."

Pops narrowed his eyes. He looked fully alert now. "Do you remember when she died? You were so young."

"That's just it, I think I do. I remember—"

Someone rapped on the door and shoved it open. Cal walked in. "Didn't expect to see you here," he said to Sylvie.

She bristled. "What's that mean?"

"You're not in the habit of stopping by."

"I work evenings."

"Uh-huh." He eyed Pops. "You look tired. It's about time to turn in, isn't it?"

"In a minute." Pops waved his hand. "Sylvie was telling me she thinks she remembers something about when your mother died."

Sylvie tamped down her temper when Pops and Cal exchanged a knowing look. Experience had taught her that they were so much alike, pushing either one usually resulted in being shut down. She'd approached Cal at least twice over the past couple of months about her mother's death and both times he'd point-blank refused to discuss that day.

Which resulted in making her even more certain they were hiding an essential piece of information from her. Such as Pops had an affair with Adam's grandmother. Except if she accepted that, then her whole concept of who her father was would have to change, and Pops had been the one rock she'd held on to her entire life. Well, and Cal and Dusty. Her brothers might annoy her to no end, but she believed they usually had her best interests at heart. But they couldn't protect her from the truth forever.

"She doesn't." Cal stood. "Come on, sis. You're keeping Pops from his beauty sleep. See you tomorrow, Pops." He held open the door for Sylvie.

Not wanting to upset her father, she kissed him on the cheek and resisted the urge to kick her brother as she walked past him out the door.

"All I needed was a few more minutes," she said, standing by his truck.

"You've been busy tonight, haven't you? First Anita, now Pops. You start that shit with him now, he'll be up all night thinking about it." He put his hands on his hips. "Look, I know things aren't going so good for you, Syl. I sympathize, really, I do. But you have to stop running round, getting everyone all stirred up."

"That's not fair. It wasn't my idea to involve Anita in

the cycling event. What is your problem, anyway? She'll go nuts if she doesn't do something. She's an intelligent woman, Cal. She needs more to do than sit at home, waiting for you."

"Has it occurred to you that my wife may not be feeling well?" he asked through clenched teeth.

"Actually, it has, Cal. She's lost a ton of weight. What's wrong with her?"

Cal sighed, wiped a hand over his face. "I promised her I wouldn't talk about it with anyone."

Sylvie put her hand on her brother's arm. "Is she…is she seriously ill?"

"She'll get better. She just needs some time and a lot of rest. Maybe you're right. She needs to get out more. I just don't want her to overdo it."

"I'll try to keep my eye on her and not let her get overtired."

Cal smiled. "Thanks, sis. Sorry to bite your head off. I'm on a short leash these days."

Like that was news. She followed him to the door of his truck. "About Mom's death," she said as he opened the truck door.

"Not tonight, Sylvie. But soon. I promise. I've got to get home now. Anita will worry if I'm gone too long."

"Cal?"

He turned back to her. "Yeah?"

"Do you stop by Pops every night to check on him?"

"Yeah. I figure you're busy at the café and Dusty's… well, Dusty."

They smiled at each other. "Thanks," she said.

"He's my dad, too. See you."

She raised her hand in a wave as he backed out of the parking lot. Interesting he hadn't offered her a drive home, although she only lived three blocks away and Collina had to be about the safest place on earth. Cal probably figured he wouldn't be able to escape her questions, being stuck in the truck with her.

She needed to spend more time with Pops. Since he'd moved she'd gotten slack in checking up on him. Seeing him at the café during the day wasn't enough.

SYLVIE CURSED THE weather. She cursed the town, her family and all of her friends. And then she cursed her dumb luck that a storm had moved in from the ocean with a vengeance. Rain drummed against the windows of the café while the wind screamed with the fury of a winter storm. She shivered and thought about lighting a fire in the stove. Might as well get cozy while she waited for all the cyclists who were *not* coming to Collina's First Great Annual Cycling Event.

The stuff memories were made from. She snorted. All that work, the hours of planning biking routes, lining up volunteers, ordering supplies, and now this. Tropical storm Hilda had downgraded from a hurricane twelve hours ago. *Hooray!* Sylvie dragged another chair closer with her foot and plopped her feet on the seat.

The door to the washroom opened and closed, and Anita ghosted into the room. In the past two weeks she must have lost five pounds. Her sister-in-law was disappearing right in front of everyone's eyes, and the only person who could stop her from wasting away was Cal. But he'd disappeared so deep inside himself, Sylvie worried he'd never find his way back.

Anita had been a trouper, showing up for all the meetings, doing a terrific job of handling the press, and even coming up with some great suggestions. The weight of the day settled more heavily on Sylvie's shoulders.

Maybe they were all cursed.

She was still blocked artistically, and she'd yet to confront Pops or Cal about her mother's death. Cal and Anita looked like they were headed for a divorce. And Adam—she rubbed her hands over her face—well, he hadn't talked to her since that night on the beach when she'd dumped all of her self-righteous bullshit on him.

He'd turned up for some of the meetings, and Teressa had talked him into helping in the kitchen on the big day. Not that Sylvie was jealous. Not much, anyway. She still thought his reaction to the news about his grandmother and her father had been out of proportion. *She* was the one who had lost her mother. *She* was the one betrayed by her family.

Even Dusty was acting off these days, sniping at Teressa without provocation, as far as Sylvie could discern.

Things were a mess, but what could she do about any of it?

So, she went back to cursing the weather.

Storms were never good news in a fishing village. Only one week into lobster season, Dusty and the other fishermen could lose most of their traps in a storm this size.

Anita drifted over to her. "I might as well go home. I think it's safe to say no one's coming."

"Looks like. You can come over to my house if you like," Sylvie offered. She couldn't imagine how tense things were for Anita at home. When she'd tried again to knock some sense into Cal, he'd told her in no uncertain terms to mind her own business. Except he hadn't stated it quite so politely.

Anita smiled sadly at her. "Thanks, but I have to go home sometime."

Sylvie pushed herself to her feet. "Thanks for all your help, Anita. I really enjoyed working with you."

Anita looked surprised. "You make it sound like it's over. Aren't you going to reschedule?"

"I hadn't thought about it. What if we get rained out a second time?"

"What have we got to lose? Most of the work is already done."

Sylvie laughed for what felt like the first time in years. "I like your attitude. Let's pick out a date right now, and you can get busy with contacting the media. Those people really love you." Anita had a knack for sounding so excited during interviews, she often infected the person interviewing her with excitement, too. Which had worked well in their favor—or would have if the weather had cooperated.

"Next weekend before we lose everyone's interest," Anita suggested.

"Works for me. Like you said, everything's ready to go. Call me tomorrow, or just drop by," Sylvie added. Anita might welcome a reason to get out of the house.

"I will."

The wind whooshed in when Anita opened the door to leave. Sylvie clamped a hand on the papers in front of her to keep them from flying around the room. Lousy storm. She sighed and looked around the empty café. As long as Anita had been here she'd almost been able to ignore the fact that not one other person had showed up.

Not the public, but townspeople. She hadn't expected anyone to make the hour-long drive from the city to Collina. But Dusty, Pops, Teressa. Heck, Beanie or Tyler even. Any friendly face would be welcome. Like a pat on the back. *Good try, kid.* But no one in the whole miserable village had made the effort to show their support, except Anita.

Not one word from Adam. Not even a phone call. She hadn't been stupid enough to expect his support, had she?

Or any of the others', really. People were still asking her when she was going back to Toronto, even though she'd told anyone who would listen that she was staying. Maybe they knew something she didn't. Like she didn't belong here. She rested her head on her arms. For all the running around she'd done, all the noise she'd made, she was in the exact same spot she'd been in since coming home. Limbo.

And God, how she missed painting. To be truthful, she hadn't at first. Or not as much as she thought she should. But now, going on seven months later, she was beginning to feel like someone with a phantom limb; a part of her that should be there, just wasn't. At what point was she going to pack up her art supplies? Or give them away.

She was struck breathless, and for the first time in a couple of weeks, panic seized her. She stuck her head between her knees and counted. In, out. The black gradually receded as the tightness in her chest eased.

She didn't look around when the door behind her opened. "Event's canceled. Café is closed," she grunted.

"I figured," Adam said from behind her.

She shot upright and twisted around in her chair, her heart thumping inside her chest. Wearing a bright yellow slicker, the rain still dripping from his face and hair, Adam looked bigger than life—and really good.

Gosh, she'd missed him.

"People are such wimps these days." She smiled, suddenly feeling giddy. "You'd think you wouldn't be able to hold people back from visiting Collina in a storm. The ocean must look awesome up at the lighthouse."

Adam smiled back at her. "Want to go have a look?"

"Absolutely." It was exactly what she wanted. Instead of trying to ignore the storm, she wanted to climb right into it.

"I hope you have rain gear."

She scoffed. "May I remind you, you're talking to

a fisherman's daughter." She grabbed her raincoat and slipped into it, a slap-happy smile still on her face. "Did you bring Romeo?"

"Not today. He's hiding under the bed. Moonbeam checks on him every half hour or so. Sylvie?"

When he put a hand on her shoulder, she glanced up. Way up. He looked so big today. Bigger than he appeared in her dreams every night.

He ran his hand from her shoulder to her elbow. "I'm sorry."

She nodded, the hard knot in her chest dissolving. "Me, too." She wasn't sure what he was apologizing for—the storm, that no one showed up, that he'd been avoiding her for the past two weeks. None of it seemed important now because he'd come when it mattered most.

"Hang on." He grabbed her hand. "It's gotten worse out."

She clung to him when he opened the door and the wind pushed her back a step. He slipped an arm around her waist and pulled her against his side as they fought their way together through the wind and the rain to his truck. She could barely form a thought, the wind howled so loud in her ears.

Adam stayed at her side until she was safely inside the cab, then made his way to the driver's side and climbed in. "Unbelievable." He pushed his hood off and wiped the rain from his face.

Sylvie bounced on the seat, supercharged from the storm's energy. "I love storms."

Adam grinned at her. "I had a feeling you might. Me, too." He started the truck. "I've never been in one this big before. It's wild down by the beach. I tried to go for a walk but the wind almost pushed me off my feet."

"Don't ever go close to the ocean when it's like this.

We get tidal waves. People have been swept out to sea, you know."

"Yeah. After a couple of minutes, I realized maybe I shouldn't be that close to the water. The waves are almost up to my front door. I called Cal to ask him if I should be worried but there was no answer."

She watched as Adam eased the truck through a river of water that was running down Teressa's driveway. "Both our houses have survived a ton of storms. We've got that rise of land between us and the beach, so don't worry. I wonder where Cal was." Out looking for Anita? Surely he knew she'd gone to the café.

"Was Anita with you?"

"She left for home just before you arrived."

He glanced over at her. "Do you like working with her?"

"Yes. She's as smart as she is beautiful. My brother's a lucky man. I hope he realizes how lucky."

Adam cleared his throat. "I've been worried about him lately. He's…not happy."

Poor Adam. Of course he bore the brunt of Cal's angry moods. They worked together every day. She sent him a sympathetic look. "He won't quit on you."

"Good to know. But I'm more concerned about him than my house. Good Lord, look at that."

Sylvie twisted to look out her window at the huge poplar tree that lay uprooted in Beanie's front yard. "Wow. Maybe we shouldn't be driving around. A tree could land on us."

Adam slowed the truck. "Want to turn back?"

She laughed. "No. Do you?"

His warm chuckle curled around her. "Nah. But if a tree does fall on us, make sure you tell your family I asked."

She pulled her gaze away from his wonderful, generous mouth. Of course she'd noticed his mouth before. But today it looked more...inviting. She licked her lips. "Want me to talk to Cal about cleaning up his act?"

"I don't think it would help. Do you?"

"I think Cal and Anita need to talk to each other."

He shot her a sideways glance, the corners of his mouth tightening. "Kind of how you tried to talk to me that night on the beach."

"Yeah, that went well." The truck shook as a strong gust hit them broadside. Her nerves stretched tight, but not because of the storm. She wanted things to be okay between them again. She wanted to be his friend. Actually, she wanted more, but what lousy timing with her life so messed up. She didn't even know for certain if she was staying. Adam was. Any idiot could see he'd already made Collina his home. And she wasn't so sure he wanted to become more entangled in her life.

She couldn't tell if the sound he made was a chuckle or a grunt. "For the record, I still don't believe my grandmother and your father were anything more than friends. Made me wonder, though. What was the age difference between your mom and dad?"

Sylvie shifted in her seat. Why did that question make her feel uncomfortable? "Twenty years."

Adam didn't say anything until he'd maneuvered the truck around a broken branch lying in the middle of the road. "That's a lot of years. Was your mom from here?"

"No. Guelph, Ontario."

"She must have loved your dad a lot to move away from everything she knew."

Did she? Sylvie strained to remember, but it had been so long ago. She'd always had the impression her mom hadn't been crazy about Collina—another thing to ask her family if any of them would talk to her about their mother. "I don't remember," she confessed.

"But you remember the night she died."

She stiffened. "Yes, I remember the night she died. Like I told you, or maybe I didn't, I'd blocked the memory. But when I heard about Pops's heart attack, it was… It all came back. The shouting, my mom crying. Pops…" She frowned. "Pops sounding mad and sad at the same time." She glared at him. "I didn't make all that up."

He reached over and covered her hands with his. "I know you didn't, Sylvie. I was just wondering, that's all."

He pulled into the parking lot a quarter mile up behind the lighthouse. The scene in front of them—the bruised sky, the towering lighthouse sitting out on a rock ledge, the angry ocean—shook something loose inside her. Like someone had pulled a wire loose and her internal circuit was shorting out. She yanked open the door and stumbled out. The rain had abated for the moment but not the wind. A monstrous creature intent on destruction, it howled and whipped around, beat the grass down flat. Far below, it picked up waves and threw them at the heavens. The energy electrified her. As if a siren were calling, she started down the path to the lighthouse and the edge of the cliff.

"Hang on, there, Peaches." Adam caught the back of her jacket and tugged her backward. "You're not going anywhere without me. And you're sure as hell not going too close to the edge."

She usually had a smart answer when her brothers tried to boss her around, but she took Adam's instructions in stride, and they walked side by side, holding hands.

"I love this!" she yelled to be heard over the wind.

Adam pulled her closer and draped an arm over her shoulders. Even through their rain gear she could feel the heat from his body. He looked down at her, his eyes shooting sparks, his mouth curled upward into a beautiful smile.

She stumbled over a shrub, and he caught her and laughed. "Pay attention."

She was paying attention, but not to the storm. She couldn't seem to look away from the straight, firm line of his bottom lip or the beautiful curve his top lip formed— she couldn't have improved on it if she'd wanted to. Which she didn't. What she did want, despite all her babbling to the contrary, was to kiss him. Feel the firmness of his lips. Taste his mouth.

They stopped to catch their breath behind the light-house, sheltered for a second from the wind. Without giving herself time to think, she stood on tiptoe and kissed him. Gently. Then harder. Then an all-out, no-holds-barred, I've-been-waiting-forever-for-this kiss. And it was as good… No, it was the best kiss she'd ever had. It was a kiss that delivered and demanded. Promised and teased. Swept her off her feet—literally.

Adam pulled her up against his big, hard body, her toes not quite touching the ground. She flung her arms around his neck and dived in.

ADAM'S HEAD REELED as he sank into the kiss. Sylvie's lips were as soft as a rose petal and sweet, like pure, clean rain. He could kiss her forever. Thank God it was storming out and they had rain gear on. It was probably the only thing keeping him from laying her down in the grass and making love to her right that minute. Drunk from the taste of her mouth, he staggered back a step, bumping into the brick wall of the lighthouse.

He should have known this magic would happen. The storm, not talking to her for the past two weeks. Watching her going to work, going for walks, going everywhere but to his house. He'd been so angry and afraid. Still was. Not so much angry as hurt that she had cut him out of her life so easily, but he hadn't yet found the courage to tell her the truth about himself.

He rested his forehead against hers. When he'd first walked into the café this afternoon and saw how defeated she looked, he'd wanted right then and there to scoop her into his arms. Wanted to wipe that look of disappointment off her face. To make her smile. So far he'd managed to do just that.

He closed his eyes and hissed in a breath when he felt her hands slip in under his rain jacket. Under his sweater and shirt. Her hands were cool and soft and inquisitive. Oh, shit.

"Sylvie," he warned and pulled back a fraction.

"Don't. Not yet." With one finger she pulled him back to her.

This time he slid his hands under her clothing, felt her warm, soft skin against his cold hands. His heart pounded as he caught her mouth with his, felt himself falling, falling, falling into Sylvie, into lust. Into love.

He skimmed the waistband of her jeans with his fingertips, traced her delicate ribs and closed his hand over her full, round breast. He groaned into her mouth as she leaned into him and brought her body up against his.

He wanted her. Now. He dropped his hands to her waist and leaned away from her welcoming heat.

She collapsed against him and laughed. "One more little kiss, and then we'll go home."

Home. The word warmed and chilled him at the same time. More than anything, he wanted to go home with Sylvie, but he never would. Not in the true sense. Not together. Never together.

He cupped her face and kissed her. He kissed her eyelids, the crinkle at the corner of each, then the spot where her lips dipped upward, and finally the tip of her nose.

And then he turned her away from him, tucked her under his arm and stepped back out into the storm. They stood wedded together, secure and immovable, his arms around her waist, she leaning back into him as they watched the storm howl around them. Finally, they turned as one and headed back to the truck.

Adam felt her gaze from time to time, but he concentrated on putting one foot in front of the other, hating himself with each step. He shouldn't have gone to the café, but he'd been so worried about Sylvie. The thought that she was probably sitting all by herself drove him crazy. He'd called Dusty and Cal, to ask them to check on her, but neither had answered their phone. When he'd gotten hold of Teressa she'd scolded him and told him to stop being such a wimp and do something.

So he'd gone. And now here he was with Sylvie looking at him with her big blue eyes like… He swallowed. Like that kiss had only been a prelude to making love. Like she wanted more.

The rain started again, coming down so hard it pitted his face. He opened the truck door and helped her inside, then ran around the other side and climbed in. The sound of rain drilling against the top of the cab was deafening.

"It's wild out."

"Yeah." Sylvie didn't look up from where she'd folded her hands on her lap.

Adam leaned his arms on the steering wheel. He shouldn't have returned her kiss. He had no right. Had no courage. He'd already made the decision of what mattered most to him, and he wasn't going to sacrifice his future to tell her about his past. He liked Sylvie. Hell, that kiss and the incredible feel of her skin would keep him awake more nights than he wanted to admit. And the way they'd stood, watching the storm as if they were one? That feeling of rightness, of belonging, would haunt him the rest of his life.

But he needed to stay focused. Sylvie was an unbelievably talented woman who would eventually go back to the life she had before. And there wasn't room for someone like him in that life. He'd be lucky if he could convince Beanie and Tyler to be his friends.

"I shouldn't have kissed you," he blurted out. Ever the smooth talker.

She looked at him then, and his heart blipped and he bit back a smile. Her eyes sparked with anger, not sadness. "I'm not good enough for you?"

He turned the key, fluttered the gas pedal. "The opposite."

"I don't get any say in the matter?"

"No." He turned the truck toward home.

"Maybe you're right."

He flinched.

"You still owe me a few cooking lessons," she continued.

He cranked his head in her direction. "What?"

She took her time looking him over. Although she was a good foot shorter, he had the impression she was looking down her nose at him. "You going to back out of that, too?"

"I didn't—"

"You did," she interrupted him. "Seems to me every time you get scared, you tuck tail and run. The least you could do is teach me how to cook a few more meals."

He loved a woman with backbone. His mother was so spineless, any breath of wind could, and often did, blow her in another direction. Sylvie was her polar opposite. If he hadn't been crazy about her before, he was now. "Fine. A few more meals. And for the record, I'm not the least bit scared of you." Liar. He was terrified.

She smiled like she had his number. "Good, 'cause it's about time you showed me how to cook the scallops Dusty dropped off."

CHAPTER NINE

TWO DAYS LATER, Adam knocked once then entered Sylvie's kitchen and flicked on the light switch before depositing his armload of groceries on the counter. The house was silent and peaceful, and the tense muscles in his shoulders relaxed. Sylvie had been serious about getting cooking lessons. When he'd stopped by the café earlier that afternoon, she'd made him promise to show her how to cook scallops tonight. And no, he hadn't gone to the café to see her. He'd come up with a legitimate reason; he'd been looking for Dusty to discuss when he was going lobster fishing. Getting to see Sylvie was a bonus. Besides, he'd done pretty good this week—he'd managed to stay away from her two whole days.

Dusty had promised to take him lobster fishing, and Adam figured getting up at four in the morning and freezing your ass off for the better part of the day while you hauled traps was a rite of passage. Practically everyone in the village had helped out on the lobster boats at some point of their lives. He couldn't wait to be inducted.

He grabbed his clean jeans and sweater and headed for the shower. He managed to banish the erotic pictures in his head, triggered by the smell of Sylvie's shampoo, by trying to gauge just how pissed off she would be this evening when she discovered they were having dinner guests. Or if she'd even care that they wouldn't be alone.

He'd made sure he mentioned to Dusty he was cooking

scallops in Pernod at Sylvie's tonight, and Dusty immediately said he was coming to dinner. When Teressa heard what was on the menu, and that Dusty had already invited himself, she called her mother to ask if she would babysit the children for the evening.

The cooking lesson had turned into an impromptu dinner party, which was exactly what he'd been aiming for.

He didn't trust himself to be alone with Sylvie. Ever since that kiss two days ago all he could think about was kissing her again. And other things. He turned off the water and toweled off hard enough to strip away a layer of skin. He pulled on his clothes, and ran his fingers through his wet hair to comb it.

He wanted Sylvie, but he couldn't have her. Hell, he'd known that the first day he saw her. He'd even tried out different ways in his head how to tell her just how much of a loser he really was. *Do you want cream in your coffee? And, oh, by the way, I have no idea how many people my father killed. And there's a good chance I inherited the killer gene.*

He grabbed his work clothes and stuffed them into his gym bag. He'd been dragging his dirty laundry around with him, doing it in the city when he was there, but soon he'd be ready to hook up the washer and dryer in his own house.

He grinned. His house was going to be a home soon. He refused to give up his dream. He needed a home. And for the first time in his life, he was beginning to believe he deserved one. So no matter what his body was telling him, he was going to listen to his head. Straight ahead. No detours.

Except maybe to the living room to look at Sylvie's seascape again. He couldn't stop thinking of her paintings since he'd seen them, and every time one of them popped

into his head, he smiled. He stood in front of the painting, his gym bag swinging from one hand. She really was
an incredible artist. Hard to believe so much energy came
from such a small woman.

He wished he could look at the painting at Teressa's
again, but he wasn't going back into her bedroom—Teressa
made him nervous. He was almost certain she'd been jok-
ing about jumping him, but in case she hadn't been, he
didn't plan to give her the opportunity.

"You brought enough for supper, I see," Sylvie called
from the kitchen.

Adam turned toward the kitchen and Sylvie. He had
the heady sensation she was reeling him in using only
her voice.

"Did you take the scallops out of the freezer to defrost
them?" she added.

He stepped into the kitchen and tripped over his feet.
Aw, hell. She must have slipped upstairs while he was
in the shower and put on a dress. She looked...incred-
ible. Slender and willowy and just...incredible. He swallowed and tried not to speculate what kind of panties she
wore that didn't leave a line. A thong? Sweat peppered
his forehead.

The emerald-green dress hugged her body like a second skin. It fell straight to her feet—her bare feet. Her red
toenails peeked out from under the bottom of the dress.
Whenever she moved the dress moved with her, caressed
her, hugging her figure in a different way each time—one
second her beautiful little behind, then her breasts that...
Don't stare. Yep, for sure she wasn't wearing a bra.

She dug through the brown paper bag he'd left on the
counter like a kid looking for treasure. "I love seven grain
baguettes." She pulled the baguette out of the bag and

waved it around like a wand, her face lit up. "What else are we cooking?"

He dragged in a breath. Time to dim the glow. He turned his back to her and searched for a corkscrew in a drawer. "Teressa's bringing dessert. A cheesecake, I think. And Dusty's bringing a couple more pounds of fresh scallops."

He forced a smile and turned back to her. His stomach cramped as he watched her carefully place the baguette on the counter.

"Well." She looked everywhere but at him. "I guess we'd better start cooking if we're having company. I'll just…um…get my book to write notes in."

He crossed his arms, lowered his head until his chin hit his chest. *Imagine*…he taunted himself, his chest tight with anger, his mouth bitter. Imagine if they were together. He and Sylvie. A couple. Loving and living together. Cooking dinner *together* at the end of a busy day. Imagine what his life could be like if he wasn't a stinking coward. Imagine if she loved him, because everything he'd done in his life to this point had made him the man he was today. He rubbed a hand over his face. *Not good enough. Quit feeling sorry for yourself.* A little pain now was going to save Sylvie a much bigger hurt later. Assuming…

He pulled himself together, lined up the veggies he'd brought on the counter and stared at them for a good five minutes, all the while straining to hear movement from upstairs. He pulled an eggplant out of the lineup and started chopping. Okay, he'd tell her. Everything. *Whack*. The whole sordid story. *Whack*.

He threw the knife in the sink. Was he crazy? They'd kissed. It had been a great kiss, but what the hell was he? A teenager? A kiss was hardly more than a handshake these days.

He could see it all now. He'd spill his guts to her, and

Sylvie would turn around and leave for Toronto, just as her family was always urging her to. Just as she should because she was so frigging talented. And he'd be left an outcast—the neighbor nobody wanted. He wouldn't even be able to sell his house for God's sake.

He splashed some wine into a glass, gulped a mouthful. He wasn't telling her. Mind made up. Move on.

Teressa charged into the kitchen, bringing the crisp night air with her. "You look like a laugh a minute. What's wrong?"

Dusty followed her in and sniffed the air. "I don't smell anything cooking."

The knot in his chest loosened. "I haven't started yet."

"But I'm starving." Dusty looked around as if food would magically appear.

"Good." He fished the knife out of the sink and started cutting more veggies. "You can cut up the baguette. And look in that bag. There's some pâté in there and cheese and olives. Find a dish and put it all together."

"I could do that. Hey, look at me, Teressa. I'm cooking."

"That's not cooking. That's taking things out of a bag." Teressa didn't look up from pouring wine into a couple of glasses. "Where's our cook-in-training?"

"Right here," Sylvie announced from the doorway. "Pour one for me, will you? Make it a big one."

Adam gripped the knife harder and continued chopping. If he turned around he'd want to take Sylvie into his arms, and that was wrong for so many reasons.

"This is my cooking lesson. I'll do that."

He inhaled her sweet scent before passing the knife to her. "Medium pieces this time." He stopped, cleared the frog out of his throat. He'd assumed she'd gone upstairs to change. He'd assumed wrong. She still wore *the dress that revealed all*. The better to torture him, he supposed.

"I wrote out the recipe for you." He slid the card in front of her. "Again, it's simple. Just stir-fry."

"Hot dress." Teressa sat at the table and toasted Sylvie. Teressa wore tight jeans and a T-shirt that had "Fearless" written across the back. "Wear it while you can. Everything goes south once you have kids."

"You could wear that dress," Dusty said from where he was doing a surprisingly good job of arranging food on the platter.

Everyone was silent for a minute until Teressa started giggling. Sylvie joined in.

"What?" Dusty look bewildered.

"Teressa's figure is a little too…womanly," Sylvie explained.

"Yeah." Dusty sounded like he was drooling. Which started the girls laughing again.

Adam relaxed against the counter and sipped his wine. He watched Sylvie bite her bottom lip as she turned back to her work and started humming a tune under her breath. Did she know something about Dusty and Teressa he didn't?

"Want me to help?" he asked.

"I think I can handle this part. What else are we having?"

"New potatoes and scallops. Could you slow down? You're trying to go too fast."

"Teressa?" Sylvie asked without looking behind her, where Teressa lounged at the table, sipping wine.

"I'm not cooking."

"I'm not asking you to. Super-chef is breathing down my neck. Distract him, will you?"

"My pleasure," Teressa purred. She leaned forward, grabbed his hand and pulled him toward her. "Come on, big boy. Come play with mama."

Dusty scowled, thumped the platter of hors d'oeuvres on the table.

Aw, crap. Were Sylvie and Teressa playing some kind of stupid matchmaking game, with him as monkey in the middle? No way. Bad enough Sylvie was ticked off at him. He didn't want Dusty on his case, too. Besides, he'd never trespassed on another man's territory. If he was right, that is, and the girls were playing some kind of game.

"I heard Beanie's daughter won two hundred dollars on the big draw today," he said in an attempt to lighten things up. "That's a lot of spare change."

"That draw doesn't work," Dusty groused. "One person sees whatever Syl has added to the mural and within ten minutes, everyone knows. They all give the same answer."

"But you don't know who's going to win," Teressa said.

"Big deal. I never do, so who cares?"

"Maybe I'll trick them the next time," Sylvie added.

Adam chuckled. "Like how?"

"That's insider information. No cheating."

"At least she painted in the lights of your house and added Romeo." Dusty turned to her. "How come you didn't paint Adam into the mural, too?"

Adam held his breath, waiting for her answer. The same question had occurred to him.

Sylvie tilted her head as she continued chopping vegetables in her precise fashion. "I guess I don't know where he fits yet."

"That's stupid." Dusty picked up an olive and popped it into his mouth. "He belongs in his house. You should paint him in his yard or, I know, looking out the window."

"I'll take that into consideration."

The room remained quiet for a few beats. Finally, Adam spoke up. "Anyone want to see the progress I've made on my house before we start cooking?" he suggested. Anyone? Everyone? Didn't matter as long as Dusty stopped glaring at him.

"Sure," Dusty agreed. "You got that new window in upstairs?"

Adam breathed a sigh of relief as he and Dusty headed for the door. "Yeah. Wait 'til you see it. It really opens up the upstairs."

Dusty turned back to the kitchen. "You coming?" He addressed his question to Teressa.

Teressa smiled. "Absolutely. I've been hearing all kinds of rumors about the love pad Adam's building."

Adam noticed Sylvie had stopped chopping the carrots. "Sylvie?" he asked. She hadn't seen the renos for the past two weeks, and he was curious to hear what she thought of the changes he'd made. Cal's mind was somewhere else these days; recently he hadn't been saying much about what he thought of the renos other than practical suggestions. Sylvie had been avoiding him as much as he'd been avoiding her, and Teressa and Dusty were always too busy to stop by. Which only left some of the locals, like Beanie, to offer their opinions and suggestions. Beanie was an okay guy, but he fixated on the plumbing aspects. Like if he was going to install a tub and how big? Or maybe just go with a shower. Adam could use more aesthetic input.

Realizing he was holding his breath, he exhaled and turned to the door.

"Why not?" Sylvie murmured from behind him.

He shoved down his disappointment that she sounded as if she didn't care one way or the other. Distance was what he'd wanted, right? Good thing because judging by her cool tone, distance was what he was getting.

As Sylvie followed the others through the dark to Adam's house, she felt as nervous about seeing the renovations he'd made as she did on opening night for one of her exhibits. Seeing how someone expressed themselves through the choices they made for their home was as personal and revealing as, well, seeing how someone expressed their feelings on canvas.

A thrill shot through her. If she ever started painting again, she'd paint a portrait of Adam. She could see it in detail already. If only the connection from her brain to her hand would start working again. Or was that from her heart to her hand? She stumbled over a piece of driftwood the storm had tossed up from the ocean. From behind her, Adam put his hand on the small of her back to guide her through the dark. The warmth from his large hand slowly worked through her dress until her body hummed with awareness.

"The door's unlocked," Adam called ahead to Dusty. "Light switch is inside to the right."

A few seconds later, light spilled out into the yard from the downstairs of the small house. How many nights had she looked across the yard to see Adam's lights on upstairs? Knowing he was there had both comforted and disturbed her. It felt right that he was living in this house, but looking across the yard at his lights made her feel lonely.

She wished he'd spent more time in Collina when he was a child, that whatever had happened to him that made him…what? Not afraid. She couldn't imagine Adam being afraid of anything. But reluctant. Cautious. She wished he could have experienced a carefree childhood and not have to bear the scars he did. But they all had scars, didn't they?

Adam rubbed a spot on her lower back. "Don't you want to go in? I'm surprised you haven't been over before now."

She moved out of his reach. It was either that or melt into his arms. "I've been busy with…everything." Not so busy she couldn't have stopped by like everyone else in the village. She held her breath as she pulled open the door. What if she hated what he'd done? What if she loved it?

"It's still a mess down here. I've kept the old staircase for the time being. But I plan to install a circular, wrought-iron staircase over here, eventually." Adam stood beside a wall that separated the old kitchen from the front room. "Cal says I can rip out part of this wall as long as I have a heavy enough beam to carry the upstairs weight. What do you think?"

She thought she could be falling in love with this man, who was investing heart and soul into creating a home for himself. "I love the idea of a wrought-iron staircase. It's perfect."

"Hey, Syl," Teressa called from upstairs amidst giggles. "Come check this out. No wonder everyone calls it Adam's love pad."

Adam smiled. "She's probably had too much wine," he said.

Sylvie gathered her courage and climbed the small stairs, acutely aware that Adam followed closely on her heels. Whatever had possessed her to wear a tight-fitting dress that required wearing a thong?

Sylvie stopped at the top of the stairs to view the large open room until Adam nudged her from behind. She walked over to the front of the house, where he'd replaced the wall with windows that looked down on the beach and ocean. Beautiful! Teressa sat on the king-size bed that sat in front of the windows. She tore her eyes away from the view and the bed and took in the entire room.

Adam and Cal had ripped out all the walls and turned the upstairs into one large room—or love pad—except where they'd built a bathroom along the back wall.

Dusty called from the bathroom. "Man, I've gotta get one of these tubs. Teressa, come see this."

Teressa jumped up and went to see what Dusty was talking about.

Adam came up behind Sylvie as she turned back to the view. "What do you think?"

"It's a beautiful space." The room felt like a beginning; full of promise but still incomplete. And it said so much about the man. The huge bed in front of the window. The white bedding. The sparseness in the rest of the room. A sensuous man who needed order in his life. Not someone who invited messiness, and heaven knew her life was a mess. She choked down a breath. Good to know. It was not like she was in love with him, anyway.

How many nights would it take to banish the image of Adam sprawled naked in his big old bed with moonlight spilling over him? She'd probably never get a good night's sleep again.

"What color do you think I should paint the room?"

She moved away from him. "You should ask Anita. She's the best at interior decorating."

"I don't want to ask Anita. I want to know what you think."

She glanced at the anger that flitted over his face. The house was his masterpiece, and she should treat it with the respect he deserved. "A light turquoise. It's a tropical color, but you have to keep it light because we don't have the hot sun to reflect a darker, more intense hue."

A smile tugged at the corner of his mouth. "And the bedding?"

"Gray. Maybe with a pinstripe of turquoise if you could find it. Satin," she added.

"Don't suppose you're planning on renting this place out once you get it done?" Dusty emerged from the bathroom. "If I found the right woman, I wouldn't come up for air for days. You gotta see the bathroom, sis. It's got a double-ender, cast-iron tub, big enough for two. Come on." Dusty grabbed her elbow and pulled her into the bathroom.

Again, the end wall was filled with windows and the cast-iron tub sat under the window. Outside, a huge maple tree shaded the house—she felt like she was in a tree house. Her brother was right, a few candles, a bottle of wine and the right person, she could spend days in the upstairs of the house alone.

"Seriously, man." Dusty grinned and sat on the toilet when Adam stepped into the room, dwarfing it. "I'd rent this place in a minute."

Adam laughed. "Glad you like it, but it's not for rent. I still have a lot of work to do."

With Adam watching her so closely, Sylvie felt obliged to say something—other than how about a sleepover. "You've done a beautiful job upstairs. I can't wait to see what you have planned for the downstairs."

Dusty hooted. "Isn't that just like a woman. Great job, but I need more. Women are never satisfied. Anyway, I'm hungry. If you're really going to cook supper, you'd better get to it."

Under normal circumstances she'd tell her brother to cook his own supper, but she wanted to get out of Adam's house as much as Dusty wanted his supper. She longed to stay and explore a whole world of possibilities with Adam so badly her body ached.

As they trooped down the stairs and headed back to her house, Sylvie realized as much as she admired Adam's house, seeing it made her feel lonely for more than one reason.

Her family home was only on loan to her. She missed her belongings. Missed spending time in her Toronto studio, as well. Though she had a studio here, maybe it was time to go back to Toronto and pack up. She was tired of living out of a suitcase. Up until now, moving back permanently had felt like such a monumental decision, but suddenly it felt like the right thing to do. To do more than simply talk about how much she wanted to move home—to actually commit to the idea.

She envied the permanence Adam was building into his life.

"You concentrate on the veggies," Adam suggested when they got back to her house. "I'll get the potatoes started. When we're ready, I'll show you how to cook the scallops. They only take a few minutes."

Sylvie smothered a laugh when Teressa beckoned Dusty with a crook of her finger, and he immediately jumped to his feet. "Let's set the table in the dining room with the good china. I love those old dishes."

Dusty stopped at the doorway. "How long before we eat?"

Adam laughed. "Fifteen minutes tops. You'll survive."

Sylvie hummed under her breath as she and Adam worked side by side.

"Think those two will ever realize what they've got going on?" Adam asked.

She glanced up at him. "You picked up on that, too?"

"Kind of hard not to."

Sylvie frowned. "They like each other well enough, but… I don't know. Dusty can be so irresponsible sometimes, and Teressa has two children to take care of. They have some pretty big obstacles to overcome."

Adam reached around her and grabbed the frying pan from its hook. She inhaled his scent and warmth and tried not to think about how big and lonely his bed had looked.

"If people want something bad enough, they find a way." Sylvie had the impression that although he kept his

gaze trained on the melting butter in the pan, he was waiting for her to say something.

"Sometimes wanting isn't enough." Her shoulders
slumped as fatigue crept in. These days, she wanted all the
things she couldn't have—she wanted too damned much.
Like her desire to get back to painting. Because although
she was beginning to understand that she needed to balance her art with…well, life, painting was an essential
part of who she was. Since she'd been blocked, she'd felt
hollow inside, like when a person eats and eats and can't
fill up. But the more she forced the issue, the possibility
of starting again felt even more remote.

She wanted Adam, too. She didn't understand what kind
of relationship she hoped for, but it would be interesting
to open that door and see what was on the other side. But
after their kiss, it was hard not to miss his back-off signals.

She hated when people ran hot and cold. Did he think
he had her hooked and she'd wait around until he made up
his mind? After being manipulated by her father and brothers, no way was she going to get sucked into that scenario.
And yet…she wasn't ready, or able, to completely close
the door between them. At the same time, she thought her
life would become less complicated if she moved home.

Dinner turned out to be more enjoyable than she'd anticipated. Her stir-fry held the right amount of crispness
and heat, even Teressa complimented her on it. The scallops, sautéed in cream with a generous dollop of Pernod,
were the best thing, hands down, Sylvie had ever eaten.
Teressa proposed to Adam three times, but that may have
had to do with the amount of wine she'd drunk as much
as how good the food tasted.

Sylvie had to admit, as she listened to Adam assuring
Teressa and Dusty, one more time, to leave the dirty dishes
because he didn't mind cleaning up, that he made a pretty

attractive package. First the beautiful home he was creating. Add to that, being a great cook. Having a sense of humor and being gracious under pressure. With a wink on the side to Sylvie, he'd promised Teressa, as solemnly as possible, that once he was ready to look for a wife, she'd be on his list of possible candidates.

Sylvie leaned against the open back door and drank in the crisp night air as she listened to Teressa sing off-key on her way to Dusty's truck. Adam stood behind her and it took all her self-control not to lean against him. Or turn and step into his arms. She'd done that already, the day of the storm, and it had taken two days before he'd gotten up the courage to even say hello to her again. He'd liked kissing her. She was certain. Did he honestly think he wasn't good enough for her? Why would he feel that way?

She stepped around him into the house and started running hot water into the sink. If she was staying here for any length of time, she'd definitely need to buy a dishwasher. "Anita has rescheduled the cycling event for this weekend."

"I heard." He sounded distracted as he put the leftover vegetables into the refrigerator. They'd cleaned up on the scallops, of course.

"Are you still available to help?" Her family and friends often accused her of being a lousy conversationalist because of her habit of drifting off in a cloud. But tonight she needed to put words, senseless chatter, between her and Adam. She wasn't ready to say all the things that needed to be said.

"Teressa has me signed up to work in the kitchen."

"If that isn't okay, I could find someone else to do kitchen duty. Mrs. Marley said she'd help if we got desperate. Her feet are hurting her, though. You could help patrol the bike routes if you'd prefer to be outside."

Adam looked up from wiping the counter clean. "The

kitchen's fine. Teressa mentioned she could really use the help."

"Okay." Sylvie plunged her hands into the hot water and started washing the dishes. As long as Teressa didn't do something monumentally stupid like come on to Adam.

Adam grabbed a dish towel and waited for her to hand him a plate to dry. "I've been thinking." He sent her a side-long glance before continuing. "What do you have planned after the cycling event?"

Sylvie tensed. If it was possible to tiptoe with words, Adam was doing it. Or trying. He was as subtle as a moose.

She caught his gaze and held it. "What's on your mind?"

"Can't get anything past you, huh?" The smile in his eyes was contagious. After a minute, he folded his arms and looked serious. "I think you should try painting again."

He put up his hand to stop her automatic protest. "Just listen for a minute. I saw the way you looked at my house. You miss being creative, don't you? How are you ever going to know whether you're still blocked or not if you don't at least try painting?"

"What makes you think I haven't?"

"Good point. Have you?"

"Not really. A sketch here and there, but a painting? No." She dragged the dishcloth listlessly through the dirty water.

"Even I can see the café has only so much potential for you, Syl. You have so much to offer. It would be a shame to—"

"Let all that talent go to waste," she finished for him, her insides curdling. "You're like all the rest. You can't wait to get rid of me." She chucked the cloth into the water.

She jumped when he slapped his hand flat on the counter. "You couldn't be more wrong. What I'm talking about has everything to do with you being happy. I'd hate it if you moved away. But if you keep running away from your problems, they'll continue to grow. You talk about your family lying to you about your parents' marriage, but, Sylvie, your mother has been dead for seventeen years. Isn't it time to let go?"

She folded her arms over her stomach. Had she thought him good-looking? Really? With that broken nose and hulking frame? He looked like someone who belonged in jail. "I haven't been harping on this for seventeen years. I just remembered seven months ago."

"Why don't you talk to your father? Get it all out instead of torturing yourself," he said in a quieter voice. "I hate to see you so unhappy."

"There's a simple solution to that," she snapped. God save her from another male who knew what was best for her. "Why don't you mind your own business? Sounds like it'll save you a lot of worry."

She could tell by the way his mouth flattened he wanted to say something else but was holding back. After a tense moment, he nodded and stalked out of the house.

She picked up the dishcloth and wrung it out with more force than necessary. Just like a man. Any excuse would do to get out of helping clean up.

What did he think? That it was easy for her to talk to her father about the possibility that he had an affair, and that her mother died tragically, running away from that truth? The topic alone made her want to run away, as well. But to confirm that Pops, her rock, was capable of betraying not only her mother but also the entire family... She didn't know if she could handle the truth.

So, maybe there was something in what Adam said. Maybe she did keep looking for reasons to delay that particular conversation with her father. And maybe, damn it, Adam was right when he said it was time to tackle the problem. She sniffed. Not that she'd tell him that. But she'd take his suggestion under consideration.

CHAPTER TEN

SYLVIE DRIFTED AROUND her studio, trailing a hand over her desk where she'd first drawn Adam's picture weeks ago. She moved to the table that held her paints and brushes, all lined up like little soldiers ready to go to war. At the moment, it felt like an apt analogy.

She continued past several half-completed canvases she'd abandoned years ago and had left at home when she'd returned to Toronto. She stopped, pulled one of the larger ones out and wrinkled her nose. She'd never mastered painting boats at sea. She shoved it back out of sight behind the other canvases and moved on, finally, to stand in front of the fresh canvas she'd stretched and sized yesterday.

After spending the entire day preparing several canvases, she'd felt fantastic, rejuvenated. It had been like old times, anticipation thrumming through her.

Nothing left to do but paint. She adjusted the two-by-three canvas. She had bigger canvases, but she hoped starting small might make creating a painting more approachable. Maybe she should have prepared an even smaller one. Six inches by six inches.

She would have laughed at the idea if she thought she could get any sound past the rock in her throat.

She usually painted big because her feelings were huge, and she needed a lot of space to express herself. But her feelings weren't big now. They were small and tight, and they burned like acid.

The rock moved from her throat into her lungs, and she started to hyperventilate. Great. Another panic attack. She sank into a chair, thrust her head between her knees. She should have seen the attack coming. Should have known her body was as anxious as her mind to betray her. She counted and made herself breathe and wiped away her tears.

She couldn't paint. She wasn't ready, and deep inside she'd known that. Sylvie dragged herself upright and leaned back in the chair, her eyes closed, tears trickling down her cheeks like a tap that wouldn't turn off.

She'd betrayed herself. Again. Just as she had over and over her entire life. Adam had asked her to try to paint, and she'd scrambled to please him. And failed.

Just as after her mother had died she'd tried so hard to please her father and brothers. The more they praised her drawing, the more she drew. Her success, even at the age of nine, gave them something else to concentrate on other than what they'd lost. She'd repeated the same pattern her whole life. First with her father and brothers. Then Oliver—the hoops she'd jumped through to please him. And now, Adam.

She made herself sick. What was wrong with her that she couldn't stand on her own two feet and get on with her life? Why did other people's approval have to mean so much? God, she was tired. Tired of being what other people wanted her to be. Of not knowing what she wanted to do.

She pressed her fingertips against the pounding in her forehead. Her family would eventually forgive her if she never painted again. Wouldn't they? Her friends in Toronto didn't care; they'd forgotten about her already. Even Oliver. Yes, she'd convinced him they were no longer a couple, but he was still her agent, and yet she hadn't heard from him in at least three weeks. And the folks here weren't really invested in her career. They barely knew her, she'd lived away for so long.

So what was the problem with not painting? People switched careers all the time. She just had to find something else to do. She squeezed her eyes shut. Pops and Cal and Dusty were going to be so disappointed. They'd get over it one day, but how she wished Pops was feeling better and they could talk. About everything. She missed her father. She needed him.

Adam would understand.

She shoved the thought away as soon as it appeared. Yes, he was good at listening, but no, she wouldn't talk to him. He was just like her father and brothers. Okay, not just like. He had more patience, but that was only because he hadn't known her long. Give him another six months, and he'd be like everyone else, telling her to stop whining and get on with it.

The real problem was not what everyone thought or wanted or said. The real problem was her fear. Fear of failing and fear of succeeding.

For all her talk about finding another career, she was an artist at heart, and the thought that she may never paint again was unthinkable. Thus the panic attacks. But slowly, she'd inched closer to the concept that succeeding was equally frightening because her idea of success had changed.

She wanted to paint only because she wanted to paint. Not to please her family. Not to distract them from their sorrow. She wanted to paint for herself, and all her life she'd been doing it for someone else. Who did she think she was to be so selfish to paint only to please herself?

Not that people would even know. But somehow the thought process had started with her not painting, and she was beginning to realize in order to succeed, she had to change. She had to find out who she was, not who everyone else wanted her to be. Was it possible to have the people you love return your love and to follow your own dreams at the same time? Could she paint for herself or not paint at all, and still have her family's and friends' respect?

Feeling drained, she pushed to her feet, waited to see if her equilibrium had returned. Sitting in her studio and feeling sorry for herself wasn't going to change anything. Thank goodness the cycling event was in a couple days. At least she could claim she'd done everything in her power to make the day a success. No relying on inspiration, just flat-out hard work.

For now she'd go to the café and talk Teressa into letting her help chop vegetables or something else equally useful.

TWO DAYS LATER, Adam squinted from the glare of sunshine on water as he paused to catch his breath on his early-morning run. Sylvie had perfect weather for her cycling event today. *Collina's First Great Annual Cycling Event.* The name made him grin every time. He prayed everything went smoothly. Sylvie had worked like a woman possessed to make sure the day was a success.

He'd heard through the grapevine she'd even mowed a couple of overgrown lawns on the main street because the owners were away. He could have done that for her. But, of course, she hadn't asked because he'd been stupid enough to make the same condemning mistake every person in her life had before him—he'd been an arrogant idiot and told her to just start painting. As if being an artist was the same as being a mechanic or a carpenter. Pick up your tools and go for it.

She hadn't talked to him since. She'd made sure she was gone when he cooked meals or caught a shower. Gone where and with whom? He didn't know. But he worried she was spending even more time by herself, and then he worried she was working too hard. At least he could help today. After cleaning up, he'd head up to the café.

He set an easier pace for the last leg of his run, enjoying the red glow of the sun coming up over the horizon. God, he loved this place. He thanked his grandmother every day for giving him the opportunity to live here. He only wished she was still alive so she could see how her little house was turning into a home. *His home.*

The upstairs was almost complete except for some cosmetic touch-ups, and Beanie had even hooked up the water for the upstairs bathroom. He'd turned the water on before going for his run, hoping the rust would disappear. If the water ran clear, he could use his own bathroom from now on. He didn't have room for a shower upstairs, so he'd have to take a bath, but at least he'd be able to avoid using Sylvie's shower. His fantasies had skyrocketed since the day they'd kissed at the lighthouse, and a man could only take so much torture. After his suggestion she try painting, he imagined the less she had to with him, the happier she'd be, anyway.

He stopped and did some stretches when he reached his front yard. He wondered if she'd tried painting, and if she had, if it had gone well for her, and what that would mean. He didn't want to think about living here without Sylvie beside him. He suspected that she'd probably leave soon because when you got right down to it, Collina didn't have enough to offer her.

And here was the woman of the hour.

Romeo, who'd been patiently waiting to go inside for a drink, let out a soft woof and headed toward Sylvie's. Adam grabbed his T-shirt from the ground where he'd tossed it. He probably stank to high heaven after his run.

Wiping the sweat off his arms and chest, he turned to say good morning to his neighbor.

And nearly choked on his spit. Hot damn! Sylvie wore tight white jeans, a minuscule white top that left more skin bared than it covered and a bright red cap. His mouth turned dry as images of an ice cream sundae with a cherry on top slammed into his mind. Every guy who turned up today would have the exact same reaction, damn it.

"You look nice," he said, managing not to ogle her as she bent to pat Romeo. "I think you'll get a good turnout."

"I hope so." She gave Romeo another pat before straightening up.

Man, she looked beautiful. Her eyes sparkled a deep sapphire blue, and she'd painted her lips a dark rose color that looked…kissable. He hadn't realized until now that she usually didn't wear makeup.

Her gaze swept over him once, the curl of her lip letting him know she didn't think much of sweaty men. Or *this* sweaty man. He rubbed his T-shirt over his chest again and hung his shirt in front of him, hoping she wouldn't notice his obvious reaction to her.

"Maybe you should change." The minute the words were out of his mouth, he knew he'd stepped into it—again.

She raised an eyebrow, her voice fringed with frost. "Into what?"

He backed up a step. "It's cold out. You're going to be cold."

"Really? What makes you think—"

She stepped in closer, the tips of her breasts brushing against him. It felt like his heart was trying to jump right out of his chest. His brain short-circuited when she tiptoed her fingers up one of his pecs.

"—that you know what's good for me?"

She pushed against him with the tip of her finger, and

he stumbled backward, tripped over his feet and fell on his ass.

She smiled and settled her cap more firmly on her head and grabbed the bag by her feet. "I think you're right. I think it's going to be a good day." Then turned on her heel and left.

Sylvie fumed as she stalked up the sleepy street to the café. Unbelievable. To think she'd been ready to forgive Adam for meddling in her life. *"I think you should change,"* she said, mimicking him. Didn't he realize a woman dressed up to bolster her confidence? He knew how much this day meant to her. How hard she'd worked to make it a success. Change-shmange. If she wanted to look hot, she'd look hot.

And dear God, talk about hot. Did the man have a clue what he looked like, half-naked and sweating? Another minute and she would have jumped him right there in the yard—and he wouldn't have minded one bit. Her lips curled into a satisfied smile. She'd seen what was going on under his jogging shorts before he'd tucked his shirt into his waistband and let it hang down. Served him right. Nope. She didn't mind it one bit if he did a bit more sweating today.

Men. They were so easy.

Teressa was already in the kitchen preparing for the day, and so, surprisingly, was Tyler. Teressa raised her eyebrows when she caught site of Sylvie's outfit.

"Hello?" she sang out. "Um, family affair?"

"I had a point to make." Sylvie pulled a long-sleeve shirt out of her bag and slipped into it. "Better?"

Teressa snorted. "If you button it up to, like, your chin. What's up with you?"

"It's hot in here already, Sylvie," Tyler interrupted, his

face flaming-red. "I don't think you really need that extra shirt."

Sylvie and Teressa looked at each other and laughed.

"Hey, sis." Dusty strode into the kitchen, a wide smile splitting his face. He went straight to Teressa, wrapped his arms around her waist from behind and nuzzled the side of her neck. "How's my girl this morning?"

Uh-oh. Sylvie frowned. What were those two up to? They were as compatible as oil and water.

Dusty grunted and let go when Teressa elbowed him in the ribs. "I'm working."

He rubbed his ribs. "I just wanted to say good morning."

"Fine." She slapped an empty muffin tin down on the counter. "Good morning. Don't you have work to do?"

Sylvie gawked. "Geez, Teressa. You don't have to be rude to him."

Teressa pointed the knife at her. "Stay out of it."

Sylvie sent her brother a sympathetic look. The wide smile he'd entered the kitchen with was now gone without a trace. Teressa was difficult at the best of times. Get her riled up, and no one was laughing. Obviously something had happened between them. She hoped no one else would get caught in the fallout today.

"Is there coffee? I haven't had any yet," she asked the room at large.

"Out front." Tyler leapt for the door. "I'll get you some. Gotta fill up the shakers, too."

"Come on, Dusty." Sylvie patted her brother's arm. "I'll show you where I need the reception table set up on the deck."

Dusty followed her outside the café. She couldn't remember him ever looking so miserable. She rubbed his back. "You tangle with the tigress, you're going to get scratched."

"Is that supposed to be funny?"

Sylvie sighed. "Apparently not. Tyler," she called through the open door. "Can you give Dusty a hand setting everything up out here, please? I want the table there." She pointed to a spot near the steps leading up to the outside deck.

"Are you sure you don't want to have the registration inside?" Dusty adjusted his cap to the back of his head. "People go inside and smell the food, they're going to want to eat."

Like she hadn't thought of that already. She squinted at him through the harsh morning glare, noting the stress around his eyes and the downward turn of his mouth. It had never occurred to her that he might actually think she was stupid. She sighed and pushed the thought away. She had enough to worry about today without adding to her list.

"I was afraid it would get too congested inside the door, and people who wanted to eat wouldn't be able to get past the lineup to register for the bike races."

"You really think that many people are going to show?"

Still with the skepticism. Obviously, her family really did believe she had her head in the clouds. Admittedly, sometimes she did wander off mentally, but that didn't mean she was stupid. And this morning she was one hundred percent present. "Just in case, humor me."

She started to go back inside, but turned around. "Where's Pops?" Cal had already warned her he didn't plan to help much, but she'd hoped Pops would come around once he saw how much time and effort she'd put into the event.

"He'll be down later, I think."

Sylvie's heart sank to her knees. "I suppose the only reason you showed up was to see Teressa."

He avoided her gaze.

Damn it. She blinked back tears. She wouldn't let her family ruin today. They'd see for themselves how good she was at organizing events and bringing in extra business. She had the skills to run the café. All she needed were some pointers on the finer details of making a business work. If she sold her apartment in Toronto, she could afford to buy the business, she'd get to stay home and the café would stay in the family. *Then* she'd be happy. Right? She closed her eyes. Why were there no guarantees in life?

"Coffee's on the counter, Syl." Tyler slipped past her to help Dusty.

"Good morning, everyone." Sylvie watched Anita approach from the parking lot. At least one member of the family had shown up. Dusty hardly counted, since he wouldn't be here if it weren't for Teressa.

Impeccably turned out, Anita wore tan slacks and a sleek brown jacket over a beige silk blouse. Not exactly biking/hiking gear, but she was here. In the morning light she appeared gaunt, and her eyes and hair appeared dull and lifeless. Even Dusty looked concerned when he saw her.

Sylvie resisted the urge to put her arm around Anita's thin shoulders and help her into the café. "Come inside and we'll synchronize our lists. Teressa has a fresh batch of muffins probably hot out of the oven by now. Let's try one with a coffee."

Anita cast a derisive glance at her before sitting at the first table and pulling her notepad out of her bag. "Cal made me eat before I left. He'll stop by later, he said."

She wouldn't hold Cal to that promise. "I'll get the coffee and muffins. Humor me and have some, too."

"Whatever you want."

Sylvie swallowed a sharp retort as she hurried into the kitchen to grab two muffins. She could almost sympathize with Cal. It must be frustrating to argue with someone who didn't offer any resistance.

She grabbed the muffins and tossed them on plates. "Everything all right in here?" she asked Teressa.

She jumped when Teressa let the oven door bag shut. "Peachy keen. Where's my kitchen help?"

"I'll send Tyler back in."

"I meant Adam. I need a real man to help me."

Sylvie leaned against the swing door. "I'm sure Adam will show up soon. Anita and I have some things we have to go over, but when we're done, I'll come back. And if you want to talk, I mean…I know you're not okay. Just give me a minute—"

"Okay?" Sylvie jumped again when Teressa banged the empty muffin sheet on the counter. "I wouldn't know what okay was if I tripped over it. I haven't been *okay* for years."

Oh, hell. The whole point of organizing the cycling event was to attract more business to the café. But with Teressa in a mood, who knew what the food would taste like? She'd probably throw an extra handful of hot peppers in the chili just out of spite. Or worse, quit. What had her brother done to her cook, and why wasn't he in here trying to fix it?

"Give me ten minutes." She pushed out the door before Teressa slammed something else.

Anita waited at the table with her eyes closed, looking like she was going to pass out. Sylvie slid the plates with muffins onto a tray and grabbed two mugs and filled them with coffee.

Okay. Her cook was one minute away from walking out on her, her sister-in-law and co-organizer looked like she was at death's door. Dusty had already aggravated the situation…somehow. She didn't even want to think of what he and Teressa had done. Together. Because everyone knew Teressa got pregnant. Period. Didn't matter what birth control she used. The only birth control that worked for her was abstinence.

To top it off, Cal was barely talking to Anita and wasn't going to show just to make a statement, and Pops… Her heart shrank into a hard fist. *Please show up.* It would break her heart if he didn't.

She'd asked for this. No one had forced her to look for ways to improve things with the café. Everyone had been happy with the status quo. Whatever happened today was squarely on her shoulders.

Through the kitchen door, she heard a deep, soothing voice. *Adam.* Adam was here and he would know exactly the right thing to say to Teressa to make her feel better, and he'd keep an eye on Anita if Sylvie got too busy. And handle her brothers and father like he tried to at the meeting. They respected him and listened to him.

She placed the tray of food onto the table in front of Anita and sank into a chair. When had she grown so dependent on him? And how did you undo something like that? Her throat tightened. Was it even possible to go back to what her life was like before she'd met Adam?

"Eat." She pushed a muffin toward Anita. "You're not going to be much help if you pass out, and I need you today, Anita. Don't let me down."

To her surprise, Anita started nibbling on the muffin. "These are good."

"Let Teressa know, will you? She's in a mood. Maybe some praise will make her feel better. Let's go over our lists while it's still quiet."

Once they'd covered what had to be done, Sylvie realized she needed a second-in-command. If they were lucky, Anita would hold it together long enough to schmooze with the press, but Sylvie needed assistance with delegating chores to the volunteers. She had hoped her brothers or father would help, but it didn't look like that was going to happen.

"Tyler." She stuck her hand out as he sped past. "Get the box out of the backseat of Anita's car. Please," she added.

"Gotcha." He saluted her and hurried out to the parking lot to return two minutes later. "Here you go." He dumped the large box on the table and headed for the kitchen.

"Hang on. I've got something for you." Sylvie ripped open the box and handed Tyler a red cap that had Collina embroidered on it in white.

"Hey, way cool!" Tyler settled the cap on his head.

"What's cool?" Dusty asked as he came in from the deck.

Sylvie tossed a cap to him. "All the volunteers get one. That way if anyone has a question, we'll be easy to find in the crowd." If there was a crowd.

"Great idea, Syl. Way to go."

"Anita's brainchild. Here you go." She passed a cap to Anita and was surprised when she put it on. They smiled at each other. If she didn't know better, she'd think she'd just made a new friend.

She'd known Anita for two years, but other than quick holiday visits, Sylvie hadn't spent any time with her. Anita was so quiet and refined, she intrigued Sylvie. She and Cal were complete opposites, and Sylvie had often felt disloyal, wondering how long their marriage would last. Watching what was happening, or not happening, between them these days, reinforced that worry.

"Okay, Tyler." She took his arm and led him over to a quiet corner to explain that she needed him to catch the volunteers as they arrived, check their name on the list and tell them what their duties were.

Tyler's eyes bugged out. "I don't have to work in the kitchen?"

"Yeah, you do. Sorry. But first, this. When customers start coming in to eat, I'm still going to need you waiting on people. You'll probably get lots of tips today, though." She glanced at her watch. "I should check with Teressa to see if everything's okay in the kitchen."

She'd rather chew barnacle shells, but if they didn't have a cook, better to know now. She grabbed two more caps and pushed against the kitchen door, a smile plastered on her face. She would be upbeat if it killed her.

Oh. She stumbled to a stop. Adam and Teressa were wound so tight around each other it hurt, actually hurt, to look at them. They looked so right together. As if they belonged.

Sylvie had gotten the wrong man. It wasn't Dusty Teressa had made love to, it was Adam, and she was in a rotten mood because she'd have to break the news to Dusty.

No wonder Adam had been avoiding her for days. He couldn't face telling her about his involvement with Teressa any more than Teressa could tell Dusty. Wonderful. When the day from hell was behind them, she could go on a bender with her brother.

Or just go. Maybe her family was right. What was she doing, playing events coordinator in a little fishing village, miles from anywhere?

Sylvie couldn't interpret the look Adam sent her over Teressa's shoulder. Not guilt, surely. She straightened her shoulders and shoved back the oncoming panic attack. No way was she going to pass out.

"Well." She stopped, cleared her throat and tried again. With *feeling*. "Looks like this problem is solved at least."

And dropped into a dead faint.

CHAPTER ELEVEN

ADAM JERKED TERESSA'S arms away from his neck and rushed across the room to where Sylvie lay in a heap on the floor. His heart hammering in his chest, he knelt down and gathered her into his arms. What was wrong with her? He gently swept her hair back off her face. Her skin felt warm, but all the color had drained out of her face. She felt so damned frail in his arms.

"It's probably a panic attack. She has them all the time." Teressa kneeled beside him and put a paper bag up to Sylvie's mouth.

Panic attack? Why had no one told him about the attacks before? "What else can we do for her? That's not working. Maybe we should call 9-1-1." His own breath stuttered in his chest. *Come on, Sylvie. Wake up.* The animation had bled out of her face; he could barely stand to look at her lifeless features. He pulled her closer to his chest as if he could infuse her with his warmth.

"Take it easy, big guy." Teressa pulled on his arm. "You're squeezing her too hard. Hold the bag over her mouth. I'll get a cold cloth."

The kitchen door swung open, and Tyler stuck his head through the crack as if afraid to enter the room. Considering Teressa's tantrum earlier and now Sylvie fainting, he didn't blame Tyler for being cautious. Except he'd appreciate some help. He was way in over his head, and the kid might have a clue what was going on.

"Aw, geez." Tyler stumbled into the room and knelt by Sylvie's prostrate body. "Did Teressa beat on her?"

"No one beat anyone," Adam snapped. "She fainted."

"Oh." He pushed back on his heels. "Yeah, she does that sometimes."

"Why has no one mentioned this to me before?"

"Everyone knows about her panic attacks. Guess we thought you did, too."

Adam didn't know whether to take that as a compliment—he was one of them and everyone assumed he was in the know—or as an insult, meaning no one cared enough to tell him.

"If she has these attacks all the time, her family must know how to deal with it. Where the hell are they?" Pops and Cal should be here along with Dusty to support her.

"I think you're supposed to slap her face. I saw that in a movie once."

When Tyler raised his hand as if to slap her, Adam knocked it away with his elbow. "Do. Not. Touch. Her."

Tyler scooted out of reach. "Just trying to help, dude. No need to get all caveman on me. I'll find Dusty."

Adam laid a hand on Sylvie's forehead. Her skin felt clammy, and her bones...man, they were so delicate under his fingers. As well as her hands. He wrapped his hand around hers. Someone like Sylvie, she was so damned ready to take on the world, it was easy to forget how fragile she could be. He cursed under his breath as he felt a suspicious prickle at the back of his eyes. *Just hell.*

"Here." Teressa shoved a cold cloth at him. "Sorry. My cupcakes had to come out of the oven. Geez, she's not usually out this long."

"Usually? How often does she get these attacks?"

"Ask her yourself. Hey, you." Teressa smiled at Sylvie. "Nap time's over. Time to get back to work."

When Sylvie tried to sit up, Adam tightened his grip. "Not so quick. I think you need a few more minutes."

Sylvie waved her hand through the air. "I'm fine."

"It won't hurt to sit still for a bit."

"Well, some of us have work to do," Teressa said. "We can't lie around all day." She stood and went back to stacking the fresh muffins in a container.

Sylvie closed her eyes again and leaned her head against his chest. "You smell nice," she murmured.

He bent his head, nuzzled the top of her head. "Beanie hooked my water up last night. I had my first bath in the new tub this morning." Why was he telling her this now?

Her eyes flew open as her forehead puckered. "That means you don't need to use my washroom anymore."

"Yeah. That's good, right? I won't be getting in your way as much." Man, he was turning into such a wuss. He felt as if he was telling her he was moving away permanently, not just giving her shower a break. When his kitchen was up and running, it was going to feel like a full-blown divorce. Not good. Not good at all. If they continued on the way they were heading, one of them was going to get hurt.

"Syl! Are you all right?" Dusty skidded through the door.

Adam reluctantly let her go when she pushed away from him. He stood and watched as her brother helped her to her feet.

"You told us you stopped having those attacks." For once, Dusty looked worried. "I'm calling Pops."

"She told you what you wanted to hear, just like she always does," Teressa commented dryly. "Don't bother your father, Dusty. You're okay, aren't you, Sylvie? Need a coffee? Did you eat this morning?"

Sylvie's mouth tightened. "I'm fine. And you?"

"In the trenches." Teressa studied her friend another minute before going back to work.

"Me, too," Sylvie agreed.

"Do you have the faintest idea what they're talking about?" Adam asked Dusty, who had moved up beside him.

"I never do."

"Hey, Syl!" Tyler burst through the door. "You gotta come see this. They're coming. Everyone's coming!"

They all filed outside behind Tyler. The sun was high in the sky now and doing its best to burn off the frost from the night before. Adam wished he wasn't committed to working in the kitchen; he'd love to go for a bike ride. And by the look of the long line of cars descending into the village, a lot of other people had the same idea.

Tyler jumped up and down with excitement. Anita had wandered out with them and smiled, a slight flush on her face, looking more animated than Adam had ever seen her. Teressa put her hands on her hips, threw her head back and whooped. Dusty scratched his head and watched Teressa. Best of all, Sylvie, standing in front of him, turned and beamed a hundred-watt smile just for him. He felt as if she'd reached up and handed him the sun.

"I guess we'd better get to work," Teressa said. "It's going to be a busy day."

BUSY WAS AN understatement. And even after three nonstop hours of chopping veggies, Adam loved every minute of it. He'd never been part of a community event before, unless gang wars came under that heading.

Sylvie's cycling day had a sweet, innocent feel to it. For the first time, he was experiencing how most people enjoyed a family day. As far as he could tell, no one was drunk or doped up or had a hate-on for the guy down the street. He knew he was being naive, but that was okay, too. People came with problems of all shapes and sizes. Just look at Teressa and Dusty, Cal and Anita, Sylvie and her family. Sylvie and him. But the way they handled their problems was different. They used their heads and their hearts to find a solution.

He'd met more villagers today than he had in the entire month he'd been here. The local folk sure could pull together when needed. When he'd commented on that to Pops, who had finally shown up around noon, the old man pointed out the community had learned to work together because when disaster struck in a remote setting like Collina, you had no one to rely on but yourself and your neighbor. Survival often depended on working together.

Pops had helped in the kitchen for the last two hours, and Adam had to admit, despite Sylvie's father not supporting her need to stay home, he admired the man. A lot. Pops was not only tough, but he was smart, and it was obvious by the number of people who poked their heads around the door to ask after his health that folks had missed seeing him around.

Adam wiped the sweat from his forehead with his sleeve for the millionth time. His eyes watered from chopping onions and garlic, but so far they hadn't found anyone else to take on the chore, so on he chopped.

Like a reigning queen, Teressa ordered her subjects to work harder, better, faster. The food flew out of the kitchen. There was no way Tyler could keep up with the orders, so Teressa commandeered Dusty, wrapped an apron around his waist and even insisted he wash his hands every time he came back into the kitchen to pick up another order. Adam had caught her bestowing a smile full of sly promises on Dusty. Those two were up to something, and Adam didn't want to know anything about it, not the what, the when or the where.

He'd tried to keep an eye on Sylvie, but it was like trying to catch a moonbeam in his hand. She was everywhere he looked and then gone. When he couldn't see her, he'd take a short break and walk around outside until he spotted her. She was usually laughing, and more often than not there was a man laughing with her.

Didn't surprise him. He hung around the back door to the kitchen for an extra minute to soak up some sunshine before reentering the fray.

The day had heated up, which meant every time he saw Sylvie, she'd undone another button on her shirt. If it got any hotter out, she'd probably take it off. And he'd be stuck in the kitchen, not even able to…what? Defend her? Like she hadn't gotten by without him up to this point?

Damn it. Tyler was right; he was overreacting, and he didn't like it. Being overprotective was not his usual behavior. But if he wasn't so busy in the kitchen, he knew he'd be practically stalking Sylvie, warding off the hungry looks he knew she must be attracting.

He was such a putz. Sylvie could take care of herself. She'd been on her own for years. And her confidence had never been more evident than today as she handled the cycling event with the ease of a seasoned social coordinator. She had probably picked up a few hints from hanging out with that perfect boyfriend of hers. What was his name? Oliver. Who named their kid Oliver unless you had some serious numbers to follow it? Oliver Something III. At least she'd dumped him, but Adam had no doubt Oliver III would be back anytime now. You didn't let someone like Sylvie slip through your fingers without a fight. Not only was she talented and funny and smart, but she was so damned sexy, she… Stop thinking about her. He had to go back into the kitchen and wouldn't that be embarrassing to have her father notice just how *happy* he was.

Adam pulled the back door open and froze as a familiar sound roared behind him. Every muscle in his body tightened, and his stomach shrank to the size of a hard pea. It was a sound that had ripped open his dreams and pulled him into living nightmares. A sound that heralded chaos and grief.

A sound that screamed, *Daddy's home*.

Adam slipped into the kitchen and willed his hands to stop shaking as he picked up the knife he'd been using.

"Wash your hands," Teressa said without looking up from the humongous pot she was stirring. "What's that noise?"

Adam took his time scrubbing his hands, hoping Pops or Mrs. Marley, a plug of a woman who had run the café for years, would say something, but no one answered. "Motorcycles," he growled.

Pops looked up from the plate he was preparing. "Harleys, by the sound of it. A lot of them, too."

Sylvie was wandering around outside, half-dressed and glowing like a flower ready to be plucked, and he was stuck in the kitchen because he couldn't risk showing his face. Because he was a coward who didn't have the guts to tell her who he really was.

Adam shoved down the panic clawing up his throat. She was safe, surrounded by friends and neighbors. This wasn't the big city; people were accountable for their actions here and held others accountable for theirs, too. Besides, a lot of people owned bikes these days. Owning a hog meant nothing. Still…

"Where's Cal?"

Pops looked up from dressing the burger on the plate in front of him. "You think we've got trouble, Adam?"

What he thought was he didn't want Pops or anyone else assuming he knew anything about bikers. Not one damned thing. Adam wiped more sweat from his face. "Probably not." He smiled at Pops. "Everyone owns a bike these days."

Teressa pulled her hairnet off and shook out her hair. She motioned Adam over to the stove. "I'll check it out. I need some fresh air, anyway. Keep an eye on things, okay? Be back in a minute."

Adam left his station and moved over to the stove. All day wherever Teressa was, Dusty wasn't too far away. The bikers were probably just a bunch of old farts. What had Dusty called them? Weekend warriors. He was obsessing.

Tyler came in and clipped two more orders on the wire. "Bunch of guys outside. They look like they're part of a bike gang, like in the movies."

Hell. Bile burned up Adam's throat. Don't get carried away.

"What are they doing?" he asked.

"Talking to Sylvie and Teressa."

He untied his apron and chucked it on the counter as his gut twisted with anxiety. "Where's Dusty?" He turned to Pops. "Call Cal."

Where was Anita? Beanie? Everyone he'd grown to like and respect? He headed for the door. He needed to gather everyone together. To protect them.

"Whoa there." Pops put his hand on Adam's arm. "Cool down. Could be they're just out for a Saturday ride. I'll check it out. You and Tyler stay put. There are folks waiting for their food." Pops patted his shoulder and ambled out to the dining room.

Adam flushed with shame. How much did Pops know about his past? Was that why he'd told Adam to stay in the kitchen? Or was this how a man took care of his family and friends? Not going off half-cocked like Adam, ready to dive into the fray, but using his head first.

But what did Pops know about handling bikers? He may be smart, and he may be tough, but Adam had street smarts. Adam talked the bikers' language. And Sylvie was outside talking to them right now. No way was he hiding in the kitchen. He headed for the back door.

"You guys take care of the orders. I'll be right back."

He slipped out the door and caught two rough-looking dudes emptying their bladders on the side of the storage shed. Adam gulped for air. *Sons of Lethe,* his father's old gang. The logo was blazed on the back of their leather jackets. Holy hell. What were they doing here in Collina?

Before he could slip back into the kitchen to think out his next move, one of the bikers turned as he was doing up his fly. He did a double take, then snickered.

"Well, God damn. You gave me a start, boy. You look exactly like your old man. Hey, Sum, look at him. Paulie Hunter come back to life."

The guy who'd first spotted him had long gray hair pulled back into a ponytail. He was a few inches shorter than Adam and had about twenty pounds on him. The second guy, Sum, was younger, taller, leaner and meaner. A tattoo with weird symbols Adam couldn't interpret ran down the back of his shaved head.

Adam's center of gravity automatically shifted lower as an acrid taste burned the back of his throat. His jaw locked in place and his hands hung loose at his sides. He watched their hands and eyes for a sign of movement; a flick of the wrist that could end his life. Pumped and primed, he was his father's son again. Would always be his father's son. And, honest to God, a part of him welcomed the edge like a homecoming.

He made himself sick.

"Sorry about your pa," Ponytail said. "Dying of a heart attack. Imagine that. Pissed off a lot of people who'd have liked to kill him." He laughed again, stopped and frowned at Adam.

"How's your ma?"

"The same."

Ponytail nodded. "She always was some strung out. Pretty lady, though. You look like you've cleaned up some. Whadda you doing living in this pissant town?"

Adam shrugged. "Letting things cool off. Had some trouble out West."

"You always was a bright boy." Ponytail squinted. "Guess if you wanted to join us, you would've already."

Adam shook his head no. He wanted them gone—now. There was a lot of rivalry between gang members, and being a member of the same gang didn't guarantee friendship. Paulie hadn't had many friends. These guys could just as easily be his father's enemies.

"What happened to Paulie's shit after he died?" Sum asked in a bottom-of-the-well voice.

"Dunno. Hadn't seen him in years. I just got out of the slammer."

Sum ran his hand over his bald head. "I liked his ride, would've liked to buy it. Some said you got it."

He hitched his thumb over his shoulder. "Listen, guys. I gotta get back to work. We've got a cycling event happening. Lots of families around today. Kids gotta eat."

"That's subtle, kid. Real subtle." Ponytail wiped his nose on the back of his hand. "You're losing your edge, living out here in the sticks. That's never a good thing." Ponytail raised his hand in a salute as he walked away with Sum.

Adam leaned against the wall and breathed for the first time since he'd spotted them. He'd forgotten how much energy it took to be tough. Like Ponytail said, he'd grown soft, and he didn't like it. Not that he wanted to be a fighter, but life threw you curves. How did he expect to survive if he got too soft and stupid? Not so long ago, he wouldn't have thought twice before busting out of a back door into an alley without checking it out first.

Pops opened the door. "If you're finished out here, we could use your help inside. Seems like everyone wants to eat at the same time."

"Yeah, I'm done." Adam tried to smile but knew he wasn't fooling Pops.

The old man wrinkled his nose. "Stinks out here. You take care of those bikers?"

"I talked to a couple of them. They're moving on."

"That's good. We don't need that kind around here." Pops tilted his head toward the kitchen. "You better come. I dragged Teressa and Sylvie inside, and there's hell to pay. They're both in a snit."

Adam unfurled his clenched fists and managed to smile. "Maybe I should stay out here a while longer."

Pops put his hand on Adam's shoulder. "You're better off with us, son. Plus it's my nap time. Who else am I going to leave in charge of all those bossy women? I think they've got Anita on their side now, too."

Adam laughed outright and followed Pops into the café kitchen. Neither were deluded that the women pretty much ran the show. He didn't have a problem with that. He liked knowing the boundaries, who was in charge, who he could trust.

There was a good chance Pops had heard some of the conversation out back. If he'd been as close to Adam's grandmother as Sylvie suggested, he'd know Paulie had been a biker, wouldn't he? Had Gram actually known about his father's line of work? He couldn't remember her ever mentioning it to him.

Well if Pops hadn't known before, he would now if he'd

overheard Adam's chat with Sum and Ponytail. He'd also know Adam had spent time in jail directly before arriving in Collina. Pops would hate a felon hanging around his family. Hell, hanging around the village, even. Like Pops had said, they didn't need that kind around here. Well, he was "that kind," and he was living beside and spending time with Pops's beautiful daughter. Hell, he'd be lucky if they didn't tar and feather him and run him out of town tonight.

But maybe Pops hadn't heard anything. Because he'd invited Adam back in to look after the women, hadn't he? Although they both knew Sylvie and Teressa didn't need any help from him.

Like the sand at the beach, his boundaries were shifting right under his feet. He no longer knew where he stood with the place he called home.

CHAPTER TWELVE

SYLVIE SWUNG HER legs as she perched on the counter by the café cooler, a bottle of beer swinging from her fingertips as she watched all her favorite people party. She hadn't known it was possible to be elated and hurt at the same time. For the past two hours, her mood swooped from exultant to despairing and back again until she worried she might get sick in front of everyone.

She placed her free hand on her stomach. It couldn't be another panic attack. Collina's First Great Annual Cycling Event was finally over. The day had been a resounding success, and everyone, even Pops and Cal and Dusty, was hanging out at the café, celebrating.

Everyone except Adam. Her stomach cramped again. Not a panic attack this time. The feeling was plain old disappointment. Adam, whom she'd confided in, who had helped her plan the event and had encouraged her each step of the way, who out of every single person in the village understood how much today had meant to her, didn't care enough to give her even a nominal pat on the back. He'd disappeared a couple of hours before the event had completely wound down.

She'd asked various people where he was, was he sick, had he said anything to anyone? Everyone had thought he was fine. Apparently he hadn't cared enough to hang around. She swallowed the stupid tears that pricked the back of her eyes.

At least the day had been a success, and wasn't that the point, anyway? No one would doubt she could run the café as well as, hell, better than, anyone else. How could they argue with her about staying home or ask her when she was leaving now? Surely, Pops would sell her the café. So why did she have that sick tickle in the bottom of her stomach? The same feeling she got when something wasn't right with one of her paintings?

She pasted on a smile as Tyler swaggered up to her, his thin arm wrapped around Beanie's youngest daughter, Regina. "Hey, Syl." He clinked his beer bottle against hers. "Great day."

"Thanks, Tyler. Couldn't have done it without you. You were amazing with organizing the volunteers." She was laying it on a bit thick. Anita had taken over his job pretty quickly when they realized no one wanted to listen to him, and he'd gone back to waiting tables. But hey, he had a girl on his arm, and he stuck it out all day, no matter how crazy it had gotten.

"Wish I could make tips like that every day."

She wondered if it would register that he'd make more tips if he showed up for work on a regular basis. "Guess we'll have to come up with another events day."

"Awesome."

"Tyler, have you seen Adam? I'm worried he might be sick." The only sick person around was her. Couldn't she give it a break?

"Geez, Syl. You already asked me that twice."

She blushed. Truly, truly sick.

"If you're so worried about him, you should go look for him. He's probably not hard to find. All the dude does is work on his house and run on the beach."

Sylvie opened her mouth to protest but caught herself. Weird. Tyler was right in a way, Adam did spend all his time working on his house, and he loved the beach. But there was so much more to him.

For one thing his house was a work of art. And the way he appreciated small things, like the village and the beach and getting to know people. The way he couldn't wait to go lobster fishing. *The way he loved his life.*

Obviously, she wasn't included in that lovefest or he would be here. Wouldn't he? Maybe she *should* check on him. Or maybe she should accept the fact that if he wanted to be here, if she was important to him, he wouldn't have left in the first place.

"There's my little Em." Pops smiled broadly as he slung an arm around her shoulders and hugged her. "You did good, darling. I'm proud of you."

Sylvie's heart lifted. Finally, Pops understood. "Thanks, Pops. How are you feeling? Not getting too tired, are you?"

"Probably, but it's been a long time since I've seen the village pull together like it did today. That was the best part. And I'd hate to have missed all the fun."

"It was great, wasn't it, Mr. Carson?" Judging by the level of Tyler's voice and the flushed color in his face, Sylvie guessed he'd reached his limit of beers. She'd have to let Mrs. Marley know. She was standing guard over the cooler that had been full of beer just an hour ago.

"It certainly was, Tyler. You were a big help today. Just make sure you don't drink too much, we're going to need you tomorrow, too," Pops gently reminded him.

Tyler puffed out his skinny chest. "You can count on me. And if those bikers come back, I'll help Adam take care of them."

She felt, rather than saw, her father go still. Adam had been in the kitchen when the bikers roared into town, hadn't he? She didn't remember seeing him outside. "Did something happen with Adam and the bikers?"

She turned to her father for an answer, but he bent over to retie his shoelace. "Nothing I know about," he said, working on the second shoelace.

Tyler looked puzzled. "He sure was hyped up about them. Don't you remember, Mr. Carson? Then he went out back after you left, even though you told him not to, and the bikers left right after he came back in. I thought, you know, that he'd taken care of them, 'cause he's so big and tough-looking. Kind of like the ones you were talking to, Syl."

A chill ran down her spine. Why would her father tell Adam to stay in the kitchen when, like Tyler said, Adam had that you-don't-want-to-mess-with-me look? He would have been her first choice to tell the miscreants to get lost. Of course, she and Teressa had been so full of themselves, they thought they could handle the situation just fine, *thank you very much.* They couldn't have been more wrong.

There'd been a moment, just before Pops and her brothers had materialized behind her, when a couple of the thugs had gotten a feral, calculating look in their eyes, and she'd wondered if she'd miscalculated.

When Pops straightened up, she leaned into him, inhaling the scent of Old Spice, and filing away the new information and questions she had. She'd ask her father about it later if she needed to, but first she'd ask Adam. He had some explaining to do.

Sylvie watched her father cast his well-versed get-lost-kid look at Tyler, the very same glare he'd used on Jerry Matthews the time the boy had asked her out for her first date at the ripe age of seven years old.

"I'm happy to see Anita out and about," Pops commented once they were alone.

"I enjoyed working with her." Anita and Cal sat together at a crowded table. Cal kept his arm along the back of Anita's seat, a man marking his territory. And so he should. Everyone may be appreciative of Sylvie that she had made the day happen, but Anita was the star. Up until today, no one had much opportunity to get to know her, but they were remedying that omission this evening. The minute one person got up from the table where she sat, another person would slip into the vacant seat. Anita looked flushed and happy, her laugh ringing out over the room.

Pops was as worried about her as the rest of them, and Sylvie knew he wanted to discuss what was happening between his daughter-in-law and son. But somewhere along the way, she and Anita had stepped over the line into friendship. Sylvie was ready to help in any way Anita needed, but she refused to interfere unless asked. Everyone had to make choices in life, and Sylvie hoped Anita made the right one. And no one but Anita knew what was best for her.

Sylvie watched as Cal squeezed Anita's shoulder and leaned over to whisper something in her ear. Anita looked distressed for a minute before her expression evened out. They both stood and headed to where Sylvie and her father sat.

It took a few minutes for them to make their way across the room with people stopping them to chat. They were such a good-looking couple. And the way Cal hovered around Anita, Sylvie knew her brother loved his wife. She hoped they stayed together long enough to work things out between them.

Sylvie hopped down off the counter and hugged Anita. "Thanks so much for everything. You were fantastic."

Anita blushed and smiled. "I had fun. Planning this day with you reminded me how much I loved working."

Sylvie grinned back at her. "Great, because I think we

should plan another event right away. Want to get together next week to discuss it?"

Cal stepped closer to Anita and took her elbow in his hand. "Anita's tired. She needs a few days to recover."

"Fine. Give me a call when you're feeling better. I can come up to your house if that would be easier."

"Now, Sylvie." Pops pushed away from the counter he'd been leaning against. "No reason to push. You have to let everyone catch their breath first."

Her heart sank. Her family thought this was a one-shot deal. Let the little lady have her fun, then send her back to Toronto. She snapped her teeth together to hold back the accusations roiling around inside her. Just because someone loved you, didn't mean they wouldn't try to bully you into doing what they wanted you to do. Her family refused to understand what she needed, and she didn't know how to make them see things her way. Maybe knocking their heads together would work.

"I'll phone you next week," she said to Anita, then put her beer bottle on the counter and marched out the door before she blew up at her father and brother and ruined the evening for everyone.

Once outside, she had no idea where to go. She didn't want to go home because the house and almost everything in it belonged to her father, and as much as she loved the place, it wasn't hers. She needed to return to Toronto and bring her belongings home.

Maybe she'd buy her own house. She needed to do something permanent, to commit herself to living in Collina. Because that was what she wanted. She picked up her pace. Would she ever get it right? Know for sure where she belonged and what she wanted to do?

Without paying attention, she wandered toward the fishing wharf, which was in the opposite direction to the house.

When she'd been a kid, the wharf had been the social center of the village. They jumped off it to go swimming. She'd tasted her first beer, her first and only cigarette, and sold her first painting here. The lot beside the wharf held a mix of old bait houses that had been converted to artists' studios and shops that did a fair trade during the height of the tourist season. Normally they'd be closed at this time of year, but today's cycling event had prompted a few to reopen their shops. She hoped they'd had good sales.

With lobster season having started last week, all the boats were in the water, tied to the side of the wharf. It was still the place to come in the early evening if you wanted to hear about the daily catch, who was having motor trouble and a myriad of tidbits of local gossip.

Sylvie stopped by the wharf head, welcoming the potent mix of salt water, ripe bait and cigarette smoke. Someone was sitting in the shadows of one of the studios, smoking. Not in the mood to talk to anyone else tonight, she turned to leave.

"If it isn't Ms. Perfect. Why aren't you at the café basking in your family's approval?"

Teressa. Sylvie sighed. Sounded like she was still looking for someone to crucify. She'd been upset about something earlier, and Sylvie supposed because they were friends, she should ask what the problem was. Only she didn't really feel like being a friend to her at the moment.

Teressa had wrapped herself around Adam this morning like a starving leech. Not that Sylvie had any claim on Adam, but still, she hadn't liked it. Besides, Teressa wasn't the only one allowed to have lousy moods.

"Why are you hiding in the dark?" Sylvie took a reluctant step toward her. The glowing red tip of Teressa's cigarette arced through the air when she flicked it into the water. With the waves slapping against the wharf pilings, and the boats chink-chink-chinking as they pulled against their ropes, the tightness in her chest loosened.

Someday, she'd like to do a painting that portrayed the kind of peace that can come from being surrounded by a familiar scene. But she'd never found an original way to express that feeling. Far too many local artists had painted the wharf, the boats, the fishermen and the old bait sheds.

"I'm not hiding. I'm thinking." Sitting on a bench, Teressa stretched and reached down to touch her toes. "You did good, Sylvie. It was a great day."

Sylvie sat beside her friend. "Your chili was a hit. Did Anita tell you, one of the people who came writes a column for a newspaper in Maine. She's considering doing a feature on the café and its talented cook." Sylvie elbowed her friend. "That would be you."

"Nothing like hitting the big time." Teressa sniggered.

"It was a compliment to your cooking."

"Yeah, I got that. But what difference does it make? Be good for the café, I suppose. But tomorrow I'll get up and do the same things all over again. And the next day, and the next."

Uh-oh. Teressa's mood wasn't just due to something as mundane as Tyler not putting the cookware back in the right place. Please, please don't let it be about Adam. "Want to talk about what's wrong?"

"I don't, but I guess I have to sometime." Teressa pulled out her pack of cigarettes, rubbed her finger across the front of the package, then tossed them into the garbage can beside her.

"No!" Hell. There was only one reason Teressa would quit smoking.

Teressa's shoulders rose, then fell. "It's too early for a home test, but…" She covered her face with her hands. "I was so stupid, Syl. I not only had sex, I had unprotected sex." She grabbed her hair with both hands and pulled. "I must be insane."

Sylvie tried to catch her breath. Teressa got pregnant if she thought about sex. So, unprotected sex? It was a done deal. She opened her mouth to ask the obvious question but couldn't get the words out. *Adam.*

That was why Teressa had been all over him this morning. And hadn't Sylvie already thought they'd make a great couple? Adam would be a fantastic father, and they could buy the café, and *poof* there was their happy-ever-after. Her stomach heaved at the thought.

Please don't let it be Adam. She'd only kissed him once, but there was something there between them. Something important. Something that needed more time to mature.

"Aren't you going to ask who the father is?" Teressa interrupted the insane chatter in her head.

"You don't even know you're pregnant yet," she said, clutching for straws.

"It was Dusty. What was I thinking?" she wailed. "If it had been Adam, I could have, I don't know, maybe built a life with him somehow. He's a good guy. But no, I had to choose Dusty. No offense, Syl, but he acts like a kid himself half the time. What am I going to do?"

Adam wasn't the father. Thank you. Thank you. Sylvie's brain slowly cleared. Damn Dusty. He knew how easily Teressa got pregnant. What had he been thinking?

"How did it happen?"

Teressa looked at her incredulously. "You want details?"

"Not like that. I mean where were you? How did you end up hanging out with Dusty."

"Oh, that. The night we had supper at your house. He drove me home, remember? Only instead of going home we decided to go for a walk on the beach over there." She nodded to the beach that started at the wharf. Her mouth curled into a smile. "We didn't get far. Look, I know he's your brother and all, but God, he's hot."

Sylvie stuck her fingers in her ears. "Too much information!"

Her friend smiled softly. "He's a great guy in so many ways. I just wish he'd grow up. God, Sylvie, what am I going to do?"

"Marry him. He has to grow up sometime. Might as well be now."

"Marry him? You know he's not going to volunteer for the position. And even if he did, what are our chances of being happy? He'd be saddled with two kids who aren't his, and the one that belongs to him he doesn't even want." She stood, crossed her arms tightly as if holding herself together. "My life is hard enough now, but to add a guy who doesn't want to be there? I'm better off alone."

Sylvie bristled. "Dusty's a good man, Teressa, and he'd be a wonderful father once he got into it. You don't know how he'll feel. When he hears you're pregnant—if you're pregnant—he'll step up to the plate. I know he will." Or Pops would kill him.

What a situation. Unless something crazy happened, like they fell in love, Teressa and Dusty had a hard road ahead. "No sense in worrying until you know for sure, and that's going to take a few weeks."

"For someone normal, yeah. But let's face facts, I'm a baby-making machine." Her cell phone peeped. "Time's up. Eliza wants to go home. Let's go." She linked her arm through Sylvie's and they walked down the middle of the road, homeward bound. "If I got pregnant using a condom and a diaphragm, it's not too much of a stretch to guess I'm pregnant now. Syl, don't say anything to anyone, okay? Promise?"

She'd love to race up to her brother's right now, yank his

beer out of his hand and yell at him for being so thought-less and stupid. But this was Teressa's news to break and handle how she thought best.

"Would you consider adoption?"

"No."

"I'd love to adopt her. Or him."

Teressa bumped her shoulder against Sylvie's. "Don't be silly. You're going to have your own babies soon."

Sylvie laughed. At least she hoped the strangled noise sounded like a laugh. "I have to find a guy first."

"There's always Oliver to fall back on, but I'm thinking Adam would have something to say about that."

"Really? I don't think so. He took off before the day wound down—didn't even hang around to celebrate its success. I think it's safe to say the only thing Adam is interested in is finishing his house."

"People are complicated, Syl. You never know what's going on in someone else's head unless you ask. And sometimes even then, you don't." Teressa hugged her. "Thanks for listening. It helped a lot to be able to tell someone."

Sylvie watched her friend drift away, the fog licking at her feet. Exhausted, she turned toward home.

As much as she may want to, Sylvie knew she wouldn't ask Adam why he hadn't stayed to celebrate tonight. She'd started to care for him. Seriously care, and that had never been her intention. She had other priorities, like getting her life straightened out, before she could consider another relationship. Which meant, as much as it hurt, and it did hurt, it was just as well Adam had made himself scarce tonight. Or maybe it wasn't just for tonight. Maybe he was sending a signal that he didn't care to get involved. Not now. Not ever.

Instead of the biking event making her life better, things seemed worse than ever. She was still blocked artistically and beginning to panic that she'd never paint again. She'd been worried before but it felt different now. It was a darkest-hour-of-the-night, soul-searching kind of panic.

She needed to paint.

That didn't mean her plan to run the café wasn't important. She'd take it on if her family let her, but chances were her father and brothers weren't one iota more open to her staying and running the café now than they'd been before. A balance would be nice. Necessary, really. All painting and nothing else was probably what had derailed her to start with. Pops's heart attack and the threat of losing her only parent had exacerbated the problem.

As for Adam, it seemed he couldn't wait to put distance between them, and she was as alone now as she'd always been. More, really. She might as well shelve the damned cooking lessons—Pops was never going to sell the café to her, and spending time with Adam was becoming more and more painful.

She increased her pace when the dark house came into view. Fine. At least she knew exactly where she stood with everyone. Now it was up to her to decide what she wanted and to move forward. Piece of cake. *Right*. Might as well create a whole new life and start over.

ADAM HOISTED THE sledgehammer onto his shoulders, counted to three and swung. Plaster dust mushroomed in the air as a section of the wall in front of him collapsed. He swung again, connected, felt a burst of satisfaction as another section folded in on itself. Die, sucker! It was the most fun he'd had in a week. He raised the hammer again and was about to swing when a sharp whistle cut the air. He turned and saw Dusty standing in the doorway.

"You planning on bringing down the whole house or just that one wall? Is it safe to come in?"

Adam lowered the hammer. "It's safe."

"Haven't seen you around since the biking event last week."

"Been busy." He wiped the sweat off his face with his sleeve. Pissed off at himself was closer to the truth, but he wasn't ready to get into that with Dusty.

"You don't believe in doing things halfway, do you?" Dusty looked around the empty downstairs.

Adam had been camping upstairs in his house the past few days while he worked on the main floor. Cal had told him what he had to do to safely take out the walls before he'd gone away with Anita to Toronto. They were staying in Sylvie's apartment and taking in the big-city sights.

Lately, Cal had been as about unhappy as a man could be, and Adam hoped the couple found some respite from their problems while they were away. Although he could have done without Cal describing Sylvie's apartment in such detail before he left—a loft apartment, with a market down the street and a café around the corner. It all sounded very cozy. He knew Cal had been trying to psyche himself up about the trip, but Adam had forgotten Sylvie had a place to escape to if she wanted to leave. He'd been in a funk since Cal had mentioned it.

He hated that Sylvie had taken pains to make herself unavailable lately, but at least he got to see her from a distance. And if he ever reached the point where he couldn't tolerate not talking to her, a point fast approaching, he could do something about it, like stand outside her door until she finally let him in.

"I don't think there's any other way to renovate down here." He dropped the hammer on the floor and went over to the old refrigerator. "Want a beer? How's the fishing going?"

"Fishing's good. Best season ever except for that storm.

Lost a few traps, but the daily haul is up, so that almost makes up for it." He grinned as he twisted the top off the bottle Adam passed him. "Want to come out again?"

Adam laughed. "Not in this lifetime." He'd puked his guts out for the first three hours before he finally got his sea legs the day he'd gone lobster fishing with Dusty.

"Don't let our little outing put you off boats. Fishing's different because we turn back into our wake, and it rocks the boat. This Sunday, though, we've got the island picnic. Everyone hitches a ride on the boats, and we go out to Cooper's Island. You've got to check out this place. It's got a rock pinnacle in the middle, and if you climb up to the top of it, you can see the whole bay." He grinned. "You can come along on my boat. I promise I'll be gentle."

Sylvie would go, too, wouldn't she? He'd get to talk to her, finally. She'd been like a ghost lately. He'd catch a glimpse of her and almost before she registered, she'd be gone. He'd cooked meals and waited hours for her to come home. No luck. He'd given up his morning run, hoping to see her leave for work, and he stayed up later at night wondering where she was when she didn't come home after the café closed. Whenever he showed up at the café, she disappeared…somewhere.

He wanted things back the way they'd been. Well, he wanted more than that, but he'd be happy just to talk to her for now.

"Okay," he said to Dusty. "But if I get sick again, I'm swearing off boats for life."

"Good man." Dusty slapped Adam's shoulder. He took another drink. "What's up with the girls lately?"

About to take a drink, Adam put his bottle back down. "What do you mean?"

"I don't know. Teressa's been… I know she can be bitchy sometimes, but she won't even talk to me anymore."

His usually sunny face turned dark. "There's been this guy hanging around the café the last two days. The girls say he's a cop from Halifax on vacation. I don't like him. He asks too many questions.

"And Sylvie's got a mad-on all the time," he continued. "She's even talking about moving, but I don't think she wants to go back to Toronto. I thought maybe one of them mentioned something to you."

Adam put his beer to one side. Hard to enjoy a cold one when he felt like he'd been punched in the gut. "I haven't seen Sylvie since last weekend, and Teressa? Yeah, I guess now that you mention it, she's been kind of glum." He'd gone to the café several times for lunch or supper, hoping to see Sylvie, but it was like they had a secret signal, and the minute he walked in, Sylvie probably slipped out the back. "I've just been—"

"Working. Yeah, we all know that. You work too hard, man. You and me, we should...I don't know. Go to Lancaster and do something. I could probably call a couple old girlfriends and cruise a few bars."

Dusty sounded as enthusiastic about checking out the bar scene as Adam felt about the offer. They were two sorry souls. "I'm not into the bar scene these days." Sylvie moving? Where? For crissakes, she didn't have to move to prove her point.

"Me, neither. Sucks getting older, doesn't it?"

Not when you had a childhood like his. He could easily imagine a better life for himself, but with Sylvie not even talking to him that was all he could do. Imagine.

"Thanks for the beer. I'll let you get back to work. Don't forget Sunday. It should be a good time."

He'd be on that boat even if there was a hurricane. He'd pick up some antinausea medication to be on the safe side, though.

What was behind the talk about Sylvie moving? Sure, she was probably mad because he'd disappeared before the cycling event was over, but no way could she be thinking of starting fresh somewhere else because of him. Hell, he'd apologize if he could find her. But how to do that without telling her everything?

Though if he thought about it, he no longer saw the point of not telling her. Either way he was miserable. The hell with it. He was going to tell her about his past. Who he was, what he came from.

She probably thought he didn't care about her, but if he told her about his connection to the bike gang, she'd understand why he had to leave last weekend. And maybe she'd give him a break. Maybe even keep all that stuff to herself until he was ready to tell everyone else. He didn't know when the best time would be but he'd recognize it when it arrived.

CHAPTER THIRTEEN

SYLVIE ROLLED HER vehicle the last few yards into her drive-way with the lights and engine off. She could have stayed at Dusty's hunting cabin overnight, but there was ridicu-lous, and then there was really ridiculous.

For the past week she'd been escaping to the cabin after work without asking her brother's permission. Dusty wouldn't care that she was using his little shack in the woods, but if she told him, he'd spread the news around, and that would be the end of her hidey-hole.

At first she'd gone to the cabin because she was so disappointed that she didn't have the energy to deal with anyone. Mostly she was disappointed in Adam. But her family had let her down, too. Not to mention Teressa. In-stead of dumping on her, Teressa should have confided in Dusty. They'd both been stupid not to use any birth con-trol. Imagine getting so carried away with passion, you'd forget something as important as that.

Not going to go there. Apparently not in reality, and certainly not in imagination.

She parked and climbed out of her four-wheel-drive vehicle. She had to concentrate on the future, keep look-ing forward.

To what?

She grabbed her purse and tramped to the house. Adam had left the porch light on for her again and probably sup-per in the oven like he had every night this week. When she'd put on her favorite jeans this morning, the waistband had been a little too snug. But honestly, who could resist the beautiful meals he left for her.

She'd scribbled furious notes, instructing him not to bother, but her instructions hadn't stopped him. She'd tried a couple of times not eating the meal he left, but her stomach only ended up growling the whole night because the house smelled so delicious.

Okay, she got that he felt bad about taking off last week. When she got right down to it, what was she being so bitchy about? He'd helped with the cycling event more than anyone else. But Adam knew how important the whole thing was to her, and at the end he'd left her hanging. His message came through loud and clear—he didn't want to become more involved. Fine. Why cook her supper every night, then?

She stomped into the dark kitchen and smelled... nothing. She sagged against the wall. That was it then. Adam had finally given up on her. For heaven sakes—she swallowed her tears—there was nothing to cry about. It was not like they had a real relationship.

Adrenaline shot through her when she heard a noise from the far corner. What the—

She flicked on the overhead light. Still asleep, Adam stirred in the armchair across the room. She clamped her hand over her heart to keep it from jumping through her chest wall.

He looked so gorgeous, his head against the back of the chair, exposing his thick, strong neck. His long legs stretched out in front of him, and his hands, his beautiful, large, work-roughened hands, hung loosely over the sides of the chair. She'd love to paint those hands. Holding something delicate, she decided. Like a baby or a flower. She grabbed the notepad and pencil by the telephone, sat and started sketching. Maybe he could be disengaging a spiderweb from a doorway.

Imagine hands like that on your skin. Rough, but warm and gentle. Large and possessive. Sliding slowly, patiently, around and over and up. She shivered at the same time sweat broke out on her forehead.

"Are you okay?" Adam's gravelly voice broke into her daydream.

She ripped the sketch off the pad without looking at it and crushed it in her hand. Never could leave well enough alone. She pinned him with a glare. "What are you doing here?"

"Waiting for you." When he stood and stretched, she watched his body move in a sensuous arc. A sculpture would be best, as she'd thought when she first met him. It would be a shame not to capture that body in clay.

He looked down at himself. "What? Am I covered in dust or something?"

She averted her eyes. "Sorry, I…" Why not just tell him what she was thinking? "I was thinking I'd like to do a sculpture of you someday."

"A sculpture?" He said the word like he'd never heard it before.

"Yeah."

"You mean like a…like a nude sculpture?" His voice deepened.

"Yes. Someday." She peeked at him, looked away. He had an intense look in his eyes like the rest of the world had disappeared except for her.

He turned away and gripped the edge of the counter. He probably thought she was nuts. He wouldn't be far off.

"Hell, Sylvie. I'm not going to be able to sleep tonight because of you saying that."

She blushed. "Oh. Well."

He turned to face her. "Shouldn't have told you. Sorry."

"No, I like that you did. Because I've been thinking that you were fed up with me or something. Which, I mean, is okay, because not everyone has to like me, and…" Babble alert! Shut up, already.

"I like you, Sylvie." He smiled a lovely lopsided smile. "A lot. But I shouldn't."

She smiled back. "Me, too—I like you. And I shouldn't, either. My life is such a mess."

"How's your dad doing these days?"

"Had a little setback. He overdid it at the cycling event, and the doctor threatened to put him back in the hospital unless he *showed better judgment* is how I believe he put it. The doc was mad at all of us." She glanced at him. "Cal probably told you."

"No, Cal's gone. He and Anita are staying in your apartment…."

"Right. I forgot. That's silly of me." Needing to move, she went over to the phone to check for messages. No blinking red light.

"Do you miss your place in Toronto?"

Chitchat. She'd thought they were past the let's-be-neighbors stage. If that's what he'd come for, fine. She was just happy to see him. Having a hard time looking at him without wanting to touch, though.

She opened the refrigerator, stared blindly inside and closed it. "I miss my own things." She looked around the kitchen. "I'm getting tired of living here. I need my own place, I think."

"You mean, go back to Toronto?"

She turned toward him when she heard the urgency in his voice. Huh, maybe not feeling so neighborly after all. "No. But I don't think I want to stay here, either."

Adam stepped toward her, then stopped and shoved his

hands in his jeans pockets. "I'm sorry about the cycling event. About leaving early. I know how important that day was to you, and you did a fantastic job, Sylvie. I was so proud of you. I'm sorry I disappointed you."

She ducked her head. *Not* going to cry. "What happened to you?"

He pulled out a chair. "You're going to want to sit down for this, Sylvie."

A chill stole over her. He looked so sad, and his voice sounded tight, like the words were stuck in his throat. She didn't want to sit. Didn't want to hear what he needed to tell her. What he'd probably been trying to tell her all week. On some level she must have sensed something was wrong; that's why she'd avoided him. But running away hadn't worked so well for her other problems. She really should know better by now.

She sat. Could that be fear that shadowed his eyes? What did he have to fear in the life he'd made for himself here?

He drew up a chair and sat in front of her and took her hands in his. "I want to get this out first. I'm crazy about you, Sylvie. I know you've got a whole life elsewhere, and you'll probably leave someday. I know there's not much chance for us, but I can't help myself."

Hadn't seen that coming. "I'm not going anywhere, Adam." She turned her hand in his so they touched palm to palm. "I've missed you."

"Me, too. That's why I've got to tell you…" He shot to his feet, gripped the back of the chair. "I'm not who you think I am."

"I don't…I don't understand."

"I'm Adam Hunter, and my grandmother spent summers here and all that. But…" She heard him swallow hard. "I'm a thief and a liar, and I almost killed a man."

The only sound in the room was the raspy sound of them both trying to breathe. "No." She managed to get the one word out.

"I did time just before I came here for beating a man almost to death with my bare hands. I learned to cook for crowds in the juvie hall. I've belonged to gangs. Know how to use a knife and a gun. I've stolen cars, booze, money."

She scrubbed at her tears. "I don't believe you. Why are you telling me this?"

He folded into the chair in front of her as if his legs could no longer hold him up. "Because when those bikers came through on Saturday, I ran into a couple out behind the café, and they recognized me. And that's why I took off. I was afraid. And then…" He looked shamefaced. "I got lost driving around. I always get mixed up on the back roads around here. There isn't a straight road in the province."

"You were afraid of the bikers?"

"Of you. This place. Everyone here. I was afraid of losing everything I've started here. Living in Collina is a dream come true for me." He rested his elbows on his knees and hung his head.

"Sons of Lethe, they're… They kill people. And deal drugs and sell prostitutes. You belong to them?" She sat on her hands to stop herself from hitting him. How dare he move here and drag all that trash to this village? How *dare* he?

"No. Never."

"But you said they recognized you."

The sigh he emitted sounded as though it had been scraped from the bottom his soul. "My dad was a member. He, uh…he was an enforcer. He killed people for a living."

"You're kidding."

"Wish I was."

Her brain turned sluggish as she tried to pick through what he was telling her. "And you lived with him? You were a family?"

He uttered a harsh, guttural sound. "In a matter of speaking. Until I was ten."

"And then you and your mother left him? Things must have gotten better after that."

"My mom's a junkie. So, no. That's why I ended up joining a gang, 'cause I had to make money to cover the bills, and on the street, it's hard to make a living without backup."

Dear God, he was talking about a lifestyle she couldn't even imagine. How could she whine about her life when he'd lived through such hell? Imagine your father being a murderer.

"What was it like living with your father?"

He shot her a look from under lowered brows. "Not good. He was a psycho. Had lots of enemies."

"He's dead?"

"Last year. Heart attack."

"And your mom?"

"She lives in Vancouver."

"Do you see her often?"

He shifted in his seat, folded his arms. "Not much. I went to see her right before I ended up in jail. I was on my way here and thought I should check on her. Found out she had this scumbag of a boyfriend who used her as a punching bag. When I saw her bruises, I lost it. I almost killed the guy."

Like a wall, the words hung between them. He was quiet for a minute, then started again. "I've always been afraid that I was a violent person just like my old man, and finally, there was the proof. So I turned myself in to the cops and did some time and they got me into a program for violence prevention. Then I came here because I wanted to start fresh. I wanted to learn to be part of a community. To be someone who mattered to other people." He wiped a hand over his face. "I guess you can't get rid of your past."

Her insides were all chewed up. "You matter, Adam. Everyone likes you."

But he'd lied to her, to the whole village, by coming here and pretending to be someone he wasn't. No, that wasn't *it,* either, exactly. "Everyone has something to hide." Except his secrets were a lot more serious than most.

He hadn't trusted her enough to handle the truth. Her heart withered. What was it about her that people, her own family for heaven's sake, didn't think she had the emotional maturity or stamina or backbone—whatever the hell she seemed to be lacking—to be treated as an equal? And yet she loved her family. Probably loved Adam, too, but she couldn't go there right now. Didn't have room in her heart for him because she hurt too much.

Had she been building a fantasy of Adam and herself together? How could they have a relationship if he didn't trust her?

He touched her hand. "I'm sorry."

"Yeah. Me, too." She got up, went over to the window and looked out at the black night. Storm clouds blanketed the sky. "You can't help who your parents are. And you did what you had to in order to survive your childhood. I understand that. I don't think you realize how good of a man you are. But we all saw it right away."

She stopped when her voice broke.

"But?" His voice sounded like beach gravel raked by the waves.

She gathered her courage and looked at him. "Why didn't you trust me with the truth? What did you think I would do? Judge you because of something that happened when you were a kid?"

"I wasn't a kid when I almost killed that man, Sylvie."

"Maybe not. But you did something about your violence, didn't you? You're not the man you were then. But my point still stands. Where do we go from here if I can't trust you and you don't trust me?" She covered her heart with her hand. "I'm hurt you think I'm so shallow that I wouldn't want to have anything to do with you or maybe even that I'd be afraid of you." With a sinking heart, she recognized the inequity. Adam holding back the truth held echoes of her dilemma with her family. Did everyone think she was weak?

He sunk his head in his hands. After a minute he straightened his shoulders. "You're right. I messed up. If there's any way I can make it up to you…?"

"I don't know. I'm locked up so tight inside right now. I should apologize, too. I knew I had to take care of business with my family before I could get involved with anyone. I've been letting it ride because I was afraid of upsetting Pops. Or maybe just afraid. But I shouldn't have let our relationship go this far. I'm sorry." The question was, how far gone was she? Head over heels in love? Or just on the cusp of falling in love? She didn't want more heartache. Didn't need it.

"The mess is my fault, not yours. Don't even think about blaming yourself for my mistakes." He stalked to the door, put his hand on the doorknob, his back to her. "You don't ever have to worry about me, Sylvie. I'd never, ever hurt you physically, and I'm not giving up on us or this place. This is my home. I'd appreciate it if you'd keep everything I told you to yourself until I can get myself sorted out, though."

She automatically reached out to him, but with his back

to her, he missed the gesture. "It never occurred to me to be afraid of you. Never."

He was out the door and gone before she could say more. She shuffled over to the armchair where Adam had sat earlier and curled into a ball. Shocked that his father had killed people for a living, she didn't know what to think. Couldn't think. The horror of Adam being dependent on the kind of man his father must have been was so huge, she couldn't imagine what he'd gone through to get to where he was today.

She'd meant it when she said he was a good man. And she even understood why he hadn't told anyone the truth about his past.

In many ways he was the bravest man she knew, because he had the guts to try to be better. But if those bikers hadn't turned up and recognized him, would he have ever come clean? And why should he feel he had to? Adam was who he was. A good man. Too bad he didn't think as highly of her as she thought of him.

SYLVIE TRIED THE door to the café, then twisted the door-knob again. Locked. She frowned at the door. Business had slowed down a bit, but to lock up on a Sunday afternoon? Her heart spiked as she pulled out her key. Holy hell. Was something wrong? Had someone died and no one told her?

She shoved the door open with her shoulder and raced for the phone. She'd holed up at the house the past three days, escaping her life the best she could by practically inhaling romance novels. Instinctually she knew she needed some time and space to let her emotions even out. The only reason she'd surfaced today was because she'd already scheduled a meeting this afternoon to plan another event, this time a treasure hunt that would take visitors all over, showcasing what the village had to offer along the way.

People had seemed enthusiastic when she'd talked to them on the phone a week or so ago, so where was everyone? And more importantly, why was the café closed?

She dialed the number at her father's apartment. No answer. Okay, she'd try Dusty. She had his cell number somewhere. She dug in her satchel and with trembling fingers retrieved her address book. No answer. Maybe if she'd gotten a cell phone like the rest of the world, someone would have contacted her. But she'd been home the whole time, a phone within reaching distance.

Anita and Cal were on their way back from Toronto, so they weren't much help. If something had happened, Dusty would call Cal right away. But not her, apparently. She whirled around when the door to the café opened behind her.

"Mrs. Marley!" The short, squat woman's face creased in a smile.

"I saw you coming in. Guess you missed the boats, eh? Me, the dampness on the water makes my bones ache. I hate to miss a good party but it's not worth it for me."

Sylvie put the phone down. "Party?"

Mrs. Marley didn't bury her surprise fast enough. "Why, the annual picnic. You know, the one they have every year."

Sylvie shivered and folded her arms around her. "Oh, yeah, sure. I've heard about it, of course." What was wrong with her these days? Why did everything make her want to cry?

"Ah, there now, dearie. They forgot to tell you, didn't they? You fit in so well, sometimes we forget you've lived away forever. I promised Teressa I'd take a turkey out of the freezer and put it to thaw in the refrigerator. She's having hot turkey sandwiches for the special tomorrow, but you probably know that." Mrs. Marley frowned as it likely occurred to her that if Sylvie didn't know about the picnic, she wouldn't know what the special was, either.

How was it possible that not one person mentioned the picnic to her? Not Pops, or Dusty or Teressa. They'd probably all thought to tell Adam. But not her. Mrs. Marley was wrong. She didn't fit in. She never had. She was dreaming if she thought she could make a life for herself here.

Sylvie followed as Mrs. Marley bustled into the kitchen, still listing names in her head. Tyler? Beanie? Hell, Mrs. Marley. Why had no one thought to tell her about the picnic?

"Look at that. You still have that old leather satchel." The older woman had stashed the turkey in the refrigerator and, obviously anxious to leave, was sidling toward the door. "What are you going to do now? Work on your mural some more?"

Work on her mural. A painting. Another drawing. She tumbled back into her childhood, Mrs. Marley smiling and urging her to draw another pretty picture for her refrigerator. They hadn't known what to do with her after her mother had died, had they? What would she have done if she hadn't had painting and drawing to get her through those years? What was she going to do now?

And again with the damned tears.

"That's top secret information." She attempted a smile. "Sometimes I think this café has ears."

"I think you're right. Can't keep a secret in this village for long."

"You think?"

"I know." She zipped up her jacket. "There's been talk about you returning to Toronto."

"Maybe for a few days." And now seemed the perfect time. She'd phone the airlines right away to see if there was a flight this evening.

"But you're not moving back to the city?"

"I don't know. I wanted to stay home but…" She blinked and looked around the empty café. "I don't know."

Mrs. Marley squeezed her shoulder affectionately. "What I do when I'm unsure about something is I let it be. Then one day I wake up, and just like that, I know. Some things you can't push."

"Thanks. That's good advice."

She patted Sylvie's shoulder one last time. "You come visit me sometime."

"I will."

After the door closed, Sylvie wrapped her arms around herself again and rocked back and forth. Thoughts drifted in and out of her head, but nothing stuck. Which was fine. Mrs. Marley was right. No sense in pushing for a decision she wasn't ready to make.

After a while, she dug the phone book out from under the counter and dialed the airline. She'd leave before everyone returned from the picnic. It would be easier, less explaining. Not that anyone would notice or care that she wasn't around. But then what else was new?

ADAM WAS THE first one off the boat when they returned later that evening. He turned down a couple offers of hanging out for a few more beers, said his goodbyes and headed for home. The day had been phenomenal, beginning with the boat ride over, to exploring the island and spending the day with his neighbors and friends, and ending with the moonlit boat ride home. Too bad he hadn't been able to enjoy a second of it.

When he'd first arrived at the wharf he asked Dusty where Sylvie was, but Dusty was too busy getting his boat ready to give him more than a vague answer. The same damned vague answer everyone gave him. *I don't know.*

What was wrong with everyone? Didn't they care about Sylvie at all?

Okay, so they'd had a situation to handle. Teressa had turned up with the new guy who'd been hanging around her, and Dusty had gone into idiot macho mode. Adam kept an eye on his bud the entire boat ride in case Dusty decided to toss the cop overboard. Neither Teressa nor Dusty had a clue where Sylvie might be, and neither seemed to care.

Pops had been on another boat, and Adam asked him about Sylvie when he arrived on the island, but Pops had been preoccupied with helping set up the picnic. He said something about Sylvie liking to spend time by herself and left it at that.

Right about then, the day went south for him. Did she like spending time by herself or was that a convenient assumption? He knew why *he* hadn't called her about the picnic. She wasn't talking to him, and he figured she needed a few days to shift through all the crap he'd piled on her. He'd been counting on being with her today, though.

In the past week, he couldn't understand how he'd gone from being thrilled to live here, to the constant small annoyances that niggled at him now. Dusty talked too much about nothing, the sun was too damned bright. And the sound of the surf? Did it ever stop? And if he had to drive one more goddamn nail into a two-by-four, he was going to go insane.

He'd turned into a grouch, and it was all Sylvie's fault.

Relief washed through him when he turned off of Main Street and heard Romeo bark in the backyard. He'd hated leaving Rom behind today, but Sylvie had probably taken him over to her house for a few hours. She loved the shepherd.

Halfway down the block he noticed the upstairs light he'd forgotten to turn off in his house, and his steps grew lighter and faster. After he checked on the dog, he planned to go over to Sylvie's and check on her, too. He needed to make sure she was okay, that she'd wanted to spend some time by herself and hadn't been forgotten.

When he turned onto Briar Lane, he stopped, his gut doing that clenching thing again. Sylvie's house sat in the dark, lifeless. He checked his watch. Only nine o'clock. She was a nighthawk and wouldn't be in bed yet. So where was she? Her car was missing, too.

Barging into her house wasn't going to tell him anything. If she wasn't home, she wasn't home. Maybe she'd gone to Lancaster. Or Cal and Anita had arrived home, and she'd gone to visit them. He went into his own house and kept right on walking through to the back to let Romeo in. Moonbeam materialized out of the dark and followed the dog inside. The two animals had been inseparable for the past few weeks.

When his phone rang, he dug it out of the small knapsack he'd dumped on the floor, but didn't find it in time to catch the call. He pressed messages and listened to Pops's voice tell him Sylvie had left for Toronto.

Left for Toronto. He whipped his cell across the room. That was it? Was she giving up and running away? From him, her family? What? Damn it, why didn't she have a cell phone so he could call her?

At least Pops had let him know. And she probably had a Toronto number. But what would be the sense of calling her? She'd obviously made up her mind about him. Just as he'd thought, no one wanted to be saddled with someone with his history. He couldn't even get mad at her for leaving.

He sat in the dark and watched Romeo nudge Moonbeam with his nose. Adam shook his head as Rom yelped when the cat swatted him with her paw. Both he and Rom deserved exactly what they got. They knew better, but they couldn't seem to help themselves.

He loved Sylvie, but he didn't know what more he could do. He thought he'd made the ultimate sacrifice for her when he told her about his past. And what had he gotten in return? A door slammed in his face.

But he wasn't going to give up on them—Sylvie was worth fighting for.

He'd been in tight spots before and regardless of his upbringing, he knew the difference between right and wrong. Giving up was one hundred percent wrong. He wanted to believe he knew Sylvie well enough to guess that she'd come back to Collina. But that didn't mean he had to sit around and wait for her to return. *Or not return.*

When he met a dead end, he usually picked the direction he thought was the right one and pushed forward. If he ever stopped, he knew he'd sink out of sight so fast. It would be easy to beat himself up about…everything. But once he started down that road…well, there were all sorts of aids to lessen the pain or guilt or whatever he got stuck on.

Look at his mother. She'd been stuck most of her life.

He wasn't going to follow her. He was better than that.

CHAPTER FOURTEEN

ADAM TURNED HIS back to the lure of the beach and entered Sylvie's house. His muscles were begging for a good, hard run, but for the past two weeks even working on his house was almost more than he could handle. Any trace of summer had vanished with Sylvie, and a cold, hard, gray reality settled over the village. The weather had put everyone on the outs.

Dusty's chatter, which used to bother him, had dried up, and now it was Adam who worked to keep the conversation flowing. Yeah, that worked well, because Adam was feeling so not friendly toward everyone at this point. Teressa was barely civil to Dusty for some reason neither of them was willing to talk about. Which was fine with him. He didn't need to be loaded down with other people's problems; he had enough of his own. Like how he'd let himself become so involved with Sylvie.

Hell, might as well call it as he saw it. He was in love with a woman who wouldn't even talk to him. After the first few days of Sylvie being gone, he'd tried calling her apartment in Toronto. He needed to hear her voice, to know that she was okay. What he got was an answering machine with a mechanical voice. Although he'd given up on actually getting to talk with her, tonight he planned to call her and leave a message.

He glanced around Sylvie's empty, lifeless kitchen and continued into the living room. Pops had asked him to feed Moonbeam, water the plants and check the message machine. A couple nights after Sylvie had left, he'd sat in front of her painting for over an hour, and every evening since he'd gone back for more. He'd even started talking to it, and yeah, he wasn't ever going to let that get out.

His tight neck muscles loosened up as he studied the seascape, remembering Sylvie's voice as she'd explained the painting to him. She'd radiated excitement and sincerity when she talked about her work. Passion. A tingling of anticipation rippled down his spine. What would it be like to have all that intensity focused solely on him, even for a short amount of time?

He didn't like feeling dependent on anyone, had avoided exactly that since…well, since he could remember. He'd learned early and fast he had no one but himself to rely on, and as far as he could tell, that hadn't changed.

He took one last look and left the room. He and Teressa had a meeting in half an hour at the café to discuss becoming business partners. He needed a plan, something else to work toward, because his house was almost completed, and sitting around twiddling his thumbs didn't interest him.

But first he had a phone call to make. He dialed Sylvie's Toronto number and left a brief message, reminding Sylvie that the annual bonfire, the one they'd all planned to attend together, was tomorrow night. She'd missed the island picnic, and if she missed the bonfire, at least someone had remembered to tell her about it.

He wanted to say so much more, like *Please come home. You were right, you belong here.* He could see the truth of it so clearly now.

At first he hoped if he gave her some time, she'd come home and they could talk everything through. But now that he'd had time to think things over, he realized there wasn't much chance of them getting together. She hadn't returned any of his calls or anyone else's, for that matter. As far as he knew, her only attempt at communication had been her email to Pops letting him know she was okay.

Didn't matter that she'd given up on him. He still wanted her home, wanted her to be happy, and he needed to look into her eyes when he told her so he'd know for sure she understood he meant it.

He left the house and wandered up to the café. It was getting dark out earlier now, winter inching closer every day. The café was empty when he arrived, except for Teressa finishing up in the kitchen. Thankfully, her new boyfriend, *whasisname,* wasn't around.

Adam had hung out with Teressa and...Jean one night. Adam couldn't pinpoint what he disliked about the guy. He seemed friendly enough, but he asked too many questions about where Adam came from and what he'd done before coming to Collina. Adam had steered the conversation away from him by throwing the same questions back at Jean. Interesting that the other man's answers were as evasive as Adam's.

"Hey, big guy." Teressa came out of the kitchen and sat across the table from him. "How are you holding up?"

"I'm good. You're looking a little tired, though. Everything all right?"

Teressa ran her hand over the table surface as if checking for dirt. "Am I allowed to mention *she, whom we shall never discuss?* I miss having Sylvie around. Crazy, eh? She lives away for years, comes home for a few months, and...I don't know. I never realized what a good friend she is." She glanced up at him. "Guess you miss her, too, huh?"

If she was referring to the constant ache he felt inside, then yeah. He kicked out his legs in front of him. "Yup."

"Everyone does. You know how many times a week someone wanders in looking for her? I caught Beanie star-

ing at the mural the other day. I think he hoped she'd secretly snuck back to surprise us with something new." She
rested her chin in her hand. "That was so great how she
put you in the mural before she left."

"Yeah." Adam crossed his arms. He didn't want to talk
about it. Couldn't without getting a damned rock in his
throat. It had been one thing when Sylvie had turned on
the lights in his house and painted a small cameo of Romeo
into the mural. But to see a tiny image of himself sitting
on the front steps of his house, watching the sunset. Man,
he'd almost embarrassed himself when Pops pointed it out
to him. Sylvie should have been the one to show him the
addition to the mural.

"I asked Pops to stop by, but I thought we should talk
first. Want a coffee or something? A beer?"

"If you're having one."

"I'll pass on the beer. I've got a pot of herbal tea in the
kitchen. I'll grab some for both of us."

Adam narrowed his eyes as he watched Teressa disappear into the kitchen. When was the last time he'd seen
her drink anything alcoholic or smoke a cigarette? Growing up around junkies and alcoholics had made him sen-
sitive to how much people imbibed. It wasn't like he was
keeping count, just something he noticed. For instance,
Dusty started drinking more right around the same time
Teressa had stopped.

He waited until she'd put the steaming mugs of tea on
the table. "I have to ask you something. Don't get mad."

Teressa picked her cup up and cradled it against her
chest. "Okay."

"Are you pregnant?"

She sipped her tea, stared at him over the rim. "None
of your business."

"It is if we're going to be business partners."

Silence closed down around them as he watched her blink back tears. "I have good pregnancies. I can work right up until a week before delivery if that's what you're worried about."

Aw, hell. If the new guy was the father, Adam was going to kill him. And if he wasn't... *Dusty.* Of course. Everything made sense now. Teressa sniping at Dusty all the time, and Dusty walking around with a stunned look on his face. Had Teressa even told him yet? "Does he know?"

"Who?"

"Dusty. Have you told him you're pregnant?"

"I didn't say he was the father. For all you know, I might not even know who the father is." Her eyes darted from the door to the window to the kitchen.

She was a lousy liar, which was probably a good asset to look for in a business partner. "You have to tell him, Teressa. He has a right to know. Besides, he'll be thrilled." After he got over the shock. Dusty would do the right thing and offer to marry Teressa, partly because he was a stand-up guy, but Adam suspected Dusty was also in love with his future business partner. He'd make a great dad. It wouldn't be easy, though. Not with having to deal with two other fathers.

Teressa slapped his hand away when he reached across the table to console her. "I didn't come here to talk about me. Let's concentrate on the café."

"Fine. What happens after the baby's born?"

"I'll hire a nanny. Look, I'm never leaving this village. I'm stuck here, and this may be my only opportunity to buy this place." Her mouth turned stubborn. "If you don't want part of the deal, I'll find someone else."

The chances of her finding another business partner were almost nonexistent. He and Teressa had slowly become friends, and he didn't know if he could forgive himself if she lost out on the opportunity to buy her own business. Plus, he'd be better off working with Dusty as a lobster fisherman and puking his guts out daily than trying to run the café alone. Which was what could easily happen once Teressa gave birth.

How often since his arrival in Collina had he heard that good help was impossible to find because all the good workers were either already employed or had moved away? Often the only option was to bring in new workers. An idea jigged in the back of his mind.

He sat forward. "Let's offer Sylvie a third of the ownership if she still wants to buy in."

"You think she's coming back? I mean, coming back to stay?"

"Don't know. But we have to include her in the deal or I'm not interested."

Teressa smirked. "Well, look at you. I had no idea you two were that serious. She can't cook, you know."

"How do you know?"

Teressa grinned. "You're nuts."

He smiled and picked up the spicy-scented tea. "You don't know the half of it. Here's what we're going to do."

When Pops arrived half an hour later, Adam was certain the older man would agree to their proposal. If everything went according to plan, everyone would get what they wanted. The only problem was the entire plan revolved around Sylvie and what she wanted. Adam assumed he knew what that was, but thinking he could second-guess Sylvie was a crapshoot. He hadn't anticipated her taking off for Toronto, and the whole idea hinged on her returning soon. To stay.

He'd never been a praying man, but he figured now might be a good time to start.

SYLVIE CRIED WHEN she first heard his message. And then played it another twenty times and cried again each time. How stupid was that? Adam hadn't said he missed her. There'd been no great declaration of…anything. Just a simple message in his deep, soft voice, reminding her of the annual bonfire.

She blinked back more tears as she coasted down the last big hill into Collina. Someone had remembered to include her. Not just someone. *Adam.*

Damn it. She slapped her palm against the steering wheel. Could her life get any messier? Toronto had been a nightmare. She'd hated everything about the city—the noise, the pollution, the constant busyness. No one had time to stop and talk to each other. Not even her friends.

Oh, she'd gone out to dinner a few times with some of them, and Oliver had taken her to the new show at a local theater and a gallery opening. He'd been his usual kind and considerate self. Hadn't pushed her about anything. Heaven help her, she'd felt so bored and…guilty. There, she'd said it. Other than a chaste kiss, nothing had happened between Oliver and her, but the whole time she'd been with him, she felt as if she were cheating on Adam. Could she get any loopier?

She'd missed him—every minute of every day. She'd missed Adam and the smell of the ocean and the camaraderie of the café, her father and even Teressa and her brothers. And she was still mad as hell at every one of them. They probably hadn't even noticed she was gone. Didn't matter. Nothing much mattered right now, except that she was home again and ready to get on with the rest of her life.

She craned her neck to count the three vehicles parked by the café. Not much going on there. By the look of the open windows in their house, Mr. and Mrs. Avery had finally returned from their visit with their daughter in Vancouver. And Beanie hadn't washed his truck since before she'd left. She stepped on the gas, anxious to get home. And, okay, curious to see what Adam had accomplished with his house since she'd left.

She turned down the side street and right away caught the solid, dusty blue Adam had painted his house. His home. Beautiful! The color probably changed with the light. In the sunlight it would look blue, but if the day turned gray, so would the house. It fit into the landscape of ocean and sky as if it had sprouted up from the earth. He may not realize it, but Adam was an artist in his own right.

Romeo bounded up to her when she pulled into her driveway. She wished Moonbeam would be as loving, but the hussy had moved into Adam's full-time before she'd even left. Lucky kitty.

She checked out Adam's house but didn't see anyone moving in the yard or inside. It ticked her off how curious she was to see what he'd done to the downstairs. She still hadn't found a way to forgive him for not trusting her enough to handle the truth about his past. Heaven knew she'd tried; she'd thought of little else while in Toronto. But she got mired down in the he-didn't-care-enough, respect-her-enough, trust-her-enough to come clean until he was forced to.

At first, okay. She understood not wanting to walk into town and tell people how messed up his life had been. But he'd had plenty of opportunities to open up to her. She even understood how important it was to him to be accepted. More important, apparently, than having any kind of relationship with her.

And yet...

Her heart lurched when she saw him running along the beach in her direction. Was there a more magnificent sight than a man stripped down to the bare essentials, straining to move a step beyond his limit, sweat glistening on toned muscles? He came up on the drivers' side of her vehicle at full speed, and all she could do was stare, awestruck by his beauty.

"Hey." He put his hands on his knees and bent over to catch his breath. "One sec." He held up a finger as he gasped a lung full of air.

His back muscles stretched and rippled as he bent over. After a minute of panting, he stood upright. Sweat dripped down his strikingly male face, followed the corded muscles in his neck, to his hardened pecs and down to his flat belly. Her mouth turned dry as her gaze touched briefly on the line of hair that disappeared into his low-riding running shorts and then dropped to his muscular thighs.

Oh, boy.

"You must have caught an early flight." He grabbed his T-shirt hanging from his waistband and rubbed the sweat off his chest, then his pits. She tried to look away, tried to cross her legs to contain the heat between them, but the steering wheel got in the way.

He stopped drying himself with the shirt. "Sylvie? Are you okay?"

She blinked. "Yeah. Of course. Just a little…" She could hardly say jet-lagged. The flight had only been an hour and a half. "Um…disoriented. It's good to be home."

She forced herself to look away and grabbed onto the first thing that caught her eye. "Nice color for your house."

"Yeah?" When he moved closer to the car to look at the house, his scent wafted in through the car window. His sweat smelled clean and sharp and…healthy, she supposed. Small wonder Moonbeam rubbed up against him every chance she got. Feeling like an idiot for sitting in her car, she opened the door and hopped out.

He moved back a couple steps. "I'm a mess. You don't want to get too close."

No kidding. Heat, and pure, distilled masculinity, rolled off him in waves. She stuck her hands in her jacket pockets to resist the temptation to trace the fascinating line of his collarbone. Or feel those hard muscles quiver under her hand.

"How was Toronto?" He kept his eyes on the house, but she could feel tense vibes radiating out from him. Small wonder. She was probably throwing off pheromones like a fireworks display.

"Loud, noisy and dirty." She looked at the ocean patiently rolling in only yards away. At the clarity of the sky and the familiarity of her home. "It's good to be home."

"Yeah? It's good to have you back. I, ah...I missed you." He shot her a sideways glance as if afraid to look at her straight on. "Come see what I've been doing on the main floor."

Without giving her time to think, he laced his fingers through hers and pulled her toward his house. "What's the news from T.O.?"

"News? Let's see. Lost the commission on the seascapes."

Adam stopped and looked down at her, his face lighting up. "They don't want any of the paintings?"

"They want the ones I finished but aren't willing to wait for the rest. You don't have to look so pleased."

"Sorry. I'd love to buy one of your paintings. Thought it might be my chance to own a Sylvie Carson original. You don't sound all that upset that the deal's off."

Lots of people wanted to buy her paintings, so why did her insides turn to jelly because Adam wanted one as well?

They stopped outside his front door, which he'd painted a startling white. Set into the blue wall, it made her think of seagulls. "You're right. It didn't upset me as much as I thought it would to lose the contract. I don't think Toronto is the best place for me right now. It's very competitive. When I start painting again, I want to concentrate on my art and leave all the hype and politics out of it."

When, not if. Somewhere along the way, her attitude had taken a positive turn. And it had nothing to do with the man beside her. Nothing.

Before she left Toronto, she'd decided to sell her apartment and move home for good. Everything else fell into place after that decision. Like her relationship with Oliver; they'd always be friends and he was a great agent but that was all. Especially now that she'd met Adam. And that was where she entered shaky ground.

It would be so easy to let herself drift—had she thought drift; how about jump?—into a relationship with him. Except she was afraid she was making the same mistake she'd made all her life, taking the path of least resistance. Letting herself follow a direction instead of actively pursuing exactly what she wanted. Was Adam the easy route or what she truly desired? She didn't trust herself to make that call, but hopefully, someday soon, she'd know. She'd reached a stalemate but decided to come home, anyway. Because…because home was where she felt the strongest. Sylvie smiled to herself.

"See your boyfriend when you were there?"

"Oliver? Of course." And bit her tongue to keep from saying more.

After a moment, he nodded and his face hardened. Damn it, what had he expected? That she'd fall into those lovely, strong arms of his the minute she arrived home? Sweat beaded her hairline.

"Are you going to show me your house?" She gestured toward the door.

"Sure. Keep in mind it's simple, nothing special."

But of course it would be. Because it was Adam's home, and he'd created it himself.

Placing a hand in the middle of her back, he escorted her in the front door. She halted just inside, struck by the simplicity of the downstairs floor.

Adam had knocked down most of the walls to make one large L-shaped room. The kitchen nestled in one corner at the back and was open to the dining area that had windows along the front with a view of the ocean. The living area continued on from the dining room with even more windows facing the ocean. The walls were painted a subtle gold, and the refurbished hardwood floor glowed. The open room had a homey, cottagey feel, and other than needing a few splashes of color and some soft touches, it was perfect. And a reflection of the man standing beside her.

She opened her mouth to compliment him but her throat muscles locked up. She wanted to be part of this…this creation so badly it hurt. Why couldn't Adam be a what-you-see-is-what-you-get kind of guy? Why did their lives have to be so complicated?

"What do you think?" The tension in his voice cut through her thoughts.

"It's stunning, Adam. I love it. You're very talented."

He grinned. "At what? Knocking down walls?"

"At this." She swept her hand in front of her, indicating the room. "Making a home." A home some other woman would eventually share with him. He wasn't the kind of man to live by himself for long.

Oh, no. Not with the tears again. "I have to go. See you around." She spun and rushed out the door. *No crying. Not now. Not later. Just cut it out.* She speed-walked across the yard and stumbled into her house.

And burst into tears when she saw the beautiful bouquet of wildflowers on her kitchen table. *Adam*. Had he known she was coming back today or had he been picking flowers for her since she left?

"Are you okay?" Adam's concerned voice came from the doorway behind her.

Sylvie hunched her shoulders. "Yes."

She heard him move up behind her. "I'm sorry if I made you cry. I hate to see you so sad, Sylvie."

"I'm not..." She gulped back tears. "I'm not crying."

His large hands slid up over her shoulders, and he started massaging her tense neck muscles. A sigh escaped before she could catch herself.

"What can I do to make it better?"

With regret, she moved away from his magical hands and turned to face him. "How did you know I was coming home today?"

"I didn't."

"When did you pick the flowers?"

"Oh." He glared at them and tucked his hands under his arms. "Yesterday. They're just, you know, from the side of the road. They looked like something you'd like."

"I do. Thank you."

"Then why are you crying?"

She jutted her chin out. "I'm not."

"Right."

"And I'm not going to fall in love with you." There. She'd said it straight-out.

"Excuse me?"

"You heard me. You can't make me fall in love with you."

He looked puzzled for a minute before a smile slowly spread across his face. When he moved toward her, she slipped back a step, bumping up against the counter.

"You know what I think, Peaches?" He hooked a finger through her belt loop and tugged her toward him. "I think you're already in love with me."

"Am not." She blushed. Could she sound more juvenile?

"Uh-huh. Tell you what. Let's try a little experiment." He tugged again. When she tipped against his chest, he slid his hand into her hair and cupped the back of her head. His mouth hovered above hers. "I'm crazy about you, Sylvie. I've tried to be a stand-up guy and give you the time you need, but it turns out I'm not all that nice. I want you in my life. Not on the edges, but smack in the middle of it, and I'm prepared to play dirty to get what I want."

Demanding, not asking. Searching, exploring. His mouth firm, almost hard against hers. Heat exploded inside her as he pressed his powerful body against hers, placed a large hand on her back and held her against him so she couldn't move if she wanted to. Which she didn't.

She knew if she asked, he'd stop and give her...whatever she asked for. Hadn't he been doing that since they'd met? And realizing that freed her to explore his beautiful mouth, investigate the hard, rigid contours of his body. Fall into him. Soak him up. Would she ever get enough?

He pulled his mouth from hers and gulped for air as if he were drowning. "We stop now or don't stop at all." He leaned down and nipped at her mouth, rubbed his lips against hers. "You're addictive."

Stop? Was he crazy? Why would they stop? He tasted like fresh apples, and his lips were so soft; she wanted to feel them on her. Everywhere. She stood on tiptoe to run her tongue along his full lower lip. Yum, apples. When he groaned into her mouth and pulled her up off her feet, she wrapped her legs around his waist, felt him hard and ready. As ready as she was for him.

Except, there'd been a good reason to stop, hadn't there?

She lost the thought for a minute when he slowly traced the plunging neckline of her T-shirt with his tongue. A delicious shiver worked its way from the top of her head down to her toes. Home had never felt so good.

Home. Right. There was that little issue of trust and respect she kept running into. She unwound her legs from around his waist and slid down his magnificent body until she was standing on her own two feet. She forced herself to unwind her arms from around his neck and stepped away. She ran a hand over her hair, straightened her clothes.

Sex would be great with Adam. Great? Heavens, she almost went blind with need when she thought about them together. But it wasn't enough. She deserved more.

"Thank you…" She stopped, cleared the debris in her throat. "Thank you for the flowers and for calling me in Toronto. I'll see you at the bonfire tonight."

She stole a peek at him. He didn't have to look so damned happy, did he? He was grinning like an idiot, like she'd just said she'd go to bed with him instead of brushing him off.

"We're going to the bonfire together, Peaches. Double dating with Dusty and Teressa. And don't think you can back out. We've got to get those two together somehow. They're driving each other, and the entire village, crazy."

She closed her eyes. "I forgot about all that."

"So you know."

Her eyes flew open. "That Teressa's…"

"Pregnant? Yeah. Didn't take a genius to figure that out. We've all suffered the sharp edge of her tongue since she quit smoking. She still hasn't taken a test or seen a doctor."

Suddenly all her qualms about returning home settled. This is what she'd missed. What she needed in her life. To have a deep connection to other people. She wanted Adam's love, too, she realized. But she needed help sorting out who she was, who she'd been and who she planned to be.

As soon as she could, she'd start with Pops. He held the clues to what happened that tragic night so long ago.

CHAPTER FIFTEEN

ADAM SNAGGED HIS down vest on his way out the door. Stars glittered diamond-cold in the clear night sky, and his breath billowed out in a cloud as he closed the door behind him, after checking one last time that both Romeo and Moonbeam were inside.

Dusty had helped him install a new woodstove in his living room a few days ago, and Adam was psyched about firing it up soon. It occurred to him as he strode across the yard to Sylvie's house that he was psyched about a lot of things these days. Mostly that Sylvie was home to stay.

She hadn't said so in so many words, but he knew—or his heart knew—that she belonged to him. He suppressed a chuckle. Yeah, it was macho bullshit to think like that, but the second he'd laid eyes on her this morning that's what he'd felt. She was his. Or he belonged to her. Didn't matter which way you looked at it, he wasn't going to mess this up. He knew Sylvie loved him, probably almost as much he loved her.

He knocked on Sylvie's back door. He'd been treating the house as his own for so long he felt silly knocking. But he didn't want her to think he was presuming anything.

When she didn't come to the door, he knocked again. Most of the house was dark except for a few lights on up-stairs. His smile faded. He'd made it clear he thought of tonight as a date, hadn't he? Their first official one. She wasn't going to screw this up, was she?

He pushed the door open and flicked the kitchen light on, straining to hear for sounds of movement. "Sylvie?" he shouted and sniffed the air. It didn't smell like she'd heated up the supper he'd left earlier.

He opened the refrigerator door. The chicken-and-rice casserole hadn't been touched. He'd had this crazy idea he could maybe seduce her with food. Hadn't he been doing that all along, anyway? But it wasn't going to work if she didn't even notice he'd left supper for her.

He went into the hallway and listened at the bottom of the stairs for a couple minutes, then started up. Faint strains of music floated down the stairs. The second floor was as dark as the kitchen and living room, and he snapped on the hall light and looked up the stairs to the third floor. He'd never been up there but knew it was Sylvie's studio.

When he'd first started using the house, Cal had cautioned Adam no one was allowed on the third floor, especially if Sylvie was working. He stood at the base of the stairs for a few minutes, weighing the pros and cons, and finally decided to go for it. He could always plead ignorance if she had a fit about being interrupted.

The door to her studio stood open, and he stepped quietly into the big open room that took up the entire third floor. The white plastered walls were bare, and wide, unvarnished pine boards covered the floor. Large windows occupied both end walls; the slant of the ceiling was sharp enough that he could stand upright only in the middle of the attic room.

Paintings were stacked everywhere. A huge table along one wall held a vast assortment of paint tubes and brushes, and an easel, holding an empty canvas, which sat by the end wall, guaranteeing that it would catch the morning light. And there, a few feet away, under the track lighting, stood Sylvie, humming along to the radio as she used a flat knife to carve some clay off the emerging figure on the table in front of her.

A thrill shot through him. Was she doing a sculpture of him? He cleared his throat to get her attention, but she didn't turn around.

"Sylvie."

She glanced over her shoulder, her expression unfocused as if not seeing him. At least she wasn't yelling at him for interrupting—yet. A streak of dirt ran down her cheek, and several clumps of clay clung to her hair as if she'd run her hands through it.

His heart did a weird flip. God, she looked so beautiful.

"Hey, Peaches."

Her expression cleared. "Adam! Brilliant. Come and take your clothes off. I need you to pose for this sculpture."

His body immediately responded to her suggestion. Yeah. Like he could sit naked for Sylvie and not embarrass himself to hell and back. "Um…it's late. You haven't eaten supper."

"Is it?" A line furrowed between her brows as she glanced out the window before she turned her attention back to the clay in front of her. "I'm not hungry. I'll eat later."

He eased into her studio, afraid of upsetting her. He liked the feeling of the room. Of course he would; it belonged to Sylvie and he could see her everywhere. In the crystals hanging in the window, in the burgundy, velvet chaise longue and matching armchair in one corner, in the two batiks pinned to the walls. But mostly in her glorious paintings. He wished she'd show him each one; there must be dozens.

"Sylvie?" he said again to get her attention. Then, not able to help himself, he kissed the back of her neck, which was exposed as she bent over her work.

"Mmm. You smell good," she said without looking up.

He peered over her shoulder. The sculpture had already taken on the rough outline of a man running. It was amazing and incredibly cool to think that he may have inspired her, even in a small way.

He hated to interrupt but maybe this was where her problems had started; people had been reluctant to let life interfere with her art. He suspected her art wasn't enough for her anymore. She needed more, and the only way for her to get more was to participate.

"We're supposed to go to the bonfire tonight, remember?"

Her head jerked up. She turned around to face him. "Bonfire?"

"The annual bonfire on the beach by the wharf. Everybody goes. We're meeting Dusty and Teressa."

"Is that tonight?" She glanced back at her work.

"It is. Look, I think it's fantastic you're working on something, but I also think it's important you go to the bonfire."

Her eyes cleared completely as she narrowed them and looked at him. "What are you doing up here?"

He grinned. "Risking my life? How about you take a shower while I heat up your supper?"

"How about you go on ahead, and I'll catch up to you?"

Adam folded his arms and planted himself a couple feet in front of her. "No way. This is our first date, and you're not going to blow me off."

Her mouth twitched. "This is a date?"

"Yup." He was taking her to the bonfire. She belonged with him, and he wanted everyone to know.

His muscles unlocked as she picked up a sheet of plastic and hung it over the clay. "I suppose if this is a date, I should get cleaned up."

Adam grinned. She didn't sound at all upset by the prospect. "Great. I'll wait for you in the kitchen. Don't take long, we're late already." He walked out and started down the stairs.

"Adam?" Sylvie called from the top of the stairs.

He stopped and turned back. "Yeah?"

She smiled. "Thanks. Again."

He gripped the railing. If he went back up there and kissed her, which is what he wanted to do, they wouldn't be going anywhere this evening. Except maybe to her bedroom on the second floor.

His heart tumbled into a free fall. "You're welcome." He smiled back and forced himself to continue down the stairs, reminding himself why going to the bonfire was so important.

THANK GOODNESS ADAM insisted she wear her down vest over her sweater. Sylvie had worried they'd look like twins, both wearing vests. But now she didn't care. It felt like November, not a mid-October night. Although the bonfire was huge and far too hot to stand close to.

From the minute they'd arrived, people had been coming up to them and hugging her and clapping Adam on the back, as if they'd accomplished something more brilliant than just showing up. Which she'd almost missed doing— again. She wouldn't be here if not for Adam.

She loved that he cared enough to drag her away from her work. Although for a minute it had been touch-and-go; no one had ever dared interrupt her while she was working. But she hadn't minded, probably because it had been Adam. Matter of fact, when she'd finally focused on him, it had taken everything not to jump him.

She'd been thinking about the beautiful, masculine lines of his body as he ran along the shore this morning.

She hadn't worked in clay much but she had a good feeling about the sculpture. And hadn't she from the first day she'd met him?

"Are you warm enough?" Adam slid his arm around her waist and pulled her close to his side. He'd been touching her in one way or another since they'd arrived half an hour ago. She knew exactly what he was doing, and although they still had problems to iron out, she didn't mind the message. After all, if another woman started hitting on him, and a few had looked interested in doing just that, she wouldn't waste time letting them know he wasn't available.

"There's Cal and Anita." Sylvie tugged on Adam's hand. "I want to see how Anita's doing. Hey, I haven't seen Teressa and Dusty yet, have you?"

"No. I meant to talk to you about that. Teressa's been hanging out with that new guy." When his warm breath tickled her ear, she shivered deliciously.

"What new guy?"

"Jean. I think she's doing it to piss off Dusty, but I don't like him, either."

Sylvie smiled to herself as they approached her older brother. Adam had said that like Teressa mattered. How quickly he'd become a part of all their lives.

"You're back." Anita hopped up from where she'd been sitting on Cal's knee and hugged her. "Did you have a good time in Toronto? I loved your apartment. We can't thank you enough for letting us stay there."

Anita looked like she'd gained a couple of pounds. It still wasn't enough, but it was a start. The minute Cal stood, he slipped both arms around Anita's waist from behind. Interesting. Cal wasn't usually so demonstrative.

"Hey, sis. Back already?"

Her glow dimmed until Adam reached down and squeezed her hand. "I'm glad you guys had a chance to stay

there because I've put the apartment up for sale," she said
to Anita. Adam squeezed her hand harder for a second.

"Really? I'm so happy for you." Anita hugged her again.

"Where are you going to go?" Cal asked from behind
Anita. Shadows obscured his face, but Sylvie could tell
by the tone of his voice he didn't approve. Tough. It was
her life they were talking about, not his.

She managed a laugh. "I've arrived. This is it. I hired a
moving company to pack everything up and truck it down
here. My stuff should arrive in a couple of days."

Anita's face lit up. "Are you interested in planning another happening for the café?"

"Of course. Are you on board?" She felt Adam move
restlessly by her side. *Please, please don't let him be another detractor like Cal.* That she'd started playing with a
small sculpture meant nothing. It was exactly that—play.
She still needed more.

"You haven't told her yet?" Cal said to Adam.

Sylvie's stomach lurched. "Told me what?"

"Adam and Teressa bought the café while you were
gone."

As her vision narrowed, Sylvie dimly noticed Anita
poking Cal in the ribs. She grappled for something to hang
on to and found Adam's hard, muscled arm. She swatted at it and swayed away. She hadn't had a panic attack
for weeks, and she'd be damned if she was going to have
one now.

Someone scooped her into their arms from behind just
before her knees gave out. Adam, of course. She buried
her face in his neck as he elbowed his way through the
crowd, reassuring people she just needed some breathing
space. He stopped a few yards down the beach from the
crowd and sat on a log with her on his lap.

"Let go of me." She pushed against his chest.

He tightened his arms. "Not a chance, Peaches. I've been trying to get you in my arms for weeks. I'm not letting you go now."

"If you think you can buy the café behind my back, think again. My father would never do that to me." She felt a measure of satisfaction when Adam grunted as she elbowed him in the gut. Growing up with two brothers had taught her how to play dirty.

"Damn it, Syl. That hurt." He heaved to his feet but kept his arms banded around her. "It isn't like Cal said."

"You and Teressa didn't buy the café?"

"We did. But there's a provision included."

"Explain."

"Both Teressa and I agreed if you're interested in becoming a partner you can buy a third of the business. Teressa needs the café," he continued. "And so do I. I'm staying, and I need work. I make a lousy fisherman, so…"

She softened her stance when he smiled down at her. "I was afraid she'd find another partner, so I said I'd buy a third. If you're not interested in owning a third, Teressa and I will go halves. And I have a couple ideas about hiring people to work here that hopefully will make it easier for everyone, but everything is contingent on what you want, Sylvie."

Tears clogged her throat. If she opened her mouth, she was going to make a fool of herself, but she had to say something. She swallowed hard. "What's your idea for hiring people?" If she concentrated on business, maybe she wouldn't break down completely.

"We hire art students."

"From where?"

"I don't know. Your old school? Any school that offers a fine arts degree. Students need summer jobs, and we need cheap labor."

"Why would they come all the way here to work for minimum wage?"

His face lit up. "Because the famous Sylvie Carson lives here, and she'll give each student one hour a week of her time for…whatever. A critique of their work? A lecture. That would be up to you to figure out."

"You think students would be interested in my opinion?"

"I think we'd have them lining up for the opportunity. You're an incredibly talented artist. You don't need me to tell you that."

She rested her forehead against his. "Will you marry me?" she whispered.

He barked out a laugh. "Yeah. Of course. Someday. But I was kind of looking forward to…I don't know…wooing you first, I guess. I want you to have the wine and roses, Sylvie. You deserve the best."

She smiled against his mouth. It was too dark to see, but she suspected he was blushing. He wanted to woo her. Wow! "Is that a yes?"

He laughed, rubbed his lips against hers. "That's a definite yes."

"And I can have a third of the café?"

"You want it all, do you?"

"Yes. I do. I don't know why, probably because of how it started, but I think I always believed I had to give up my family life to succeed in art—like I had to pay for my success." She slipped her hands around his neck. "But you make me believe it's all possible. And if I never paint again, well, we'll just have to have tons of kids to make up for it."

He chuckled and pulled her closer. "I'm going to love being married to you."

She sought his lips and kissed him. In the dark, surrounded by him, all things seemed possible. "Let's go home," she whispered into his mouth.

"Another very good idea. I can't wait to hear what else you come up with."

She giggled and kissed him again, her happiness spilling over into the night. She'd found her way home, hadn't she?

POPS'S RAISED VOICE from the edge of the crowd made Adam jerk away from Sylvie. Would he ever not feel guilty about…whatever? Take your pick. He put his arm around Sylvie's shoulders and pulled her closer than was comfortable, trying to get back to where they'd been only a minute ago, but the moment was lost. Sylvie had tensed up; she dropped her arm from around his waist and managed to put a couple of inches between them.

Okay, they still had things to work out, mostly his coming clean with her family and friends. He knew it was past time for that confession, but he'd be damned if it was going to happen now. Tonight was about him and Sylvie. Or so he'd hoped.

"Something's wrong." Sylvie pulled him in the direction of the fire. More raised voices, Pops's and maybe Dusty's, rose above the murmur of conversation. Sylvie and Adam started running when they heard a shout and the sickening thud of flesh hitting flesh.

They broke through the circle of people that had moved even farther back from the fire to make room for the two men facing off against each other. Hell. Adam could have guessed Dusty and the new guy, Jean, would get into it. He'd hoped Teressa had the sense not to invite Jean to the bonfire.

Adam caught the back of Sylvie's vest as she started to march into the fight zone. "Not a chance, Sylvie. I'll take care of this. You go to your father and make sure he's okay."

He took in the scene in front of him. Jean had got in a good punch already; Dusty was bleeding from the nose. Not that Dusty seemed to care. He stumbled and swung wildly at anything that moved near him. Jean, on the other hand, looked cool and alert, one eye on Dusty, the other assessing the crowd. He stopped his appraisal when his gaze lit on Adam. He raised his eyebrows, flicked him a smile. The guy knew how to fight and recognized that Adam did, too. Because Adam was doing the same thing, calculating his odds and looking for an escape route before he stepped into the ring.

Adam hadn't liked the guy since he'd first appeared and now he knew why—Jean reminded him of himself. When Cal ducked into the ring opposite Adam and made a grab for his brother, Jean stuck his foot out at the last second, and Cal crashed to his knees. The mood of the crowd switched from excited curiosity to anger.

Five feet away, Pops pushed forward, Sylvie hanging on to his arm, and all Adam's systems flared into high alert. He rushed Dusty from behind, wrapped his arms around him and swung him out of the cleared area and into the arms of his father. Letting go of Dusty, he swiveled on one foot while shifting lower, finding his center of gravity. Without thinking, he'd assumed a tai chai stance. His focus narrowed to the man standing on the other side of the ring.

Jean's eyes lit up for a moment, as if delighted to have a worthy opponent, but then he held his hands up. "Hey, man. I was just defending myself. Guy was swinging at me. I'm not looking for more."

Adam could tell from the way Jean handled himself that he was a fighter, and a dirty one at that. Adam wanted the guy gone from the village.

His tension slowly dissipated as Jean turned away and disappeared into the crowd. Cal climbed to his feet and Anita put her arms around him as she sniffled back tears. Adam's stomach twisted into an ugly knot. The fight had been over before it even started, and yet people were still upset, disturbed. If they reacted so adversely to one little punch in the face, how would they feel when they found out he'd almost killed a man? They'd never accept him for who he was because the world he grew up in was as foreign to them as living on the moon.

"Thanks, man." Cal shook his hand.

"Guy's a dirty fighter," Adam reassured him. No one liked to eat dirt in a fight.

They turned as Dusty started shouting again. Pops and Sylvie each held on to one of Dusty's arms, trying to hold him back. The idiot was stupid drunk and spoiling for a fight.

"We've got to get him out of here," Cal said, following Adam as he rushed over to restrain Dusty. Pops let go when a couple of other men stepped up and grabbed Dusty, but Sylvie held on.

Adam stepped in front of Dusty. "Take care of your father, Sylvie." He glared at her until she let go. She didn't look happy with him.

"Dusty." Adam got right in his face and yelled. He didn't want to deck the guy, but he would if he had to. Alcoholic fumes bathed his face when Dusty turned his bullish glare in his direction.

"Dusty, my man." Adam smiled. "Party's over. Time to go home."

Dusty stared at him with a dazed look on his face. "S'not over," he finally slurred.

"Yep. Cal and I are going to take you home now." He took hold of Dusty's arms. "Let's go."

Adam sighed when Dusty pulled his arm free. He was going to make this as hard as possible. "Where's Teressha? I want Teressha."

Good question. Where was the lady of the hour? "Tell you what." Adam took Dusty's arm again at the same time Cal grabbed the other one. Together, they frog-marched him to the edge of the crowd. "We'll take you home, then find Teressa for you."

Dusty grinned sloppily at him as he swayed into his brother. "You're a good guy, Adam. Isn't he a good guy, Cal?"

"The best. Come on, bro. Hop up into the truck."

Dusty braced himself against the truck door and refused to budge. "Where we going?"

"Your house. Get in," Cal said.

Adam could tell by his clipped tone, the man was losing patience with his younger brother.

"Don't want to. Too lonely."

Adam stepped forward when Cal put his hand on Dusty's back to push him into the truck. Drunks never responded well to force. "How about you come home with Sylvie and me? We'll have a party at your old place."

"Where's Teressha?"

"I'm going to find her as soon as we get you home, remember? Let's go, bud. Cal, you want to get Sylvie for me?"

"Done this a time or two, have you?" Cal asked as they steered Dusty into the backseat.

"You could say that. Dusty's a pussycat comparatively." Especially as he'd passed out already. Getting him into bed was going to be a challenge, though.

"Here they come." Cal tilted his head toward Sylvie, Pops and Anita, who were walking toward them. "You want me to follow you?"

"I've got it. Pops looks like he needs to hit the hay."

"It doesn't take much to wear him out these days. Thanks, Adam. Appreciate the help."

"Not a problem."

He watched Sylvie kiss her father and Anita good-night. He stepped forward and shook the old man's hand and was pleasantly surprised when Anita gave him a small peck on the cheek.

Sylvie bounced on the seat beside him when they headed for home. "You were like a ninja warrior."

Adam rolled his eyes. "Right. That's me all over."

"I'm serious. You were incredible. I guess…" Her voice turned thoughtful. "You're probably used to fighting."

He reached across the cab and took her hand in his. "Not by choice."

She squeezed his hand. "Of course not."

"Too bad the bonfire was a bust. We'll have to try again next year." Who'd have guessed that the thought of going to a bonfire a year away would make him feel as if he'd won a million bucks?

"I've never seen Dusty so drunk. I think Teressa broke his heart," Sylvie whispered.

As if on cue, Dusty stirred in the backseat. "Where's Teressha?"

"Don't start with that again," she scolded over her shoulder.

"You shut up," Dusty slurred.

Adam gripped the steering wheel with both hands. The guy was skunk drunk and Sylvie's brother, so he'd give him a break. If it happened again, though, he'd need to have a talk with Dusty. Brother or not.

ADAM STARTED BREATHING easier when they pulled into Sylvie's driveway. Just a few more minutes. They'd dump the guy in a bed, and then he and Sylvie could get back to where they'd left off. Which had been one short step from heaven. He barely refrained from whistling as he hustled around the truck to help Dusty out of the backseat.

"Why don't you just ask Teressa to marry you? You know that's what you're going to do in the end, anyway." Sylvie glared at her brother as he stumbled out of the truck.

Adam closed his eyes. Crap. Didn't she know better than to antagonize a drunk, angry man?

Dusty leaned against the side of the truck despite Adam's best effort to propel him toward the house. "You don't know shit," Dusty spit out at his sister.

"Hey, there." Adam shook his arm. "Go easy."

Dusty slung his arm around Adam's shoulders and staggered toward the house. "She doesn't. She thinks our mother wassa saint. But she wasn't." Adam shifted his balance to absorb more of Dusty's weight as he leaned against him.

"Mom was running away with some asshole."

Sylvie scooted around in front of them and shoved her brother with both hands. Both Dusty and Adam staggered backward. "She was not. Take it back."

"S'was. Oops. Forgot it's a secret. Shhhh." He put his finger to his lips. "Can't tell our little prinshess."

"You're lying." Adam's heart hurt when he heard the tremble in Sylvie's voice. One good fist in the face would end this right now. Too bad Dusty was her brother.

A moment of clarity crossed Dusty's face as he looked at his sister. "Shit. Sorry, sissy. I'sa idiot."

"Why would you say something like that?"

But Adam could see from the blank expression on his face that Dusty had slipped back into his drunken stupor.

Sylvie shoved her brother again.

"Why would he say that?" she demanded of Adam. Tears shimmered in her eyes.

"I don't know, baby. Let's get him in bed, then you can phone Cal." Tempted to drop the SOB right in the driveway and leave him for the night, Adam yanked Dusty's arm tighter around his neck and walked them into the house.

Unfortunately, what Dusty had said made sense. He'd known all along his grandmother would never hurt anyone deliberately. And he'd heard the occasional veiled reference to Sylvie's mother's discontent. After all, she'd married a man twenty years her senior and moved to an isolated village where she hadn't known a soul. Had to be a story in there somewhere. Not that he was going looking for it.

He dumped Dusty on the couch in the living room, pulled his boots off and covered him with a crocheted blanket from the back of the couch. He heard Sylvie speaking tearfully into the phone and made himself go into the bathroom and pour a glass of water for Dusty. Sylvie probably needed a couple of minutes to herself to process the new information. What did you say to someone who just found out her mother had run away from home? Isn't that what Dusty had implied?

One thing he knew for sure, he could kiss his plans for a romantic evening goodbye. Way to go, guy. Not exactly the time to be thinking about *his* needs, now was it?

Finished with Dusty, he straightened his shoulders and cracked open the kitchen door to be greeted with a wail of despair.

CHAPTER SIXTEEN

ADAM HAD BEEN wrong about a lot of things in his life but he'd never been more wrong about how Sylvie would react to hearing her mother had walked away from her family. When he opened the kitchen door, Sylvie flew across the kitchen and burrowed into him.

"Let's go to bed. You want to make love to me, don't you?"

Adam folded her into his arms, felt her soft body mold to his at the same time every cell in his body screeched to attention. Oh, yeah. No question about what he wanted. He inhaled the enticing scent of peaches and the delicious, underlying hint of woman, thinking of where he'd start, where he wanted to end up. And why he shouldn't.

"More than anything in the world, Sylvie. But now is maybe not the best time."

She pulled back and eyed him with suspicion. "Why not?"

Not able to stop himself, he leaned down and tasted her pouty bottom lip. Her tongue darted out to touch his briefly before disappearing again. A growl rolled out of him as he cupped her firm behind and pulled her hard against him, then lost himself in her taste and the silkiness of her mouth. He loved how her body was soft where his was hard, how her curves blended into his angles, how her fragility matched his strength.

She was much stronger than him in so many ways.

Strong enough to stand up for what she wanted, to demand integrity from the people she loved, and to allow herself to be vulnerable. Isn't that what she did with her art, open herself to the whole wide world? He wondered if what she received in return made it all worthwhile. And if he could, in some small way, add to that.

Summoning his last speck of sanity, he dropped his arms and stepped away from her. When she came after him, he held her at arm's length. "Hold on, Peaches. We need to talk before my brain stops functioning."

"Talk? Really? I had other things in mind. Like this." She pulled his T-shirt out of his jeans and skimmed her hands over his chest.

Adam sucked in a breath. *Think. Kitchen. Her father's house.* Not a— He sucked in another breath when she found his nipple and tweaked it. He grabbed her hands through his shirt and hoodie, dragged his gaze away from the way her breasts moved up and down, as if she'd been running and was short of breath.

Where was he? Kitchen. Right. And—

"I don't want to take advantage of you. I don't think the timing is right, Sylvie, and you know it, too. I love you and I want you, but you're hurting, baby. You need to settle this thing with your family." He took her hand. "Come on, I'll drive you to your father's."

She leaned her forehead against his. "I'm scared. What if Dusty is telling the truth? What if my own mother didn't want me?"

"You don't have all the facts. But what I do know is people love you. You'd be surprised at how many folks stopped by the café while you were in Toronto to ask when you were coming home. Even Teressa admitted she missed you."

"And you?"

"Every minute you were gone. Next time you leave, I'm going with you. But I know you won't leave for long, because you belong here."

"Yeah, I do." She squeezed his hand and sighed. "You're right. I can't put this off any longer. Time to talk to Pops."

POPS WAS STILL up when Adam left her outside the door to his apartment. Sylvie walked into her father's open arms and rested her head on his shoulder. He was such a great dad. It had thrown her world off-kilter when he'd had the heart attack. Nothing had been the same since.

"I remembered the fight," she said, knowing he'd understand which fight she was referring to. "But I remembered it wrong." She stepped back and took in his expression. His eyes held a lifetime of sadness, and his broad shoulders slumped, as if worn down by life. She'd never thought of her father as old until now.

He pushed a curl back away from her face. "Your mother loved you, Sylvie."

She caught his hand. "You don't have to cover for her anymore. The important thing is you stuck with us. I love you, Dad."

Pops cleared his throat. "You never called me Dad before."

What else had she been remiss in doing? She tugged him into the living room, and they sat side by side on the couch. "Tell me about my mother."

He squeezed her hand. "The first time I saw her I was a goner. I was in Ottawa. A bunch of fishermen had gone there to protest—I don't even remember about what now. Quotas, probably. Your mom was visiting her cousin. We were both on a tour of the parliament buildings, and I didn't waste any time introducing myself."

A smile played along his lips. "I talked her into having

coffee with me. The next day, we went out for dinner. Then I invited her to come visit Collina, and she did."

He was silent a minute. "I never should have married your mother. She didn't belong here, and I knew that. But I was so crazy in love with her, I couldn't let her go." He picked up Sylvie's hand and played with her fingers. "She was happy at first. Happy to have babies and her own house. She was the only child in her family, and her parents had died in a house fire the year before we met. They were farmers, a poor family, and she liked having pretty things, and I liked giving them to her.

"After a few years she got...restless, and Collina..." He looked around the room, as if viewing the entire village. "There aren't many options here. So we bought the café, and she named it Plain Jane's because she knew she was easily the most beautiful woman around these parts. She liked that her looks made her a little different from most folks around here."

He smiled at her. "That's why I let you run wild like a little tomboy. Looks are fine and dandy, but life can get pretty shallow if that's all you've got. Even though you're as beautiful as your mother, turns out I didn't have to worry about you."

"Because of my painting."

"Yes, that, too. But I meant because you've got such a big heart, and you always were as sharp as a whip.

"She'd have come back," he said after another pause. "If she hadn't gotten into that accident, she'd have come home. She loved you and your brothers. She wouldn't have left you all behind."

Sylvie gave up trying to stem her tears. She laid her head on her father's shoulder and sniffled until the lump in her throat grew small enough that she could speak.

"Thank you, Pops. I think I've been afraid all these years that you'd leave me, too."

Pops nodded. "I knew it. Not at first, and by the time I realized what all the drawing and painting was about—trying to please me and your brothers—it was too late. You were gone. And I'm sorry for that. But it hasn't been so bad, has it? We've had to do without you, but look at the beautiful and accomplished woman you've become. I'm so proud of you, Sylvie. And I'm thrilled you want to stay home."

Smiling, she darted a look at him. "But you don't want me to run the café."

Pops laughed. "You've got me there. Talent like yours is a gift that shouldn't be wasted. But if it makes you unhappy to paint, then so be it. Matter of fact, I've got something for you."

He lumbered to his feet and disappeared into the kitchen. When he returned a couple minutes later, he held a notebook in his hands.

She clamped a hand over her mouth. "Oh, Pops." It was his famed recipe book, crammed full with tried-and-true recipes he'd collected over a lifetime.

He sat and passed her the much-thumbed book. "Adam's not the only one who can teach you a thing or two in the kitchen. You pick out some recipes, and you and me can cook up a few good meals. That is, if you're still interested."

She beamed at him. "Of course I am. Thank you, Pops."

He cleared his throat. "I'm giving you the house, too, if you want it. The boys both have their own places, and I'm happy here at the seniors center. If you're staying, you should have your own house. I imagine you'll be fixing it up to suit you."

She launched herself into his arms. "Thank you. I love

that house so much. Maybe I can get Adam and Cal to help me with a few changes."

"Speaking of Adam, do I have to ask him what his intentions are?"

She giggled. "He intends to marry me. It's just…" Her smile slipped off her face. "I'm not sure what I want. I love him, but…is it possible to love a person too much? It feels like for the first time in my life I'm free to do exactly what I want, and Adam has such definite ideas about where his life is headed. What if I can't say no to him?"

"There's no such thing as too much love, darling." He ran his hand over her head. "Has it never occurred to you the reason everything's fallen into place for you is not in spite of Adam, but because of him?"

ADAM DIDN'T OFFER any resistance an hour later when Sylvie appeared at his door and launched herself into his arms. He'd managed twice to hold her off, but he didn't have the stamina to be noble a third time. He'd imagined Sylvie in his bed with the moonlight spilling over her naked body more nights than he cared to count. And now she was offering to fulfill that fantasy.

After assuring himself her father had answered the questions she needed answered, they stumbled up the stairs, neither willing to take their hands off the other. He struggled with his hoodie half over his head and thought he might lose control completely when he felt her hands on his belt and zipper. When he finally fought his way out of his sweatshirt, Sylvie was kneeling in front of him. The picture was beyond erotic, and he recited the measurements for his kitchen cupboards that still needed to be built as she skimmed her hands over his naked butt and down his legs. Any diversion. Anything at all to slow things down.

His body roared with need and his knees started to buckle as she pressed her face against his thigh.

"Sylvie," he croaked.

She ran her hand down his other thigh and followed the quivering outline of his leg. "You're so...male. So beautiful."

He reached down and hooked his hands under her arms, raising her up to eye level. "I'm much more interested in you than me." He managed to get rid of her sweater and shirt, stopped to trace the top of her lacy purple bra before attacking the clasp. When her generous, round breasts sprang free, he scooped them reverently into his hands.

So soft. Her skin was like cream. He lowered his head and took her into his mouth, a sigh escaping as he settled into her softness. There was nothing subtle about her body; her curves were bold and striking. Tempting. The dip of her waist and the lovely roundness of her hips; her body was designed to allure and tantalize, and he filled his hands with her, ravenous and impatient.

SYLVIE HAD NEVER known greed before, but she recognized the driving need inside her as Adam lowered her to the bed. She arched her back and offered herself to Adam. She wanted more. She wanted to explore every inch of his body. She wanted to own him, to make him hers.

Even knowing it was wrong to feel that way, she couldn't control herself. Didn't want to. A sigh of pure pleasure rippled out of her as he ran his large, rough hands down her sides and around to cup her behind. His smell and warmth enveloped her. She opened her legs, ready for him, wanting him. No, needing him. Now.

A strangled sound escaped her as he pulled away, and she arched up again to follow. He brought his mouth back to hers. "I need a minute." He fumbled with the small foil package, finally opened it and covered himself. Then stopped and looked down at her open and waiting for him. The hard edge of desire in his eyes softened as he smiled at her, and he leaned forward to take her mouth again. "I love you," he murmured against her lips.

Then slid home, their rhythm growing, expanding, stretching, until Sylvie clung to the edge of the world. Swinging wild and free. Up, up, and with one last thrust, her world shattered, a starburst of colors exploding inside her.

ADAM STIRRED, KNOWING without coming fully awake that the world, his world, had changed. He smiled as images of how he and Sylvie had explored each other's bodies—*worshipped* each other's bodies, long into the night—flicked through his mind like an erotic dream come true.

His body hardening before his brain fully engaged, he reached for her. And came up empty. His eyes jerked open. He checked the right side of the bed. Not an erotic dream. Sylvie had been there. And now she was gone.

He sat up, strained to hear her move around in the bathroom or downstairs. Nothing. For the first time since he'd moved into the upstairs, he cursed the bright morning sun that needled into his eyes.

Last night had been perfect. She'd said she loved him, hadn't she? For sure she knew he was crazy about her. And she'd asked him to marry her.

He sat on the side of the bed and scrubbed a hand back and forth through his hair as if somehow he could stimulate his brain to work.

Okay, so he'd have preferred waking up next to her, but they'd both lived alone for a long while. So, yeah, perfectly understandable she needed some space. He'd make her breakfast. Blueberry pancakes, her favorite. Then take her back to bed. Or wherever he found her—the taking being the important part.

After showering and rummaging for clean clothes, he rustled up the ingredients for pancakes and made his way over to Sylvie's house. Snores from the living room greeted him when he entered the kitchen. He poked his head in the other room and saw Dusty still passed out on the couch. He must have come to at one point because he'd drunk the water that Adam had placed on the table beside him—too bad Dusty hadn't left when he'd woken to do so. Hard to have a romantic breakfast for two with a disgruntled, probably half-drunk brother hulking around the house. It was easy to see the Carson family could prove to be more of a liability than an asset at times.

Adam slipped past Dusty and took the stairs two at a time. The clothes Sylvie had been wearing last night were strewn around her bedroom like she'd ripped them off in a hurry. He smiled and glanced over his shoulder, a reflex action knowing her brother was downstairs, then picked up her purple bra and rubbed the silky material between his thumb and fingers. It was nearly as soft as Sylvie herself.

He continued upstairs and eased the door open to her studio. His throat constricted. With her back to the door, Sylvie was standing at her easel, painting. The sun created a halo of her blond curls. He stuck his hands in his pockets to stop himself from crossing the room and running his hands over her form-hugging yoga pants. A powerful and bold naked male form was emerging from her canvas.

A full-body flush flashed over him. She wasn't painting him specifically, was she? He frowned at the painting. It could be any guy, right? His stomach dipped to his knees at the same time that he smiled. It was kind of cool. But not. He wasn't sure how he felt about everyone seeing him in the buff.

"Hey," he called softly from the door, suddenly not sure of anything.

Sylvie glanced over her shoulder. She looked puzzled for a second before her eyes crinkled at the corners and her face relaxed into a smile. "Hey, yourself."

Reassured, he crossed the room and settled his hands on her waist. "Oh, man, Sylvie. That's incredible."

She leaned back into him. "Think so? I call it Sand-man."

He peered closer at the painting. It wasn't close to being finished but he could see where she was going with it. A naked man raced along the beach, but Sylvie was slowly blending him into the sand and sky. If he understood what she intended, when the painting was completed, you'd have to look several times to see the man.

"He's part of his environment," he said spontaneously. "Same as the other painting. The seashell."

She smiled up at him. "Exactly. He's as elemental as anything else in his environment. He belongs, in the same way the seashell belongs."

He felt a warm glow inside. *He belongs.* That was good, right? Or was she saying he was dumb as a rock?

Deciding to leave the art comments to someone who knew what they were talking about, Adam pulled her back against him and nuzzled her neck. "Are you hungry?"

When she didn't answer he checked her expression. She continued to stare at the painting then picked up a tube of red paint and squirted a drop on her palette. She dipped her brush in the paint and with what looked like painstaking care, applied a touch red on the horizon.

Adam let go of her waist. He'd take that as a *not right now.* His stomach growled as he descended the staircase. Might as well make breakfast while he was here. At the

very least he'd slip a cup of coffee on her worktable before he left.

As he assembled the pancakes he couldn't help but re-
call the meals he and Sylvie had cooked together. He knew
he should be happy. For her to start painting again was
monumental. It was a safe bet to say he'd been instrumen-
tal in helping remove whatever had been blocking her, so
why did he feel so lousy? Maybe because it wasn't the
morning he'd hoped for or had planned. How long would
it take her to finish the painting, and would she be as preoccupied the entire time?

"Morning." Dusty shuffled into the kitchen, looking
as pasty as the dead fish that had washed up on shore the
other day. He didn't smell much better.

Adam handed him a coffee without saying anything.

Dusty made a sound that could have been a thank-you
but came closer to a grunt. Adam put together the ingredients for pancakes and started cooking them. Dusty was
in a tight situation, but at some point he had to man up.
All of which he was probably well aware of and he didn't
need any advice on from Adam. Especially this morning.

When Dusty finished his coffee, he went for a second
cup, then settled into the old armchair in the corner. "How
bad did I mess up last night?" he finally asked.

Adam considered the question. Where he came from?
Not much at all. But considering they were talking about
Collina… "I didn't see Teressa around."

Dusty stared down into his coffee. "That would be because I insulted her before I took a swing at Jean. I don't
remember anything after that."

"Cal and I broke it up. Sylvie and I brought you here.
Hungry?" He sat a plate of pancakes in front of his friend,
knowing he'd feel better if he ate—if he could keep the
food down.

Dusty tucked into the food and Adam sat down with his own plate and ate without talking. Once Dusty had polished off the pancakes, he pushed his empty plate away and sat back.

"Thanks."

Adam nodded.

"Guess you know." Dusty wiped a hand over his face.

Adam looked up. "Know what?"

"Teressa's pregnant." He choked out the words.

"For sure?"

Dusty shrugged. "Probably. I'll have to marry her." More a question than a statement.

For waking up so damned cheerful, Adam's morning was taking a serious downturn. Adam pushed his food away and folded his arms. Shouldn't Dusty's father or brother be having this conversation with him? "I thought you liked her."

Dusty put his mug on the table and rested his head in his hands. "I do."

"How much?"

"A lot. Ever since I was...I don't know, ten, twelve? She had these wild red curls when she was little. One day this boy named Al, who's since moved away, was making fun of her hair. She started crying, so I told him to lay off." Dusty glared at him as if expecting Adam to make a smart-ass comment. "And she kissed me, you know? This little-girl kiss right here." He pointed to his cheek. "And then she put her little hand in mine, and I walked her home. I've been crazy about her since."

He gulped his coffee as if he were parched. "First time she got pregnant, I went mental. Hightailed it off to Toronto and camped out in Sylvie's apartment for a month until she kicked me out. Second time..." He frowned out the window. "The kids are nice enough, but hell, what a nightmare dealing with the fathers. One's a hundred percent scum, and the other one took off two years ago and hasn't come back since. But what if he shows up someday and wants his kid? Three kids." He cursed under his breath. "I'm not ready for one. What am I going to do with three?"

There was no easy answer to that one. "You've got to talk to Teressa. She's probably scared, too."

Dusty looked up. "I hadn't thought about that. I tried to talk to her all week, but she kept shoving that SOB between us. Why is she hanging out with him? I don't get it."

Denial and avoidance probably had a lot to do with it. "Teressa's the only one who can answer that."

"Yeah." Dusty looked around the kitchen. "Where's Sylvie? She's usually stuck to your side like glue when you're cooking."

A pain shot through Adam's stomach. The good old days. "She's painting."

Dusty's gaze sharpened. "No kidding."

Adam stood. "I'm going to take a coffee and a couple of pancakes up to her. I doubt she'll notice, but she might get hungry."

"Wow. Sylvie's painting again. That's huge."

Maybe he was getting the flu because he was beginning to feel lousy all over. Amazing that just a few short weeks ago he'd dragged his feet when Sylvie had begged him to teach her how to cook. He was glad she'd started painting again. Really. But did the gates have to open this morning? Couldn't they have stayed closed a few more days and given them time to explore their new relationship?

Hell. He was thinking about himself while Sylvie was creating a masterpiece. Could he be more selfish?

Actually, he could, but he wasn't going down that road. Dusty wasn't the only one who had to deal with reality. The minute he'd woken and found Sylvie gone this morning, a voice in his head had started nagging him. He wasn't good enough for her. Hadn't he known that all along? But that wasn't going to stop him from trying to become worthy of her. He couldn't hide anymore. It was time to be honest about his past, and if it cost him his future, what future did he have without Sylvie, anyway?

"Um…I need to talk to you and Cal and Pops. Are you going to be around today?"

Dusty hesitated as he started to put his plate in the sink. "Sounds serious. Everything okay?"

"Yeah, I'm good. I just…need to talk to all three of you."

"I'd planned on avoiding Pops and Cal for a few days." Dusty sent him an apologetic smile. "I've heard all their lectures before. But, okay. If you need me, just let me know when and where."

Dusty was such a great friend. Would their friendship survive Adam telling him what a badass he'd been? He said goodbye to Dusty, loaded Sylvie's tray with everything he thought she might need and slipped it on a table just inside her studio door. She didn't look around this time.

ADAM PACED HIS living room, stopped and looked around to make sure everything was in place and started pacing again. Pops, Cal and Dusty were due to arrive any minute now, and he felt as nervous as…well, he'd never felt as nervous as he did right now. That was saying something, considering the knee-knocking jolts of adrenaline he used to get before hijacking a car.

He decided to ask the Carsons to come to his house, thinking that if they saw he'd made a home for himself, it might help his situation. That had to count for something, right? But now he wished he'd asked to meet anywhere else but there, because regardless of the renovations, his home was still a dumpy old house. So what if he'd knocked out a few walls and painted the inside? Not everyone would see the place the same way he did.

His heart pounded when he heard a vehicle pull into his driveway. All three had come in Dusty's truck. Not able to stop himself, he glanced up at the lit window in Sylvie's studio. He'd caught himself looking over at her house far too often only to catch her shadow occasionally moving past the window.

He greeted the men when they came to the door and was thrown off his stride—not hard to do tonight—when they all followed him to the kitchen and sat at the table. He'd thought they'd sit in the living room. It was all one room anyway and didn't really matter, but sitting in the kitchen made the visit feel less formal. He should have known they'd park themselves here. Hanging out in the kitchen was a Maritime tradition.

"I haven't seen your house for a couple of weeks. I like what you've done." Pops accepted the beer Adam handed him. "Your grandmother would have loved how you opened up the downstairs. She always complained about the small rooms."

Adam brought three more beer to the table, passed a bottle to Cal and one to Dusty, and sat. "The rooms as they were probably weren't so bad for a summer place, but because I'm planning on staying for the winter, I needed more open space down here."

"You'll be needing a few cords of wood," Dusty said. "Mrs. Marley's brother-in-law is selling some cut and dried and delivered for two hundred a cord. I'll give you his phone number if you like."

"Sounds good. Thanks."

"What's this about Sylvie painting?" Pops leaned forward, his face full of hope.

"She started this morning, and as far as I can tell, she's

still at it. I took some food up for her, but we didn't talk the last two times I went up. From what I saw…" He stopped and choked on the sudden lump in his throat. "She's really something, isn't she?"

"Usually she locks the door when she's hot into something. It probably didn't feel like it, but her even letting you into the studio is a big deal," Cal said.

It should have made him feel better that Cal understood how he felt left out, but he didn't want anyone's pity. He dragged in a deep breath and looked at all three men. "There are some things I need to tell you about myself. I've lived a rough live and I've done things I'm not proud of. I didn't tell you before now because…because I wanted to start over, and I didn't know if anyone would give me a chance if they knew about my past."

"You've lived a hard life, Adam." Pops sounded sad and tired, and Adam was sorry he had to burden him with the truth, but he didn't see any other way.

"Pops told us about your dad and all that. It sounded pretty crappy." Dusty took a drink. "What?" he said to his father and brother, who both looked exasperated. "That's what you were talking about, right?" he asked Adam.

"Yeah, I just didn't think… I thought you didn't—"

"Your grandmother kept in touch even after her heart prevented her from traveling," Pops said. "She probably didn't know everything, but she knew a lot about what happened in your life. I won't lie and say she didn't worry about you because she did, but she always said you had a good heart. That's why she gave you this house. She wanted you to know you always had a home to go to no matter what happened."

Adam clenched his teeth so hard he worried one of his teeth might crack. Damned if he was going to snivel in front of the Carson men. He swallowed hard, swigged some beer. "I should have told you when I first came."

"None of our business," Pops said. "We already knew because of your grandmother. But beyond that—none of our business." He put his hand on Adam's shoulder and squeezed. "You're a good man, Adam. Regardless of where you've been, this is where you've ended up. The community is lucky to have you. And I think…" He looked around the table. "That this can stay inside the family. All anyone needs to know is that you're here now. I also think I need another beer after that speech."

They all laughed, and Adam got up to grab a few more beers, thankful for so many things. That he hadn't broken down, which he'd come perilously close to doing. And that his grandmother had seen his potential and believed in him. But mostly because he had friends, who someday may become family if his luck held.

SYLVIE MADE HERSELF put down the paintbrush in her hand. She walked to the other side of the room and viewed the painting from a distance, then drifted over to the door and leaned against it as she studied the painting from another angle.

Not bad. Different from her other work, but it was definitely a Sylvie Carson. A thrill shot through her. Thank God things were back to normal. She reached down and absently grabbed the second half of a scrumptious grilled veggie sandwich Adam had brought up hours ago. She'd have to ask him if it could be added to the menu at the café. As she munched on the sandwich she allowed herself a few more minutes to study the painting, then dropped the crust on the tray and went to the window to look out at her world.

The night was black without a star in the sky. She'd

been painting for hours, and for the first time ever, she acknowledged there were more pressing things than her work to attend to. She shouldn't have bolted from Adam's bed this morning. It wasn't inspiration, but fear, that had sent her flying across the yard to her home.

Adam was an amazing person—smart, kind, considerate. And his body. She sighed. What kind of guy used the word *woo?* How romantic was that?

So why was she feeling excited and scared at the same time? She'd asked him to marry her, and he'd said yes… *but.* Yeah, big, big *but.*

He had his life all mapped out. He knew exactly what he wanted to happen, and wasn't it fantastic that he wanted her to be part of his plans. But…she had plans, too, though not as definite as his, which could be a problem. He knew what he wanted and was pushing forward to reach his goals. She knew what she didn't want and was slowly backing out of those things.

The problem, she decided, the reason she ran when she woke this morning, overcome with love for him, was her fear of falling into the same old trap of wanting to please the people she loved. Although she was afraid she'd sacrifice her dreams and needs to make Adam happy, she wanted to believe that she wouldn't lose her focus. So far she'd managed to stand up to her father and brothers; she was still here, wasn't she? She'd put her apartment up for sale and arranged to have all her belongings shipped home. Taking control and making a definitive move were the actions of a strong woman, right?

And then Adam had phoned and she'd caught the first flight home. She rested her head against the cool windowpane. And then she'd asked him to marry her, jumped into bed with him first chance that presented itself and *pow!*—all she wanted to do was trail around after him and beg for more.

She'd escaped to her studio to retrench, and all the angst that had held her back evaporated, and she was back, painting again. For a second, she guarded the thought close to her heart.

But what was she supposed to do with what she'd learned about her mother? Everything had begun to fall into place the minute Dusty had spilled the truth. On an unconscious level, she'd probably known all along that her mother had abandoned her. That would explain why she feared losing the people she loved, and why she was always so anxious to please them at the expense of her own happiness. She did not want to repeat the same mistake with Adam. She wouldn't.

Maybe she shouldn't have made love to him. Now they were tied together, because what had happened last night had been about a lot more than a quick romp. He'd imprinted himself on her, and she was pretty sure she'd done the same thing to him. How ironic that she'd become unblocked the morning after.

She went back to her worktable, picked up her brushes and started cleaning them. One thing she knew for certain, she wasn't going to hide behind her art this time. She wanted a rich, full life filled with family and friends, and, she prayed, with Adam.

CHAPTER SEVENTEEN

SYLVIE CAME TO him in the night. Slipped into his bed, into his arms, into his heart. And was gone when he woke every morning. Adam's body craved hers. He was drunk on her taste and scent, and a lifetime wouldn't be enough to satiate his desire.

He kept busy during the day, finishing his house, working at the café and initiating gradual changes he and Teressa had agreed to. But they were all distractions to get him through the day. He lived for the night, to feel Sylvie's softness and vitality and hold on to her for a few short hours.

She allowed him into her studio, with the unspoken rule that he not interrupt when she was painting. And, God, how she painted. If her talent had been incredible before, it was truly awe-inspiring now. He'd counted three new pieces completed, which was amazing considering how detailed they were, and two more that were roughly sketched in. The sculpture had disappeared, and he didn't feel comfortable enough to poke around her studio to look for it.

Two weeks later he woke, alone again, and the pain that had been growing in his gut knifed through him, making it almost impossible to get out of bed. He finally rolled out and staggered to the window when he heard several vehicles pull into the yard. From his upstairs window, he watched several reporters spill out of their vans and onto her lawn with their cameras. A few minutes later, a sleek sports car swept into her yard, and a slender, elegant man exited the car and walked into Sylvie's house without knocking, as if he belonged. Mr. Perfect had arrived.

He'd known from the minute he'd met Sylvie that this was where they were headed. What had he been thinking to believe, even for a second, that he was good enough for her? He was an ex-con, the son of a killer, for God's sake, and there was no place—*no place*—in her life for someone like him. Sylvie had known it, too, and she'd kept their relationship exactly where it belonged. In the dark, like it was a dirty secret.

Adam struck out with his hand and punched a hole in the wall beside him. What the hell good was the house to him now, anyway? He couldn't stay here and watch Sylvie live her life without him. Yeah, he'd try to talk to her, if he could get past her groupies. But what good would talking do? It wouldn't change who he was.

He squatted down when Romeo slunk into the room, his tail between his legs, as if he were afraid of Adam. "Hell. Come here, boy." When he held out his hand, the dog moved closer and started wagging his tail.

"What are we going to do, Rom? You're not going to be too happy about leaving Moonbeam behind, are you? You love it here, too, don't you?" He scratched behind Romeo's ears.

He'd come too far, fought too hard to make his life better, to let go of his dreams. He and Sylvie needed to talk. He had to find a way to make their lives work together.

He jumped in the shower, threw on some clean clothes and stomped across the yard to Sylvie's house. He didn't bother knocking.

"Hey." Mr. Perfect, Oliver III, spun around from the toaster when Adam strode into the kitchen. "You're—" he swirled the butter knife in a circle "—the guy next door. Sorry, I forget your name."

"Where's Sylvie?"

"She's working and can't be disturbed."

Adam continued past him and up the stairs, ignoring Oliver's protests. Without knocking, he thrust open the door, and his heart turned over with a thud. She looked so beautiful, standing in the sunlight. He closed the door behind him and locked it. It was a full minute before she looked up.

"Adam!" A guarded look closed down her expression.

"Sneaking over to see me every night isn't enough. I deserve better than that. I want to get married, and I want to wake up beside you every morning. I want you to have my babies and I want to be involved in every part of your life. If you can't give me that, then it's over. It's all or nothing with me." He didn't know where the words had come from, but it was exactly what he was feeling.

She picked up a cloth and wiped the paint off her hands. "It's not that I don't love you."

He folded his arms over his chest. She was going to say no. No to him, to their life together, to his dreams. "You're talking about lust, not love. If you loved me, you wouldn't be ashamed of me."

"I'm not ashamed of you." She threw the rag down on the table. "I'm overwhelmed. I'm afraid you're going to take over my life, and I can't handle that. Please don't push me."

He clenched his teeth against the pain. "How much time do you need to recognize what you already know? You think what's between us could happen with anyone else? You love me, Sylvie, I know you do."

She looked down at her hands, her voice so low he had to lean forward to hear her. "*I* don't know if I do...."

He jerked his head in a nod. "If you ever figure it out, come find me." And turned and left because there was nothing left to stay for.

"You look like week-old fish guts." An hour later, Teressa surveyed Adam from head to toe when he entered the back door of the café.

Adam slouched over to the coffeepot and filled a mug. "Can't say the same for you," he commented over the rim of his cup. "You're glowing."

Teressa pulled the dough she'd been kneading toward her and punched the white lump with her fist. "Potential pregnancy becomes me." She didn't make it sound like a good thing. "You better start taking care of yourself, partner. I'm counting on you."

"I'm okay."

"You've lost a few pounds in the past couple of weeks, and you look like you haven't slept for a year. And while I'm at it, that three-day beard makes you look like a mugger." She wiped her hands on a cloth and went over to stand in front of him. "I know you love her, and I know what she's like when she's 'creating.'" Teressa made parenthesis in the air. "If I were you, I wouldn't hold my breath that she's going to change. And now that the perfect Oliver is here...." She shrugged and went back to the dough.

"I was delusional to think Sylvie would be interested in someone like me. Stupid."

"Don't sell yourself short, partner. You're a great guy. Hell, I'd ask you to marry me if I wasn't pregnant. I mean possibly pregnant."

He sighed. "How much longer are you going to drag this out? When are you going to find out for sure?"

"Haven't decided."

"Have you talked to Dusty yet?"

She darted him a venomous look. "Only if you count the marriage proposal he left on my machine last night."

Adam groaned. What a doofus. "I take it you're not interested."

"If I was nineteen and single, yeah. But twenty-seven, with a possible third child on the way? Not a chance."

Adam winced when she walloped the dough. "You could have a good life with him if you gave him a chance."

"The only reason he offered to marry me is because he thinks I'm pregnant. That's no basis for a marriage."

He opened his mouth to protest but changed his mind. It was Dusty's job to convince Teressa to marry him, not Adam's. The best he could do, if marriage was what Dusty really wanted, was encourage the guy to try harder than leaving a frigging message on a machine.

He braved putting a hand on Teressa's shoulder. "Things will work out. Have faith."

She pushed his hand away. "No, they won't. They never do, not for me. And fair warning—if Sylvie doesn't smarten up, I'm going to hound you to marry me."

Adam shuddered. He liked Teressa well enough, but she kind of scared him sometimes.

He washed his hands, rolled up his sleeves and selected his favorite knife for chopping. "What's up with Cal and Anita? Since they got back from their trip, they can't keep their hands off each other."

"I noticed that, too. I guess they've decided to try for another baby."

"Oh." Shame washed over him. He was glad they both seemed happier, but whatever they got up to was none of his business.

"Too much information for you?" Teressa hooted.

"Something like that. So…" he said after a minute. "I'm putting my place up for sale."

"What?"

He lined up some cleaned carrots and started chopping. "I just talked to Sylvie. She doesn't want me." He stopped, gave himself a second. "I can't live beside her. It'll kill me."

"You're not thinking of leaving!" Teressa rushed over and slugged him in the shoulder. He reeled back a step.

"Cut it out. That hurt."

"What's going on?" Dusty entered the kitchen and stepped between Adam and Teressa. Hard to tell who he was protecting.

"Adam's selling his house because your sister can't see beyond the end of her nose. I know Sylvie's your sister, but she pisses me off. What am I telling you for?" she yelled at Dusty. "You Carsons are all the same. You're emotionally deficient. You think you know what love is, but you haven't a clue."

The door between the kitchen and dining area squeaked open a couple inches. Tyler stuck his nose in through the crack. "Is it safe to come in now, 'cause people are waiting for their food."

"I'll take your orders," Adam offered and turned back to Teressa. "Why don't you and Dusty continue this conversation out back?" Maybe they could resolve some of their problems if they just talked.

"I'm not going anywhere with him." Teressa ripped off a handful of dough and slapped it into a ball.

Tyler sidled closer to Adam. "What are they fighting about?"

"I'm right here. I can hear you," Teressa said in a singsong voice. "Adam's selling his house."

Tyler looked from Adam to Teressa. "Why?" he asked the room at large.

"'Cause Sylvie's got her head stuck up her—"

"Cut it out, Teressa." Dusty moved in front of her. "Be mad at me, but leave my sister alone."

"You can't sell your house, dude," Tyler said to Adam. "It's so cool now that you've fixed it up."

"Who's selling their house?" Pops strode into the kitchen through the back door. He'd been showing up a lot lately to help out.

Adam glared at Teressa before turning to Pops. "I'm *thinking* about it. Things haven't worked out between me and Sylvie."

"You can't sell your house," Pops protested. "Give her more time—she'll come around."

Cal, with Anita trailing behind him, entered from the dining room and stood quietly by the door as if sensing the tense mood of the room. Beanie followed close on their heels. Ignoring Adam, they all started discussing the merits of whether he should put his house up for sale or not.

Adam leaned against the workstation and watched, amazed as the discussion heated up. Even Cal got into it. It was almost as if…as if they really cared what he did. Incredible. Was this what it felt like to have a family? A lot of well-intentioned people meddling in your life? A smile slowly spread across his face. He loved the fuss, loved every single person in the room, warts and all. No way was he giving this up.

Which meant he had to find a way to convince Sylvie that she loved him. What was it Teressa said, that the Carsons wouldn't know love if it came knocking? Could that be true? Yeah, Sylvie had said she loved him, but she'd retracted the words almost as soon as they were out of her mouth. Could Sylvie be in love with him and not recognize the emotion? Only one way to find out.

He put his fingers in his mouth and whistled. Everyone

stopped talking at once and turned toward him. "Listen up," he said. "I think I've got a plan."

SYLVIE STOOD AT the kitchen window and stared across the yard at the for sale sign in Adam's front yard that had been swinging in the wind when she woke this morning.

The simple sign struck terror into her heart. What had she done?

The reporters had left yesterday, so there was no reason she couldn't go outside and investigate. But her house and Adam's felt like an ocean apart. How many days had it been since she'd seen him? Three? Five? She didn't know for sure. All she knew was that she ached inside, like an essential part of her was missing. The only time she could escape the feeling was when she painted.

So she'd kept on painting because she needed time to think, to feel her way forward. The first night that she'd crept across the yard and found Adam's door locked had been like a slap in the face. She'd stumbled back, crept into her own bed and cried herself to sleep. Sylvie rested her forehead against the window.

It wasn't that she didn't understand. Adam wanted more than just an occasional nocturnal visit. He wanted the Full Monty—marriage and children and the happy-ever-after. And she wanted...well, that was the problem, wasn't it?

His house had stood dark every night since. He'd gone away. Surely she'd have heard if he'd left for good? But how to find out where he was staying? She'd called Teressa, her first line of information, but her friend refused to talk to her. Which meant Dusty wouldn't, either, and he was usually the easiest to worm information out of. Even her father had made himself scarce, and Cal... Cal was suddenly too busy to take her calls.

"Sylvie? You haven't answered my question. I have to

go back to Toronto. Are you coming with me?" Oliver asked from the doorway to the living room. He'd been his usual patient and understanding self the past few days. Unlike Adam, who'd put his beloved house on the market and stormed off. Or slunk away. How badly had she hurt him? Damn it. She couldn't believe he was selling his house. Not just his house. His home. She had to find him.

She looked one more time at the ominous sign in Adam's front yard and turned to Oliver. First things first. "I sold my apartment."

"Darling, you know you can stay with me. It'll be fabulous. What we always wanted."

What *he'd* always wanted. She'd never wanted, truly wanted anything, until she'd met Adam. Although she hadn't seen him for days, she could still taste him on her tongue. Still feel his large, work-roughened hands claiming her.

"Sylvie." Oliver grabbed her by the shoulders and gently shook her. "My God, you're even worse than usual. It's impossible to have a conversation with you."

She rubbed her forehead. "Sorry. I'm not going back to Toronto, Oliver." The thought of returning to the city made her ill. This was her home, where she belonged, and she was finally, *finally,* free to do as she liked.

Oliver's face tightened. "But you'll come for the opening of your show? That's in two months from now."

"I promise." She slid her arm through his and walked with him to the door. He'd already loaded his luggage into the rental car. "Thank you for coming all the way down here to see me. You're a good friend, Oliver, and a great agent."

"Are you sure you're making the right decision? It seems so…limited here."

She smiled. He was so wrong. Life in Collina was rich with possibilities. If she wasn't too late.

It didn't occur to Sylvie to clean the paint off her hands or change into something more appealing than her torn jeans and Cal's old flannel shirt until she arrived at the café. If the parking lot was anything to go by, most of the village was here. What was going on?

Suddenly nervous, she opened the door and slipped inside. Anita, dressed for high tea as usual, stood at the front of the room, printed handouts neatly arranged on the table in front of her. She stopped talking when she saw Sylvie, and everyone in the room turned and stared at her. Her eyes swept the crowded room. Adam wasn't here.

"What's going on?" Her voice sounded far too wobbly for her liking.

Anita beamed at her. She'd gained a bit more weight and she looked…purposeful. "We're planning another event for the village. A treasure hunt."

Sylvie stepped farther into the room. "But that was my idea."

Teressa twisted in her chair to glare at her. "So?"

Sylvie put her hands on her hips. "So I want to help, too."

"Sure you're not too busy?" Sylvie tried to remember why she'd thought she and Teressa were friends.

She looked at Anita. "Anything I can do to help, let me know. Where's Adam?"

The room went dead quiet. "Oh, come on, someone must know where he is."

Teressa studied the fingernails on one hand and, if Sylvie wasn't mistaken, had sunk her other hand's nails in Dusty's arm. He kept his eyes on the floor. Anita shuffled a pile of papers. Cal leaned forward and rested his arms on his knees, his gaze glued to the floor. She didn't see Pops anywhere. Tyler looked at her, his face lobster-red.

"This isn't funny," she said. The wobble was back in force.

"He's at Dusty's cabin," Anita said quickly, as if afraid someone would stop her.

"Anita!" Teressa admonished her. Dusty grinned, as did Cal.

She beamed at Anita. "Thanks." And flew out the door.

AT FIRST SHE didn't recognize the man in black leather sitting on the gleaming Harley with his back to her. But she recognized his fluid grace when he moved to climb off the bike. She'd left her car down the road, afraid of getting stuck in the deep puddle, and walked the rest of the way in. Sitting with his back to her, he hadn't seen her approach. Admiring the strong lines of his body and his feline grace, she waited for him to notice her.

She could have sworn she hadn't moved a muscle or made a sound, but he stiffened suddenly and looked over his shoulder.

"Sylvie." A smile flashed over his face before it slid into a neutral expression.

"Who's bike?"

Adam ran his hand along one handlebar. "My dad's. His name was Paulie Hunter. He left me the bike."

She sidled closer. "It's beautiful. I didn't know you had it."

"I only told Dusty."

"And he kept it secret?"

"He probably forgot about it. Thought I should take it for a spin first to make sure everything was working before I sell it."

She shoved her hands in her jeans pockets. "You're selling your house, too."

"Yeah."

"I'd like to buy it."

"What?" That got him looking at her.

"I want to buy your house, if you're selling. I'm going to call it the honeymoon cottage and rent it out."

"No." He swung off the bike, and as he stood in front of her, she was reminded of all that he was. The son of a biker, an ex-con, a grandson, a fascinating, hardworking, good, good man.

"Why did you come out here, Sylvie?"

She took a deep breath, and prayed she hadn't blown it. "To give you this." She held out the sculpture she'd wrapped in a towel before racing out the door.

She hopped from one foot to another as she watched him slowly peel the towel back. His face softened as he studied the sculpture. "It's me."

"Yeah."

"And Romeo and Moonbeam." He turned the small piece in his hand. "I was afraid you were doing a nude of me." He laughed self-consciously.

"I still have the nude but I wanted to do this first. I call it 'Hero.'"

He cleared his throat. "It's beautiful. The more I look at it, the more I see."

She smiled. "Exactly. That's how I feel about you. I do love you, Adam. Not just the person you want everyone to see. I love all of you. The frightened little boy who had to leave everything in the night and flee, the smart-ass teenager with a chip on his shoulder, the son who cared enough about his mother to try to protect her, and the man who came here so full of dreams and made them happen."

She stopped to blink back tears. "I pick you," she said,

looking deep into his eyes. "I love you, and I want us to make a life together here."

Instead of pulling her into his arms and kissing her, as she'd hoped, he leaned against the bike, away from her, and carefully balanced the sculpture on the back tray of the bike. "What's changed?"

"Nothing. Everything. You know how you see something the same way forever, then one day—*bam!*—you get a jolt and suddenly everything looks different?" She stuck her hands in her pockets. "Just like you said, it doesn't matter what happened all those years ago. I'm an artist. Would probably have been one regardless of what happened. My mother's death just fast-tracked everything.

She stepped closer until she was standing between his outstretched legs. "I know now that I don't have to do anything to be loved. I just have to be me. And if I'm very, very lucky some gorgeous, funny, clever man will love me just as I am. I thought that guy might be you."

His face lit up, and he laughed. "Only one way to find out, isn't there, Peaches."

She took one final step closer, and his arms banded around her. She rested her hands on his chest. "We should write down a list of expectations so we both understand clearly what the other person wants." She'd thought the idea inspired on the way here, but now that she said it out loud, it sounded stupid.

Adam cupped her behind and lifted her closer to him. "I expect we'll have two or three kids, and that I'll build a beautiful studio for their famous mother." He nuzzled her neck. "Yum. You smell good enough to eat." When he sank his teeth into her earlobe, her breath caught. "I expect we'll live in my house while I renovate your family home, and we'll move there in about a year because you'll be pregnant."

He pulled back far enough to rub noses. "But I'd like to keep my house. We can escape there when our kids get to be rowdy teenagers."

"Are you done?" She smiled at his hiss as she tucked her hands under his T-shirt and ran her hands up over his chest.

"Not nearly. Let me see. I expect Teressa and I will do okay running the café as long as you and Anita keep us in line."

"Anita?"

"She's a natural manager. We need her. I expect I'll get my sea legs someday and be able to go lobster fishing like a man."

He smiled against her mouth when she giggled. "And I expect we won't make it inside Dusty's cabin before we get rid of most of our clothes."

If Adam's other expectations were as accurate as his last, Sylvie mused a few minutes later as they grabbed their scattered clothes and the sculpture and raced for the cabin, raindrops chasing them inside, then she and Adam had a full life ahead of them.

As for *her* expectations, the only difference between her list and Adam's was that he'd said his first. They both wanted the same things.

Except for the children part. She thought four was a better number. But she was willing to negotiate.

* * * * *

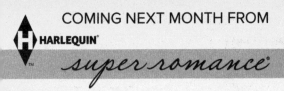

COMING NEXT MONTH FROM

HARLEQUIN

super romance

Available October 1, 2013

#1878 HIS BROWN-EYED GIRL • by Liz Talley

Lucas Finlay is completely out of his league looking after his two nephews and niece. Luckily assistance is next door. Addy Toussant manages to make order from the kid chaos. She's also sparking an out-of-control attraction in him!

#1879 A TEXAS FAMILY
Willow Creek, Texas • by Linda Warren

Jena Brooks returns to Willow Creek, Texas, to find the baby who was taken from her at birth. Will Carson Corbett stand in her way...or does he hold the key to solving the mystery?

#1880 IN THIS TOGETHER
Project Justice • by Kara Lennox

Travis Riggs is a desperate man. So he does something a bit crazy: he kidnaps Elena Marquez. His only demand is that Project Justice review his case, but things get complicated when Travis starts falling for his hostage!

#1881 FOR THE FIRST TIME • by Stephanie Doyle

Mark Sharpe has been torn about JoJo Hatcher since he hired her. Yes, she's a great investigator. Yet she tempts him to cross the line between boss and employee—something he's never done. But when his teenage daughter is threatened, JoJo is the one he trusts to find the truth.

#1882 NOT ANOTHER WEDDING
by Jennifer McKenzie

Poppy Sullivan intends to stop her friend from marrying the wrong woman. Problem is her first love—and heartache—is the best man, and he wants a second chance. But there's no way she's giving Beck Lefebvre the opportunity to break her heart again, no matter how charming he is!

#1883 BECAUSE OF AUDREY • by Mary Sullivan

Audrey Stone and her floral shop are thorns in Gray Turner's side! All he wants to do is wrap up his family's business holdings in Accord, Colorado. But every move he makes, she's there...in the way. Worse, now he can't get her out of his mind!

YOU CAN FIND MORE INFORMATION ON UPCOMING HARLEQUIN® TITLES, FREE EXCERPTS AND MORE AT WWW.HARLEQUIN.COM.

HSRCNM0913

Poppy Sullivan's teenage fling with
Beck Lefebvre happened so long ago it isn't
worth remembering...until she runs into him
at a wedding she's trying to stop. He's still
good-looking, but her pride takes a hit when he
doesn't seem to recognize her! What's a girl to do?
Pretend she doesn't recognize right back....
Read on for an exciting excerpt of

Not Another Wedding

By Jennifer McKenzie

"So?" Beck's voice drew Poppy's attention, caused her to turn
before she thought better of it. "Aren't you going to ask how
we know each other?"

Oh, he'd like that, wouldn't he? Though she might not have
seen him for years, she knew his type. He prided himself on
being unforgettable to women. Well, it was time he learned
a lesson.

"No." She couldn't help noting how good he looked. Really
good. However, she'd give up chocolate before admitting it.

She turned on her heel, intending to return to the party and
find someone—anyone else—to talk to, but his hand caught

her bare arm above her wrist. His fingers were warm.

"I guess I've changed. You're as gorgeous as ever, Red." His blatant appraisal of her body should have ticked her off. She was not his to behold, but the attraction sizzling through her was impossible to deny. Poppy shook the thought off. She did not want him looking at her. Not even a little. He'd lost that privilege years ago and a bit of sexy banter and warm hands didn't change anything.

"If you'll excuse me." She pulled her arm free and hurried away before he got a chance to stop her again. As she made her way through the crowd, Poppy did her best to ignore the knocking of her heart. When she sneaked a glance back, Beck was still watching. He even had the audacity to raise his glass toward her as though to toast her running away.

Fabulous.

Will Poppy be able to avoid Beck?
Or is he determined to renew their acquaintance?
Find out in NOT ANOTHER WEDDING
by Jennifer McKenzie, available October 2013 from
Harlequin® Superromance®.

REQUEST YOUR FREE BOOKS!
2 FREE NOVELS PLUS 2 FREE GIFTS!

HARLEQUIN®

super romance®

More Story...More Romance

YES! Please send me 2 FREE Harlequin® Superromance® novels and my 2 FREE gifts (gifts are worth about $10). After receiving them, if I don't wish to receive any more books, I can return the shipping statement marked "cancel." If I don't cancel, I will receive 6 brand-new novels every month and be billed just $4.94 per book in the U.S. or $5.24 per book in Canada. That's a savings of at least 14% off the cover price! It's quite a bargain! Shipping and handling is just 50¢ per book in the U.S. and 75¢ per book in Canada.* I understand that accepting the 2 free books and gifts places me under no obligation to buy anything. I can always return a shipment and cancel at any time. Even if I never buy another book, the two free books and gifts are mine to keep forever.

135/336 HDN F46N

Name	(PLEASE PRINT)	
Address		Apt. #
City	State/Prov.	Zip/Postal Code

Signature (if under 18, a parent or guardian must sign)

Mail to the **Harlequin® Reader Service:**
IN U.S.A.: P.O. Box 1867, Buffalo, NY 14240-1867
IN CANADA: P.O. Box 609, Fort Erie, Ontario L2A 5X3

Are you a current subscriber to Harlequin Superromance books and want to receive the larger-print edition?
Call 1-800-873-8635 or visit www.ReaderService.com.

* Terms and prices subject to change without notice. Prices do not include applicable taxes. Sales tax applicable in N.Y. Canadian residents will be charged applicable taxes. Offer not valid in Quebec. This offer is limited to one order per household. Not valid for current subscribers to Harlequin Superromance books. All orders subject to credit approval. Credit or debit balances in a customer's account(s) may be offset by any other outstanding balance owed by or to the customer. Please allow 4 to 6 weeks for delivery. Offer available while quantities last.

Your Privacy—The Harlequin® Reader Service is committed to protecting your privacy. Our Privacy Policy is available online at www.ReaderService.com or upon request from the Harlequin Reader Service.

We make a portion of our mailing list available to reputable third parties that offer products we believe may interest you. If you prefer that we not exchange your name with third parties, or if you wish to clarify or modify your communication preferences, please visit us at www.ReaderService.com/consumerchoice or write to us at Harlequin Reader Service Preference Service, P.O. Box 9062, Buffalo, NY 14269. Include your complete name and address.

HSR13R

They say there's always a first time for everything

Mark Sharpe has been torn about JoJo Hatcher since he hired her. Yes, she's a great investigator. Yet she tempts him to cross the line between boss and employee—something he's never done. But when his teenage daughter is threatened, JoJo is the one he trusts to find the truth.

For The First Time
by Stephanie Doyle

AVAILABLE OCTOBER 2013

Love the Harlequin book you just read?

Your opinion matters.

Review this book on your favorite book site, review site, blog or your own social media properties and share your opinion with other readers!

Be sure to connect with us at:
Harlequin.com/Newsletters
Facebook.com/HarlequinBooks
Twitter.com/HarlequinBooks

HARLEQUIN®

A *Romance* FOR EVERY MOOD™

**Stay up-to-date on all your
romance-reading news with the
Harlequin Shopping Guide,
featuring bestselling authors, exciting new
miniseries, books to watch and more!**

The newest issue will be delivered right to you
with our compliments! There are 4 each year.

Signing up is easy.

EMAIL

ShoppingGuide@Harlequin.ca

WRITE TO US

HARLEQUIN BOOKS
Attention: Customer Service Department
P.O. Box 9057, Buffalo, NY 14269-9057

OR PHONE

1-800-873-8635 in the United States
1-888-343-9777 in Canada

Please allow 4-6 weeks for delivery of the first issue by mail.